From the Pest Zone:
The New York Stories

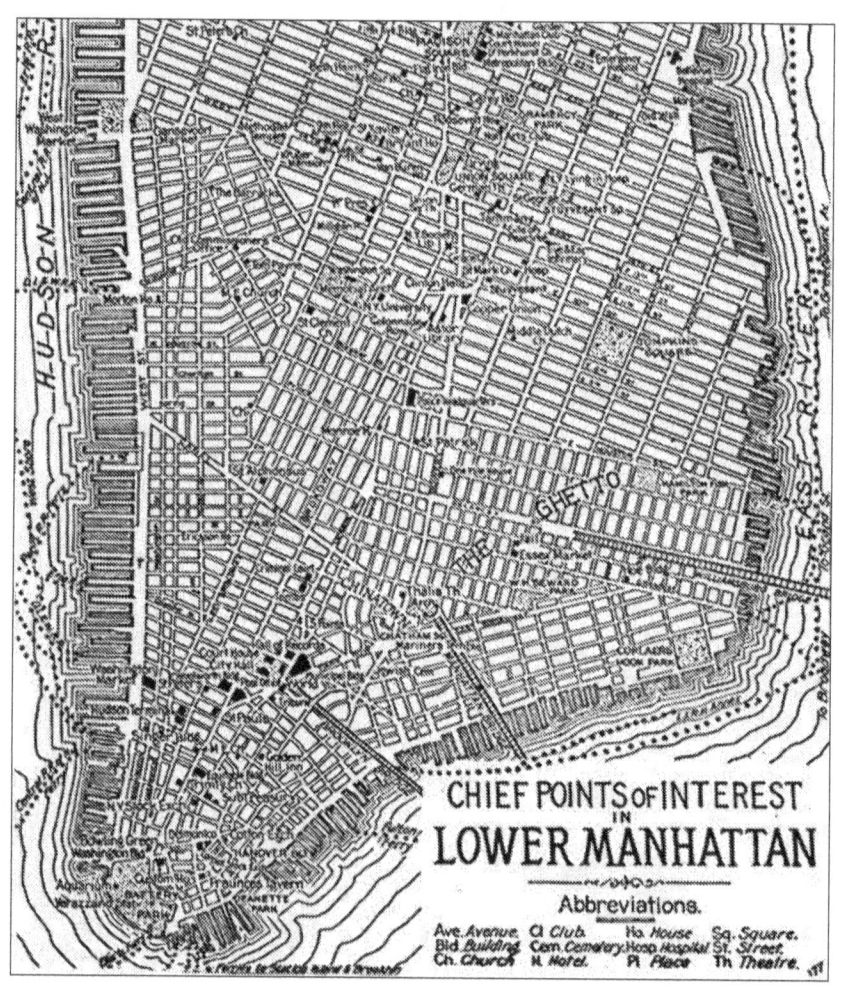

CHIEF POINTS of INTEREST
IN
LOWER MANHATTAN

Abbreviations.

Ave. *Avenue*   Cl *Club*   Ho *House*   Sq. *Square.*
Bld. *Building*   Cem *Cemetery* Hosp *Hospital* St. *Street.*
Ch. *Church*   H. *Hotel.*   Pl *Place*   Th *Theatre.*

H. P. Lovecraft

From the Pest Zone:
The New York Stories

Edited by S. T. Joshi and David E. Schultz

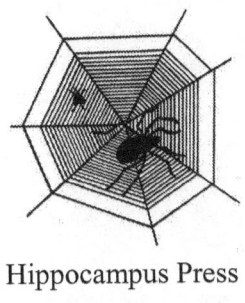

Hippocampus Press

New York

Published by Hippocampus Press
P.O. Box 641, New York, NY 10156.
http://www.hippocampuspress.com

Cover illustration by Sean Madden.
Cover design by Barbara Briggs Silbert.
Photo credits: Ron Breznay, pp. 78, 96; Donovan K. Loucks, pp. 34 , 88;
Steven Mariconda, p. 59.
Hippocampus Press logo designed by Anastasia Damianakos.

First Edition
1 3 5 7 9 8 6 4 2

ISBN 0-9673215-8-1

Contents

Abbreviations

AT   *The Ancient Track: Complete Poetical Works* (San Francisco: Night Shade Books, 2001)

CB   *Commonplace Book* (West Warwick, RI: Necronomicon Press, 1987); entries also in *MW* as numbered

D   *Dagon and Other Macabre Tales* (Sauk City, WI: Arkham House, 1986)

DH   *The Dunwich Horror and Others* (Sauk City, WI: Arkham House, 1984)

FFY   *Fungi from Yuggoth* (in *AT*)

HM   *The Horror in the Museum and Other Revisions* (Sauk City, WI: Arkham House, 1989)

JHL   John Hay Library, Brown University

LL   S. T. Joshi, *Lovecraft's Library: A Catalogue* (New York: Hippocampus Press, 2002)

MM   *At the Mountains of Madness and Other Novels* (Sauk City, WI: Arkham House, 1985)

MW   *Miwscellaneous Writings* (Sauk City, WI: Arkham House, 1995)

OED   *The Compact Edition of the Oxford English Dictionary* (Oxford: Oxford University Press, 1971 [reprint of 1933 ed.])

SHL   *Supernatural Horror in Literature*, ed. S. T. Joshi (New York: Hippocampus Press, 2000)

SHSW State Historical Society of Wisconsin

SL   *Selected Letters: 1911–1937* (Sauk City, WI: Arkham House, 1965–76; 5 vols.)

Introduction

My coming to New York had been a mistake. . . .

The final year of the life of H. P. Lovecraft was marked by almost unendurable hardship. His later years had been marked by grinding poverty—the high price not only of artistic freedom and personal integrity, but also of youthful disinclination to prepare for the future and perhaps an unwillingness to recognize, until too late, that genteel poverty could neither shelter nor feed him forever. But the ultimate twelve months were the most difficult of all. Lovecraft and his closest surviving blood relative, his aunt Annie E. P. Gamwell, had combined households in May 1933 to reduce expenses, but to little avail. Lovecraft's broken confidence in his ability to write good fiction, stemming from the crippling rejection of his novel *At the Mountains of Madness* in 1931, declined further in subsequent years, save for a single flash of self-assuredness in late 1935 when, after learning of the acceptance of two stories submitted to *Astounding Stories*—one by a fledgling literary agent, the other surreptitiously by a friend—he immediately tried his hand at one final tale, "The Haunter of the Dark." Even though Lovecraft refused after 1931 to submit his work to the professional magazines, he mechanically sent batches of stories to book publishers, only upon request, only to have them predictably returned. The few items he allowed to be published—grudgingly perhaps, since many were not his very best work—were either (in his eyes) ruthlessly butchered or ineptly bungled. Either way, the work whose integrity he struggled so diligently to maintain was botched in the hands of insensitive but well-meaning enthusiasts, or merely misunderstood. The discouraging setbacks in Lovecraft's literary career and his precarious finances—newly assailed in 1936 by expenses related to Annie's bout with breast cancer—were exacerbated by his own worsening health and its financial implications.

But despite these misfortunes, Lovecraft withstood them more serenely than he did the period he referred to as his "New York exile" of 1924–26, for at least at the end he was amid the familiar background of his beloved Providence. To be sure, Lovecraft's "exile" was self-imposed. Following the death of his mother in May 1921, he became increasingly attracted to the circle of amateur journalists who lived in the New York area. He impetuously married fellow amateur journalist Sonia H. Greene on 3 March 1924, and the two took up residence at her apartment at 259 Parkside Avenue in the Flatbush district of Brooklyn. The plan was for Lovecraft to find work there to augment Sonia's independent income, although at first they would have to depend on that income for their needs.

In the years following his brief residence in New York City, Lovecraft made no secret of his profound loathing for the city that never sleeps. His youthful correspondents must have felt that Lovecraft's references to his "exile" were made with his typical humor and self-deprecating exaggeration; but he undoubtedly felt at the time that he truly had been banished. That exile was his choice, although by silence he implies that it was not—that he was urged, somehow, against his will to move to and then stay in New York. We will not attempt to address why a grown man in his mid-thirties, felt that way; or why he did not simply leave when it became obvious that residence there was not meant for him, but instead endured twenty-five painful months waiting for that final reprieve to come from his aunts.

Once safely restored to Providence, Lovecraft could jokingly dismiss the ordeal: "Two years to the bad, but who the hell gives a damn? 1923 ends— 1926 begins! . . . What does a blind spot or two in one's existence matter?"[1] But his letters to his aunt Lillian, of which the following is only one minute extract, depict a man at the end of his tether:

> I am unable to take pleasure or interest in anything but a mental re-creation of other & better days—for in sooth, I see no possibility of ever encountering a really congenial milieu or living among civilised people with old Yankee historic memories again—so in order to avoid the madness which leads to violence & suicide I must cling to the few shreds of old days & old ways which are left to me. Therefore no one need expect me to discard the ponderous furniture & paintings & clocks & books which help to keep 454 always in my dreams. When they go, I shall go, for they are all that make it possible for me to open my eyes in the morning or look forward to another day of consciousness without screaming in sheer desperation & pounding the walls & floor in a frenzied clamour to be waked up out of the nightmare of "reality" & my own room in Providence. Yes—such sensitivenesses of temperament are very inconvenient when one has no money—but it's easier to criticise than to cure them. When a poor fool possessing them allows himself to get exiled & side-tracked through temporarily false perspective & ignorance of the world, the only thing to do is to let him cling to his pathetic scraps as long as he can hold them. They are life for him.[2]

In any case, before the reprieve came and before Lovecraft made the deliriously ecstatic return to his true home, he managed, somehow, to write a few stories and poems—not his greatest by any means, but signposts pointing toward them.

---

1. HPL to Frank Belknap Long, 1 May 1926 (*SL* 2.46).
2. HPL to Lillian D. Clark, 8 August 1925 (ms., JHL).

Lovecraft had first visited New York City in April 1922, and although he had been profoundly moved by the first stunning visual impression of the distant skyline at night, the city close up repelled him utterly. Even well into 1925, he still extolled the fairylike qualities of the Manhattan skyline; indeed, a few of his descriptions of Manhattan rival his numerous rhapsodic descriptions of Providence. Consider the following, probably written at a time when he already knew he would be moving to New York but had not yet disclosed the fact to his friends:

> As you know, I am very much enamour'd of the skyline of New-York, & believe it hath an ethereal beauty which only a fabulous Dunsanian city beyond the east cou'd equal. 'Tis a beauty unique and original, & I can understand Samuelus' adjective of "flowerlike" which he applied to the faery coral growth which springs up out of violet waters to disport with the stars & win the moon's argent admiration. That such a coral growth shou'd be the work of vile human insects, matters not in the least to me. I hate the insects but admire their mineral deposit—so that when I look at that spectacle of majesty & loveliness from Manhattan Bridge I cannot believe that it holds anything so base and nasty as organick life. . . . New-York is very beautiful—it is the only town on earth which fascinates me as Providence does. There are really two New-Yorks—the increasingly Georgian New-York of the ground, which passengers on the streets see— the New-York of Minetta Lane and Fraunces Tavern—and the elfin, heaven-scaling New-York of the air—the New York which rears Babylonian pinnacles for admiration afar off, and is brother to the thin delicate clouds of vernal dawns. The architecture of the future seems design'd to perpetuate this duality of beauty, and none may say what unheard-of forms may not rise into unsuspected reaches of aether as the decades pass—until the final decadence comes. This flowering of ambitious stone will be utterly original, and will form America's only genuine and spontaneous contribution to the architecture of the world. With such ecstasies of wild beauties above them, I do not see how New-Yorkers can think sordid, circumscribed thoughts, or remain in the bestial wallow which ingulphs not only them but most of the rest of mankind. Beauty and aether should breed beauty and aether![3]

What made Lovecraft think that he could thrive in, or even abide, New York? Was his plan to endure New York for a brief time, until he could persuade his wife to move back to Providence with him? This is unlikely, for Lovecraft took with him all his belongings, mostly furniture and books, for the purpose of re-creating Providence wherever he might dwell (surely he did not imagine he would leave 259 Parkside Avenue in Flatbush to live alone at 169 Clinton Street in Brooklyn Heights). It seems that, bol-

---

3. HPL to Frank Belknap Long, [February 1924] (*SL* 1.293–94).

stered a few early successes as a professional writer, Lovecraft honestly felt he could make a career of writing in the nation's publishing capital. The previous year he had published several old stories in *Weird Tales*, to the enthusiastic response of the magazine's editor and readers. As Lovecraft headed for New York, he had just been paid $100 for "Under the Pyramids," a story ghostwritten for Harry Houdini, who seemed a good client for Lovecraft's services. Lovecraft also had been approached about assuming the editorship of *Weird Tales*. *That* would have meant a move to Chicago, which would have been even more repellant than moving to New York, and so Lovecraft declined. Even so, his rosy future changed when Edwin Baird, the editor of *Weird Tales*, who had favored his work, was replaced by Farnsworth Wright. Lovecraft was somewhat taken aback to find that his work was no longer accepted instantly, and that in order to ensure the sale of his work he was expected to cater to the demands of the editors—and readers—of pulp magazines. This may have provided the first inkling that his coming to New York had indeed been a mistake.

In a short-sighted way, it would be difficult to imagine the situation otherwise. Lovecraft's profound dislike for New York and its inhabitants, and the fact that he was creatively stifled by his surroundings, seemed to indicate that he had made a grave error in uprooting himself from Providence and trying to settle in an environment completely antipodal to his likes and sensibilities. And yet W. Paul Cook, somewhat distanced from the whole matter, provides acute insight into Lovecraft's New York experience:

> Lovecraft never became thoroughly humanized, he never became the man we love to recall, until his New York experience. To the very end of his days, he hated New York with a consuming passion. I mean the city itself, not the many good friends he had there. But it took the privations, trials, and testing fires of New York to bring his best to the surface. And it took personal contact with those cultured, clever, sophisticated New York amateurs and semi-amateurs to make him look out and not in, to broaden him so that he could cultivate an artistic tolerance, if not entirely altering his viewpoint.
>
> Certainly there was hardly anything that could possibly happen to anyone that did not happen to Lovecraft in New York. The closet in his rooming house was even raided and his entire wardrobe stolen with the exception of what he was wearing at the time—and he was not wearing his best clothes. At the time this happened he was at his very lowest ebb of material fortune. His income was almost nil, he was reduced to about twenty cents a day for food—and he usually spent that for stamps. With a pride which of course he *would* show, he concealed his circumstances from his friends, and only by chance did some of those friends hear of them. Thereafter on various pretexts he was lured to call at times when a meal could gracefully be served. His aunts in Providence were notified, and

they despatched a truck which brought Howard back to Providence lock, stock, and barrel. He came back to Providence a human being—and *what* a human being! He had been tried in the fire, and came out pure gold.[4]

The details have been disputed, but the basic observation is no less valid. The self-imposed exile, bitter though it was, had results that none, including Lovecraft himself, could foresee. As Cook notes, Lovecraft gradually came to look outward rather than inward, but in more ways than one. The callow, somewhat self-absorbed and inexperienced young man (mentally, at least, for at thirty-three, the sheltered Lovecraft behaved like someone much younger) matured after being "tried in the fire," and not only did his personal outlook benefit therefrom, but so, too, did his writing. *That* is the subject of another book. Our hope here is to illumine the five stories of Lovecraft's days in New York—works that, although not among his very best, contain glimmerings that shone forth in his later great achievements. Although Lovecraft expressed reservations about these stories, it is telling that he repudiated none of them and that, late in life, he conceived of a possible collection of stories, to be titled *The Colour out of Space*, that would contain, among others, three of his New York tales.[5]

The Shunned House

The last story Lovecraft wrote in Providence, in late October 1923, was "The Festival." It was eight months before he attempted another work of fiction, and when he did, he pursued it most circuitously.

Lovecraft appears to have contemplated a story about his "shunned house" as early as 1922, for there is an entry in his commonplace book that he acknowledged as its inspiration: "Horrible Colonial farmhouse & overgrown garden on city hillside—overtaken by growth. Verse 'The House' as basis of story."[6] An earlier entry (c. 1920), perhaps from the time when that poem was written, reads: "Shapeless living *thing* forming nucleus of ancient building."[7] But neither of these images, nor the various literary sources identified in our notes, were the primary inspiration for the story. William Fulwiler has conjectured that "The Shunned House" is the story that Lovecraft had contemplated writing in February 1924, to be titled "The House of the

---

4. W. Paul Cook, *In Memoriam: Howard Phillips Lovecraft: Recollections, Appreciations, Estimates* (1941), in *Lovecraft Remembered*, ed. Peter Cannon (Sauk City, WI: Arkham House, 1998), pp. 115–16.

5. I.e., "The Horror at Red Hook," "In the Vault," and "Cool Air." Had not "The Shunned House" been printed as a separate (although uncirculated) booklet, that, too, may have numbered among the book's contents.

6. *CB* 95; see "The House," *AT* 45-46.

7. *CB* 80.

Worm."[8] Less than a month before Lovecraft's marriage, he wrote Frank Belknap Long at length about his numerous recent exploits with the editor (Edwin Baird) and owner (J. C. Henneberger) of *Weird Tales*—the acceptances, his work for Houdini, and the latter's extremely flattering comments about Lovecraft's "The Rats in the Walls"—saying "I've been getting so many inside glimpses into [*Weird Tales*] of late, that I feel as though I own'd it!" He also mentioned that "Henneberger wants a novel or a novelette from me—something unspeakably terrible, and over 25,000 words in length. I think I shall comply with his request, developing a monstrous and noxious idea which has for some time been simmering unwholesomely in my consciousness—a ghastly thing to be intitul'd 'The House of the Worm'."[9]

After seven months in New York, Lovecraft had become painfully homesick. His somewhat maudlin poem "Providence," written about the time he wrote "The Shunned House," is evidence enough. But what was the direct impetus for his writing about the spectral house on Benefit Street in Providence? He reveals the answer in a letter to his Aunt Lillian, telling of his visit to Elizabeth, New Jersey:

> The Andrew Joline house, built in 1735, is wholly hidden from the street by shops, but stands in a spectral courtyard, with its back on the river bank. And on the northeast corner of Bridge St. & Elizabeth Ave. is a terrible old house—a hellish place where night-black deeds must have been done in the early seventeen-hundreds—with a blackish unpainted surface, unnaturally steep roof, & an outside flight of steps leading to the second story, suffocatingly embowered in a tangle of ivy so dense that one cannot but imagine it accursed or corpse-fed. It reminded me of the Babbitt house in Benefit St., which as you recall made me write those lines entitled 'The House' in 1920. Later its image came up again with renewed vividness, finally causing me to write a new horror story with its scene in Providence & with the Babbitt house as its basis. It is called 'The Shunned House', & I finished it last Sunday night.[10]

In referring to the house as the "Babbitt" house, Lovecraft means only that at one time it was once the home of a Mrs. C. H. Babbit (so cited in the 1920 census), with whom Lillian had lived as a companion in 1919–20.

---

8. See Fulwiler's letters to the editor re "The House of the Worm" in *Crypt of Cthulhu* No. 19 (1984): 59 and No. 23 (1984): 53–54. *Worm:* "Any animal that creeps or crawls" (*OED*). The title itself brings to mind *The Lair of the White Worm* (1911) by Bram Stoker (1847–1912), which HPL borrowed from W. Paul Cook and read in October 1923. The writer Merle Prout coincidentally published a story in *Weird Tales* titled "The House of the Worm" in October 1933 (containing elements borrowed from Lovecraft's "The Call of Cthulhu").

9. HPL to Frank Belknap Long, 7 February 1924 (*SL* 1.304).

10. HPL to Lillian D. Clark, 4–6 November 1924 (ms., JHL).

More properly, the house at 135 Benefit Street is known as the John Mawney House (built c. 1764).

If the composition of Lovecraft's story of horrors in Providence was somewhat roundabout, its publication was no less so. "The Shunned House" sat in manuscript for nearly a year, although Lovecraft circulated it among his various colleagues. (Samuel Loveman was so enthusiastic about it that he wished to show it to an editor at Alfred A. Knopf but apparently never did so.) Then, when it finally was submitted to a publisher in July 1925, it was not, as might be expected, sent directly to *Weird Tales*. Instead, Lovecraft sent it to Edwin Baird for use in *Detective Tales*. It is not known if he wrote the story expressly for Baird's use, but in any case it was rejected.[11] Undaunted, Lovecraft declared that he would attempt another story more to the magazine's liking, and he submitted "The Shunned House" now to *Weird Tales*, only to have it returned again. Lovecraft offhandedly informed his Aunt Lillian that Farnsworth Wright, "by the way, rejected 'The Shunned House' as beginning too gradually, though he extends it high personal praise."[12] Wright had suggested that the story be cut in order for it to secure berth in *Weird Tales*, but Lovecraft demurred: "I shan't spoil 'The Shunned House' by abridging the introductory parts—it's easier to write a new story for the magazine & keep this one in what I consider its more artistic form."[13] Ultimately, Lovecraft gave up trying to land the story professionally and instead offered it to fellow amateur-journalist W. Paul Cook for a new magazine.

This time publication seemed certain, although the issue of payment was less so: "My 'Shunned House' will be published next spring in W. Paul Cook's proposed magazine, *The Recluse*, which he may or may not try to launch professionally."[14] Probably because the issue had already become quite large, the story did not appear in *The Recluse* (1927), which contained Lovecraft's celebrated essay "Supernatural Horror in Literature." Cook's new plan was to issue the story as a booklet with a preface by Frank Belknap Long (see Appendix). In April 1928 he began setting type for it. Lovecraft received proofs for it in mid-May and completed the work in early June. Within weeks he had read the page-proofs. Lovecraft declared to correspondents that, having read the proofs *five* times, the book was completely error-free. Cook printed the book before the end of June, and it looked as though it soon would be available. Unfortunately, *The Shunned House* never was fully distributed in Lovecraft's lifetime. For years Lovecraft told friends and correspondents that the printed sheets had been stored away, waiting only to be

11. HPL to Lillian D. Clark, 8 August 1925 (ms., JHL).
12. HPL to Lillian D. Clark, 23 September 1925 (ms., JHL).
13. HPL to Lillian D. Clark, 4 October 1925 (ms., JHL).
14. HPL to Lillian D. Clark, 2 December 1925 (ms., JHL).

bound in order for the story to be available. Various misfortunes suffered by Cook, both financial and personal, first postponed the binding of the book, then ultimately shelved the entire project.

In May 1933, August Derleth had the story on loan from Lovecraft. Derleth mentioned to Farnsworth Wright that he had the tale in hand, and Wright told him he did not recall reading it previously and asked to see it. When Derleth sent it to Wright, Wright remembered having read it before and once again declined to publish it, but not without reservations. Lovecraft wrote to Derleth, "I hardly thought Wright would want it again. As for abridgment—I'd do it if Wright would add a note stating that the version is an abridged one, & forbidding anthologies from copying the text as printed. But probably he wouldn't."[15] Later that year, it appeared that another amateur journalist, Walter J. Coates of Vermont, editor of *Driftwind*, might be able to bind the book, although in a less elegant fashion than Cook had intended; but by January 1934 that plan, too, had failed. Upon learning of the second failed attempt to have the story published, Lovecraft's ambitious (perhaps overzealous) young correspondent R. H. Barlow decided he would attempt to complete the job. The binding of 250 booklets proved beyond the abilities of even the capable Barlow, and only a few of his hand-bound copies and also loose sets of pages were distributed to friends. Barlow's presentation copy, inscribed "For H P L—Who only wrote it—With the compliments of the binder. R. H. B. June 9, 1935. On the occasion of his second visit," was bound in full leather, and hand-tooled with raised bands.

Following Lovecraft's death in March 1937, August Derleth took it upon himself to secure magazine publication of various of Lovecraft's professionally unpublished works, and he largely succeeded. Wright, who had rejected "The Shunned House" twice before, accepted the story in May 1937 and published it in the October issue of *Weird Tales*. The best of Lovecraft's New York stories was, for all intents and purposes, unpublished in his lifetime, and only his death could secure its publication. The unbound sheets of Cook's aborted booklet that had been in Barlow's possession ultimately came into Derleth's hands. He bound and sold them through Arkham House, and today Lovecraft's "first book" commands extremely high prices.

The Horror at Red Hook

More than nine months elapsed before Lovecraft undertook another work of fiction. Like "The Shunned House," the new tale originated in notes found in his commonplace book. The most pertinent one dates to 1925: "DELRIO asks 'An sint unquam daemones incubi et succubæ, et an ex tali

---

15. HPL to August Derleth, [May 1933] (ms., SHSW).

congressu proles nasci queat?'" It is one of two notes that he acknowledged as sources for the story. The other dates considerably earlier, to
1920, and had been in his book for perhaps five years before it was used
for a story: "Hideous cracked discords of bass musick from (ruin'd) organ
in (abandon'd) abbey or cathedral." Lovecraft acknowledged both as influ-
encing the story, and yet neither is a direct result of his New York experience—the subject of the story—and both represent only minor bits of
color. Other, broader impressions served as the impetus for the story. The
following, to his aunt Lillian, is quite succinct:

> Saturday, August 1st, I was up in the afternoon; &, responding at last to
> the relief occasion'd by the final transfer of amateur responsibilities to
> younger shoulders, commenc'd the writing of a new hideous tale, "The
> Horror at Red Hook", wherein I tell of hellish happenings amongst the
> mongrel Satan-worshippers that lurk in a slum district of Brooklyn, be-
> twixt Clinton St. & the waterfront. A gentleman of ancient Dutch family,
> in Flatbush, goes down amongst these folk & becomes their leader in ter-
> rible rites—after which he meets a loathsome end. And a Dublin-born
> detective, who investigates the decaying rookeries of the noxious crew,
> sees things which shatter his nervous system & give him such a horror of
> old brick houses that he has to seek retirement in Chepachet, R.I., where
> there are no brick houses. Once, in Pascoag on a walk, he sees a brick
> building & falls in a convulsion![16]

The following later account, written well after his escape from New York,
sheds considerable light not only on the origins of the story, but also on
Lovecraft's daily routine in New York and the means by which he coped
with being uprooted and displaced from Providence.

> Let me thank you exceedingly for the copious account of Red Hook
> decadence which you so kindly sent, and which interested me so much on
> account of my close view of the accursed region in 1925. . . . I'd like to get a
> squint at the future articles dealing with individual gangs which your cutting
> promises—for I am sure that I must have encountered some of these
> primitive tribal survivals at first hand as they careened from cafeteria to
> cafeteria in the squalid reaches of Court Street beyond Borough Hall. How
> well I recall that night in the Tiffany when a party of plain-clothes men en-
> tered and searched a party of young roughs for firearms! Every pair of
> hands shot up as if by instinct—for clearly, these worldly-wise striplings
> were no strangers to the technique of constabular inquisition. And then that
> unforgettable overheard conversation in Johnson's Coffee-Pot, when a se-
> lect group of hackney-coachmen exchanged naive recollections of bygone
> durance at Blackwell's Island and Sing-Sing; whose inconveniences they
> vowed were grossly exaggerated, and whose cuisine they extolled to the ex-

---

16. HPL to Lillian D. Clark, 6 August 1925 (ms., JHL).

treme disadvantage of their host's—a most damnably tactless and indelicate
sort of comparison to make out loud in the presence of the sensitive Athe-
nian behind the buffet that gleamed so splendidly with the glory that was
Grease. . . . My knowledge of Red Hook was not one of seriously studied
details, but one of impressionistic observation and overheard fragments
linked together by the thread of fancy—and yet it was essentially a first-
hand one. I saw these gangs with my own eyes as they loafed near Borough
Hall, and would have been blind if I had not noted the coarse degeneracy of
the physiognomies—a kind of pervasive local decadence and brazen inso-
lence peculiar to the region, and so characteristic that it nearly overrode the
marks of race and gave a sinister quality in common to every sort of gang
from Nordic to Oriental. Their language and manners were such as I had
never encountered before and have never encountered since; and to hear
them through open windows in the night, howling afar like wolves at a
spectral moon, or piping loathsomely on cracked mouth-organs in melodies
whose words and meaning must have been of the pit, was to gain a sort of
spiritual insight into gulfs of underlying horror that no mere trip through
the district would ever have supplied. My own post of observation, at the
corner of State and Clinton Sts., was of course on the mere fringe of the
worst parts; but I took several walks of exploration around the waterfront
rookeries and acquired a very fair pictorial and aural image of the whole
blight, even in its extremest phases. There was an evil hush—a dramatic
tension—about the entire sprawling fester; and a hideous element of pu-
trescent homogenity seemed to spread all over the brooding expanse,
wearing down the line of demarcation between the various national colonies
and the various architectural areas—which latter differ all the way between
the crumbling mansions of vanished aristocracy and the dingy frame tene-
ments of autochthonous slumdom. Clinton Street is of hidden rottenness
and masked abomination. It has still its noble skyline of fine old roofs and
church-towers which the twilight restores to pristine alluringness, and some
of its intersections are truly lovely to the charitable eye in the dark. It was
this quality which deceived me so completely on the winter nights when I
was hurriedly seeking a bargain in large rooms. This is not Red Hook
proper, but that district itself—beyond Atlantic Avenue and toward the
pier—has some quaint brick houses that were very modest and lovely in
their day. The actual waterfront, of course, is like all other waterfronts; . . .
whilst the Gowanus section near the canal, where the growing town overtook an old Dutch village, has always been a "tough" region of factories,
warehouses, and shipping. Gowanus has always had a rough-and-ready,
chip-on-shoulder sort of pride and self-respect lacking in other slums; because it has so far resisted the foreigner (who does not take kindly to vigorous physical exertion and adventurous sea-concernments) and preserved its
original blue-eyed and tow-headed virility, spiced with husky accents and
cauliflower ears. . . . Ah, me, what colour and mystery it all takes on in retro-
spect! Surely, its wild squalor was not without a certain wry, Baudelairian
sort of beauty; because it represented a natural and strictly local growth,

with some of the adaptation of life to landscape which makes for authentic character. It was a study in genre—and some day a real artist may catch its spirit more suavely and effectively then I could do in my brief hymn of hate—written whilst still there, and therefore without the effect of spatial and chronological perspective. I believe I could write of the place better now than I did then.[17]

And it seems that, sprung from the confines of Brooklyn, and more emotionally detached from his captivity, Lovecraft wrote much better about his experience than he had in the story itself.

In writing to Clark Ashton Smith about the completed tale, Lovecraft explained its genesis in part, confessing that the magic trappings were somewhat less than imaginative:

> I have a nest of devil-worshippers & devotees of Lilith in one of the squalid Brooklyn neighbourhoods, & describe the marvels & horrors that ensued when these ignorant inheritors of hideous ceremonies found a learned & initiated man to lead them. I bedeck my tale with incantations copied from the "Magic" article in the 9th edition of the *Britannica,* but I'd like to draw on less obvious sources if I knew of the right reservoirs to tap. Do you know of any good works on magic & dark mysteries which might furnish fitting ideas & formulae? For example—are there any good translations of any mediaeval necromancers with directions for raising spirits, invoking Lucifer, & all that sort of thing? One hears of lots of names—Albertus Magnus, Eliphas Levi, Nicholas Flamel—&c., but most of us are appallingly ignorant of them. I know I am—but fancy you must be better informed. Don't go to any trouble, but some time I'd be infinitely grateful for a more or less brief list of magical books—ancient & mediaeval preferred—in English or English translations.[18]

The story never benefited from more than Lovecraft's "encyclopedic" knowledge of incantatory magic.

Like "The Shunned House," "The Horror at Red Hook" seems to have been intended for a detective magazine. Lovecraft's original title for the story was "The Case of Robert Suydam," and its themes were reexplored at length in the short novel, *The Case of Charles Dexter Ward* (1927), which he conceived as a detective novel. It does not appear that he submitted the story to *Detective Tales,* however; rather, he sent it to *Weird Tales.* He inundated Farnsworth Wright with "Red Hook" and the new "In the

17. HPL to Bernard Austin Dwyer, 26 March 1927 (Arkham House transcripts; not included in letter 265 in *SL* 2). This lengthy letter (see n. 44) contains still more information concerning about HPL's New York days and the genesis of "Cool Air."

18. HPL to Clark Ashton Smith, 9 October 1925 (*SL* 2.28).

Vault" (q.v.), along with "Polaris," "Beyond the Wall of Sleep," and "From Beyond" from the trunk, and also Sonia Greene's "Four O'Clock" and Clark Ashton Smith's "The Abominations of Yondo." By 24 October he learned that of his tales only "Red Hook" had been accepted, but oddly it wasn't published until January 1927.

In later years, Lovecraft was not proud of "The Horror at Red Hook," and yet it achieved a minor recognition in its day. Christine Campbell Thomson promptly selected it for *You'll Need a Night Light* (London: Selwyn & Blount, 1927), which went through four printings. It was then published without permission in November 1928 in *Not at Night!* edited by Herbert Asbury. Not only did the book plagiarize the contents of several of Thomson's anthologies, it also lifted its title from the overall series. The publisher, Macy-Masius (later The Vanguard Press), had brought out numerous books with weird themes in the later 1920s. (Indeed, the publisher approached Lovecraft in March 1932 about a possible collection of his work.) Lovecraft had found out about the book's appearance at second hand:

> I also noticed the *Times* review.[19] . . . It is amusing how people become famous for writing which they themselves despise. . . . It rather tickled me to see this Herbert Asbury claiming *editorship* of a book which he merely took as he found it—but maybe he changed the punctuation in some of the tales. I suppose "Red Hook" must be in it—& if so, I am wondering if I ought to get any royalties. . . . I'd like to see the volume anyway, to get an idea of its mechanical appearance.[20]

Asbury made several comments that raised Lovecraft's hackles, stating that the average reader merely wants shocks and thrills, and is "inclined to resent what he calls 'fine writing,' and considers that an author who so indulges his muse not only obscures his story and retards the action, but makes an offensive effort to air his learning." He also wrote:

> Most of the authors represented in this collection appear to be comparatively unknown in this country (Seabury Quinn is the only one whose work I have ever seen before), and scholars and critics will look in vain for evidences of the skill and erudition displayed by such masters of the horror story as Edgar Allan Poe, Ambrose Bierce and Algernon Blackwood. But any such comparison would be manifestly unfair, for the only

---

19. [Unsigned], "Horror Tales in the Nth Degree" [review of *Not at Night!*], *New York Times Book Review* (25 November 1928): 36.

20. HPL to August Derleth, "Monday" [late November or early December 1928] (ms., SHSW).

criteria applied in selecting these tales from the many which were available were shock and gruesomeness.[21]

Writing to August Derleth, Lovecraft kidded, "Asbury's geographical mistakes are somewhat amusing. Really, I'll have to emigrate to the States if there's a chance of getting well known over there some day! Beastly fog, this—I can hardly see St. Paul's dome from my Bloomsbury upper window as I write!"[22] But later he wrote:

> I . . . did not care much for Asbury's slighting reference to the artistic & scholastic merit of the contents. I was tempted to answer his slur about scholarship by pointing out that his own lordly erudition was not sufficient to detect & delete the mispunctuation which destroys the sense of the quotation from Delrio—the comma after *tali* which the British anthologist stupidly copied from the original misprint in *Weird Tales*. (In the copies sent to you, I have carefully scratched out the intrusive comma with a penknife.) I'm not sure yet whether or not I'll buy the book.[23]

Lovecraft was never paid for the appearance of "The Horror at Red Hook" in *Not at Night!* and ultimately Macy-Masius withdrew the book from the market rather than pay royalty or damages to *Weird Tales*, which had threatened to taken legal action against the publisher because the magazine had granted book rights to the stories only to Selwyn & Blount.

He

"The Horror at Red Hook" strikes a reader familiar with Lovecraft's work as a story unabashedly written to cater to the audience of pulp thrillers, but "He," written only ten days later, is an anguished cry from the heart. And like "The Horror at Red Hook," "He" had its origins in poignant fact. Consider this account of a voyage of exploration in Greenwich Village undertaken by Sonia and Lovecraft in August 1924, almost exactly a year before he wrote the story:

> Falling into a conversation with [a] chrysostomic gentleman of leisure [. . .], we learned much of local history; including the fact that the houses in Milligan Court were originally put up in the late 1700's by the Methodist Church, for the poorer but respectable families of the parish. Continuing his expositions, our amiable Mentor led us to a seemingly undistinguished door within the court, and through the dim hallway beyond to a back door. Whither he was taking us, we knew not; but upon emerging from the back door we

21. Herbert Asbury, "Introduction" to *Not at Night!* (New York: Macy-Masius, 1928), p. 11.
22. HPL to August Derleth, 14 December [1928] (ms., SHSW).
23. HPL to August Derleth, 26 December 1928 (ms., SHSW).

paus'd in delighted amazement. There, excluded from the world on every side by sheer walls and house facades, was a second hidden court or alley, with vegetation growing here and there, and on the south side a row of simple Colonial doorways and small-pan'd windows!! It was beyond words—it is still beyond words, and that is why I cannot do it justice here! Buried deep in the entrails of nondescript commercial blocks, this little lost world of a century and a quarter ago sleeps unheeding of the throng. Here stretch worn pavements which silver-buckled shoes have trod—here, hidden in cryptical recesses which no street, lane, or passageway connects with the Manhattan of today! Two dim lamp-posts illumined the scene—that elder and mysterious scene for which the uninitiated search in vain, though scouring every linear inch of New-York's visible streets. Transported, I paus'd to reflect and let my fancy run riot. What awesome images are suggested by the existence of such secret cities within cities! Beholding this ingulph'd and search-defying fragment of yesterday, the active imagination conjures up endless weird possibilities—ancient and unremember'd towns still living in decay, swallow'd up by the stern business blocks that weary the superficial eye, and sometimes sending forth at twilight strains of ghostly music for whose source the modern city-dwellers seek in vain. Having seen this thing, one cannot look at an ordinary crowded street without wondering what surviving marvels may lurk unsuspected behind the prim and monotonous blocks. . . . Gad's death, if ever I get an unworried moment to write another story, I vow 'twill deal with some such embalmed street, or square as this nameless inner court within a court.[24]

Again, Lovecraft gives a detailed account of the story's conception:

Monday the 10th [of August], I rose late, was swamped by correspondence all the afternoon & evening, & at the close of the latter turned to the business of fictional composition. I was not, however, able to produce anything—being bored with the sameness, regularity, colourlessness, & poison-like quality of the usual round & scene. Thus feeling it necessary to recover the psychology of independence & individuality—to feel that I could go where I darned please when I darned pleased, & imbibe the visual piquancy & variety of colonial sights as dictated by my mood,—I set forth on a nocturnal pilgrimage after mine own heart; beginning at Chelsea, the village overtaken by New-York in the 'forties, west of 7th Ave. between 18th & 24th Sts, & working south toward Greenwich amongst the curious houses, imagination-kindling streets, & innumerable kitty-cats whose graceful presence called back to memory the wholesome long-departed domestick life of the village. Circling round by the ancient quadrangle of the Union Theological Seminary, & dreaming dreams of the old days, I worked slowly southward in the light of a misty waning moon, & eventually struck the borders

---

24. HPL to Lillian D. Clark, 20 August 1924 (AHT). Cf. *CB* 149: "Evil alley or enclosed court in ancient city—Union or Milligan St.—Fungi."

of Greenwich. There I threaded anew the well-loved & tortuous labyrinths which I have described in so many previous travelogues, doubling frequently on my course & saturating myself with the colonial atmosphere that means mental life for me—old iron-railed steps, Georgian knockers, or steep gables, dormers, & gambrel roofs in black silhouette against the half-clouded sky. . . . My Greenwich peregrinations included Abingdon Square, Grove St., Grove Court, Barrow & Commerce Sts., the Minettas, Milligan & Patchin Places, Gay St., Sheridan Square, & Charlton St., & embraced many marvellous glimpses of the old times. Once I saw a colonial doorway lighted up, the traceries of transom & side-lights standing out softly against the mellow yellow gleams inside. From Greenwich my route led south along Hudson St. to old New York, (across Lispenard's Meadows & the filled-in swamp) & I noted the colonial square at the intersection of Canal. Later crossing to Greenwich St., I descended into the most ancient district; noting the Planters' Hotel, Tom's Chop House, & the like, & emerging on Broadway to salute St Paul's & plunge down Ann St. into the heart of Golden Hill—Irving's boyhood neighbourhood, & the seat of much disturbance during the late disastrous revolt against His Majesty's government. I passed under the Brooklyn Bridge to Vandewater St., & noted with horror the replacement of a fine colonial row by a damnable new garage, (other excellent colonials have vanished in Greenwich, at Barrow & Hudson Sts.) & doubled back through New Chambers & Pearl, noting beside the former a colonial smithy which had always appealed to me. Proceeding along Pearl toward the Battery, I viewed all the ancient houses & waterfront panoramas as I passed them—remarking incidentally that the old Harpers publishing house has been newly razed. At Hanover-Square, seat of the best British gentry before the Revolution, I lifted my hat in honour of King George the Third; then passing on by the Queen's Head Tavern—Fraunces', that is—to those regions of Battery Park where one or two colonial mansions yet linger. It was now five o' the morning, & I had so fully thrown off melancholy by my free & antique voyage, that I felt exactly in the humour for writing. The clouds were dissolving, & another day was done. Should I drag it away in New-York, & lose the keenness of my mood, or keep on in my dash for liberty—gaining fresh strength as I kicked aside the irritating fetters of the usual? The sea was before me—the clean, salt harbour beyond which lay a white man's country—& a Staten Island ferry rode at anchor. Who, possessed of any imagination whatsoever, could pause for an instant? So I planked down my nickel, boarded the ship, & in a few moments was riding the billows under a dawn-paling sky. Whither bound? The New-Englandish soul within me suggested the nearest substitute,—ancient Elizabethtown—so upon my landing in the grey twilight I took the proper trolley & rode in ecstasy past seashores & hills turning pink & gold with the sunrise. At the Elizabethtown ferry I saw the burnished copper disc of the sun gleaming gloriously on the waters, & by 7 a.m. I was in the central district of the village, gravely saluting the old colonial spire that towers—as you will remember—above the shady churchyard. At a small shop I bought a dime composition book; & having a pencil & pencil-sharpener (in a case, which S H gave me) in my pocket, proceeded to select a site for literary creation. Scott Park—the triangular space we passed in going to look at those rooms in East Jersey St.—was the place I chose; & there, pleasantly intoxicated by the wealth of delicate un-metropolitan greenery & the yellow & white colonialism of the gambrel-roofed Scott house, I settled myself for work. Ideas welled up unbidden, as never before for years, & the sunny actual scene soon blended into the purple & red of a hellish midnight tale—a tale of cryptical horrors among tangles of antediluvian alleys in Greenwich Village—wherein I wove not a little poetick description, & the abiding terror of him who comes to New-York as to a faery flower of stone & marble, yet finds only a verminous corpse—a dead city of squinting alienage with nothing in common either with its own past or with the background of America in general. I named it "He", & had it nearly done by three, when my Leeds-Loveman engagement called me back to Babylon. Finishing the tale en route, I would have been in ample time to receive my messages had transportation been normal; but alas! at the water's edge I found a broken ferry! For an hour, amidst the profanity of draymen & other prospective passengers, the red boat was held up for tinkering; when it did start I was foredoomed to lateness. The rest of the trip was pleasant, & in the evening at home I polished my story before an early retiring. I trust Leeds has forgiven me for my apparent remissness—Loveman has, for he telephoned this afternoon & made an engagement here for tomorrow night. He has not been feeling well, he says, & did not attend the gang meeting last night. Tomorrow I shall read him my newest story & discuss the prologue for "The Sphinx". At present, no one but myself has seen "He".[25]

Lovecraft submitted the story to *Weird Tales* in early October 1925, before he submitted the previously completed "Horror at Red Hook," presumably because it was much shorter and could be more quickly typed. By 8 October, he had learned of its acceptance, and it appeared in the issue for September 1926. Acceptance of the story buoyed Lovecraft's spirits somewhat, for he wrote Lillian, "The one thing that encourages me is the fact that two of my new tales ('He' & 'Red Hook') have been accepted, a circumstance which indicates that age has not as yet considerably impaired my powers of authorship."[26] But feelings of self-doubt plagued Lovecraft for the rest of his life.

In the Vault

"In the Vault" surely is one of Lovecraft's least Lovecraftian stories. It is easy to see why. Well into his exile, he wrote the story at the suggestion of Char-

---

25. HPL to Lillian D. Clark, 13 August 1925 (ms., JHL).
26. HPL to Lillian D. Clark, 7 November 1925 (ms., JHL).

les W. "Tryout" Smith, editor of the amateur journal, *The Tryout*. The suggestion may have been a sympathetic gesture meant to help a struggling friend, for Lovecraft may have confided to Smith in a letter a sentiment later articulated so poignantly to Frank Belknap Long: "I couldn't form a single well-defined thought in that damnable Clinton Street pigsty,"[27] even though he had found himself full of new ideas "clamouring for expression."[28] Lovecraft must have gotten the idea from Smith around August. To Lillian, he wrote: "I hope to write some more stories shortly—but I must get rid of my superfluous amateur letter-writing. Any incubi or responsibilities detract disastrously from one's creative imagination, & I must cultivate the stimulating impressions of freedom, novelty, & strangeness. Meanwhile I must finish the two stories I sketched out roughly last month—the short thing developed from C. W. Smith's tomb notion, & the longish novelette involving antique horrors risen from the sea."[29] Lovecraft wrote "In the Vault" on 18 September and quickly thereafter typed it—perhaps, in light of his detestation of typing, because it was the shortest of his most recent efforts, or perhaps because he felt it was the most salable of the bunch. When he lent the story to Clark Ashton Smith, he wrote: "The enclosed was written up from an idea given me by an interesting old fellow in Massachusetts—the idea of an undertaker imprisoned in a village vault where he was removing winter coffins for spring burial, & his escape by enlarging a transom reached by the piling-up of the coffins. This is all my venerable friend suggested—the *motivation* & denouement, together with the actual writing, were all my own. I tried to employ a homely, prosaic style more or less in harmony with the theme."[30] But the story does not quite seem to ring true, as does "The Picture in the House." Given his difficulties in writing fiction, it is perhaps just as well that Lovecraft did not attempt to write "The Call of Cthulhu" (the "longish novelette" whose plot he had already recorded in detail at this time) while in New York, but waited until he had returned to Providence.

Lovecraft submitted "In the Vault" to Farnsworth Wright on the heels of Wright's acceptance of "He" and "The Cats of Ulthar"—but only after first passing the story to his aunts. As usual, he sent it with a batch of other stories. He was confident the story would be accepted, noting that "it ought to be as acceptable to Wright as anything of mine."[31] Lovecraft received Wright's verdict on 27 October, noting that he rejected "'In the Vault' as

27. HPL to Frank Belknap Long, 26 October 1926, *SL* 2:80.
28. HPL to Lillian D. Clark, 8 August 1925 (ms., JHL).
29. HPL to Lillian D. Clark, 8 August 1925 (ms., JHL).
30. HPL to Clark Ashton Smith, 20 September 1925 (*SL* 2.26).
31. HPL to Lillian D. Clark, 4 October 1925 (ms., JHL).

being too horrible for the censors."[32] Ironically, Lovecraft himself may have been responsible for the story's rejection, since it was "The Loved Dead" (which he ghost-wrote for C. M. Eddy) that had gotten *Weird Tales* into trouble with the censors the prevous year. Lovecraft now felt that his only recourse was to send the story to Tryout Smith, who had suggested it, and Smith dutifully published it in the November 1925 number of *The Tryout*. Despite Lovecraft's proofing, the story was marred by many misprints.[33]

Because *Tryout* was an amateur paper, Lovecraft had no qualms about later trying to find a paying market for his story. In 1926 he included it among a batch of stories submitted to J. C. Henneberger, who at the time was attempting to launch a new magazine, but that venture came to naught. Another five years passed before Lovecraft attempted to find a berth for the story. He wrote to August Derleth in the spring of 1931, "I have also sent 'In the Vault' & one other old MS. to [Harold] Hersey for G.S. consideration . . . . with similar expectations of rejection,"[34] and, as predicted, *Ghost Stories* rejected the tale. The same thing happened when he submitted the story (once again with other manuscripts) to Harry Bates of *Strange Tales of Mystery and Terror*. In September 1931, Lovecraft lent the story to August Derleth at the latter's request. The story promptly was returned, but as a clean, newly retyped manuscript (with "improvements"):

> A thousand & one thanks for your generosity in typing "In the Vault"—a job I wouldn't have undertaken myself for any amount! . . . Your alterations are all right, except that in certain places I like to use a semicolon, for the sake of neatness & balance, where others are apt to use a comma. "Old Father Death" was distinctly affected—shewing the difference between what I wrote in 1925 & what I would write now. "Soul", however, is commonly used in rural New England in the sense of "person" . . . . 'good soul', 'a lazy soul', &c. &c. &c. No one here could possibly find any lack of fitness in the expression as used. The mythological connotation would not even be thought of. . . . I doubt if it would do much good to send it again to Wright—I hate the cheapening involved in persistent peddling. But I'll think the matter over—& am meanwhile more grateful than I can say for your kindness in saving the tale from probable total annihilation. Now that its lease of life is extended, it may yet find a home some day.[35]

Although Lovecraft was disinclined to send the story to Wright, Derleth volunteered to do so. Lovecraft acknowledged Derleth's offer, writing:

---

32. HPL to Lillian D. Clark, 27 October 1925 (ms., JHL).

33. "I enclose a *Tryout* with my 'In the Vault' so badly printed as to be almost illegible." HPL to Lillian D. Clark, 2 December 1925 (ms., JHL).

34. HPL to August Derleth, [late March or early April 1931] (ms., SHSW).

35. HPL to August Derleth, 24 September 1931 (ms., SHSW).

"About 'In the Vault'—well, since you went to all the bother of typing, it would be churlish in me not to accede to your wish for its re-submission to Wright; so here it goes! It will probably come back—although as you say, Wright was rather more afraid of really weird stuff in 1925 than he probably is now"—that and the threat of confiscation of the magazine. This time the story was more warmly received, and its sale netted Lovecraft fifty-five dollars. Lovecraft must surely have noted with wry bewilderment and irony that as his great novel of 1931 reposed unpublished in his files, one of his lesser efforts, a piece not at all representative of his current aspirations, was awarded second honors for the annual O. Henry Memorial Prize of 1932.[36] Derleth's inexplicable fetish for the story earned it the opening berth in the Lovecraft omnibuses he edited and published, *Best Supernatural Stories* (1945) and *The Dunwich Horror and Others* (1963).

Cool Air

Between the writing of "In the Vault" and "Cool Air," Lovecraft was detoured into another project, one that may have kept him from slipping over the brink as he awaited the opportunity to leave New York. In November, W. Paul Cook invited him to write "an article . . . on the element of terror & weirdness in literature"[37] for publication in Cook's now legendary *Recluse*. Not only did Cook's invitation result in the composition of one Lovecraft's most significant essays, it also resulted in the crystallization of his cosmic perspective—the essence of what most readers most respond to in his fiction. Only upon completion of the bulk of the research on the essay and the final return to Providence did the shift from a macabre to a cosmic point of view become complete. The reading that occupied Lovecraft during much of the winter of 1925–26 exposed him to concentrated doses of the great writers of weird fiction. Upon the completion of most of his research, and even much of the writing of "Supernatural Horror in Literature," Lovecraft finally undertook his best realized New York tale, "Cool Air." Not only was it the last story he wrote while in New York, it also was the last story specifically set in New York.

It is not certain when Lovecraft wrote "Cool Air," but his letter to Lillian Clark of 5 March 1926 suggests that he completed the story only shortly before that time, probably in late February. His letter indicates that at that time he was already thinking seriously of returning to Providence, for he wrote: "Glad you liked 'Cool Air', & hope I can turn out some more material when this addressing siege is over. I'd like to concoct something

---

36. *O. Henry Memorial Award Prize Stories,* ed. Blanche Colton Williams (Garden City, NY: Doubleday, 1932).
37. HPL to Lillian D. Clark, 11–14 November 1925 (ms., JHL).

which would bring in a fortune at one bound, so that we might settle down in that apartment you mention. As a location I choose that reclaimed Colonial section around Thayer St. which Theodore Francis Green is developing!" Lovecraft's exile was nearly over. His letter of 27 March records his ecstatic, near-orgiastic, reply to Lillian's invitation asking him finally to return home. Perhaps the liberating anticipation alone makes "Cool Air" stand out as the most successful of Lovecraft's New York stories.

Although "Cool Air" is only one of several stories of life after death (such as "Herbert West—Reanimator," *The Case of Charles Dexter Ward*, "In the Vault," and, in a way, even "The Whisperer in Darkness"), its genesis is somewhat unexpected. One indisputable source is the entry Lovecraft identified in his commonplace book: "Man's body dies—but corpse retains life. Stalks about—tries to conceal odour of decay—detained somewhere—hideous climax."[38] As with the notes that suggested "The Horror at Red Hook," this important note antedates the immediate influences upon the story by several years; and the source of Lovecraft's note in his commonplace book is not known, although the note seems to coincide roughly with the period during which he wrote another tale about the reanimated dead, "Herbert West—Reanimator." Some have suggested that "Cool Air" was inspired by Poe's "Facts in the Case of M. Valdemar," which is reasonable considering the similarities in subject matter, Lovecraft's fondness for Poe, and the fact that he had been working on the Poe chapter of "Supernatural Horror in Literature" around the time he wrote "Cool Air."[39] But Lovecraft himself gives this genesis for the story:

> The house described in "Cool Air" is an actual one—in which a friend of mine once had quarters. As to the source of "Cool Air"—while "M. Valdemar" has always been a favourite of mine, I don't think it was the primary element behind the tale. The genesis was less direct. One idea was to embody the general repulsiveness of New York's run-down sections—a theme also manifest in "He" & "Red Hook". That place in 14th St. is a portrait from life of a seedy joint on whose ground floor my friend George Kirk had a book shop (he still conducts the business—long ago moved to 58 W. 8th St.). More than that—I wanted somehow to embody the terrible (though

---

38. In May 1934, when HPL presented his notebook to R. H. Barlow in exchange for a typescript prepared by Barlow, HPL appended the entry the notes "Cool Air" and "1922?" (written initially as 1921). HPL clearly was uncertain about when he had made the entry, and no evidence has been found thus far to date it unequivocally to either 1921 or 1922.

39. HPL to Lillian D. Clark, 5 March 1926 (ms., JHL): "My article is now dealing with Poe, & in preparing it I am re-reading whatever I describe in detail, in order to achieve perfect accuracy. What a marvellous yarn 'Arthur Gordon Pym' is!"

not wholly new) idea of a person needing some constant artificial aid in order not to lapse into some grotesque & hideous state. If any one tale unconsciously influenced me, it was probably Machen's "White Powder" (in "The Three Impostors") rather than "M. Valdemar". Yes—I think the idea of *decadence from some familiar norm* tends to be more horrible than that of *sheer alienage to the normal. Decay* links the horror more closely to the familiar world around us, & to the beings of that world.[40]

If the unconscious influence upon the story was Arthur Machen's "Novel of the White Powder," it is possible that the note in Lovecraft's commonplace book dates to the summer of 1923, when he first became acquainted with Machen's work. But on the other hand, the note could have been inspired by anything, and only the rereading of Machen in late 1925 as part of Lovecraft's research for "Supernatural Horror in Literature" helped the idea to gel into an actual story.

To be sure, other entries in Lovecraft's commonplace book seem to have exerted some influence on "Cool Air":

16 The walking dead—seemingly alive, but—
53 Hand of dead man writes.
65 Riley's fear of undertakers—door locked on inside after death.
112 Man lives near graveyard—how does he live? Eats no food.

Dr. Muñoz literally is a walking dead man. He is the dead man who leaves the scrawled note at the end of the story. He does not fear undertakers, perhaps, but he acknowledges that he is a sworn enemy of death; and he does lock his apartment from the inside at the story's end. And while he is not guilty of necrophagy, he does "live" without sustenance. More tellingly, Lovecraft considered *himself* to be not unlike a dead man during his exile, as evidenced in his celebrated homecoming letter to Frank Belknap Long: "Who am I? What am I? Where am I? I—a corpse—once lived, and here are the signs of resurrection!" And as he observed the scenes of home on the train ride to Providence, he rejoices, "GOD, I AM ALIVE!"[41]

The setting of the story is the brownstone at 317 West 14th Street occupied by George W. Kirk, both as a residence and as one incarnation of his Chelsea Book Shop. Kirk had formerly occupied the apartment above Lovecraft's at 169 Clinton but left there as early as May 1925. He settled at the 14th Street boarding house in August but stayed there only until October before moving again. Lovecraft had access to the brownstone for only

---

40. HPL to Henry Kuttner, 29 July 1936 (transcript, SHSW).
41. HPL to Frank Belknap Long, 1 May 1926 (*SL* 2.45–46).

two months or so, but even so he "knew [it] very well—my friend George Kirk having a bookshop on the ground floor."[42]

> Kirk has hired a pair of immense Victorian rooms as combined office & residence. . . . It is a typical Victorian home of New York's "Age of Innocence", with tiled hall, carved marble mantels, vast pier glasses & mantel mirrors with massive gilt frames, incredibly high ceilings covered with stucco ornamentation, round arched doorways with elaborate rococo pediments, & all the other earmarks of New York's age of vast wealth & impossible taste. Kirk's rooms are the great ground-floor parlours, connected by an open arch, & having windows only in the front room. These two windows open to the south on 14th St., & have the disadvantage of admitting all the babel & clangour of that great crosstown thoroughfare with its teeming traffick & ceaseless street-cars.[43]

The story, however, is also suggested by Lovecraft's own apartment at 169 Clinton Street.

> Naturally I would have shunned a lodging which seemed to savour of coarseness, but here again unusual conditions conspired to deceive me. I still think that none but a seer and prophet could have escaped error, and that the house *had* until almost that precise time been of the quality I thought I had found. My guess is that its decay had just set in, owing to the spread of the Syrian fringe (all unsuspected by me) beyond Atlantic Avenue. The man having my room before me was a N.Y.U. professor, and there was still in the house a splendid young chap who knew people that I knew in Providence. The landlady was a refined-looking woman with two prepossessing youths as sons, and with a British accent of such absolutely authentic caste that there can have been no mistake about her tale of better days—the usual thing—and her claim of being the daughter of a cultivated Anglican vicar in Ireland, educated in a private school in England. Poor old Mrs. Burns! Only later was I to learn of her shrewish tongue, desperate household negligence, miserly watchfulness of lights and unwatchfulness of repairs, and reckless indifference to the class of lodger she admitted! I think her decadence must have been a gradual one—probably she wanted good lodgers, for she seemed naively impressed with the traditions which my books and furniture and effects seemed to imply, and vowed that they gave her wistful memories of her childhood home at the vicarage in Ireland; but she must have stopped asking references when the sinking of the neighbourhood made the house harder and harder to fill with people of the right sort. I was soon disillusioned—and with what a thud! Voices came from the next room—and *what* voices! Of course poor Mrs. Burns apologised for these particular roomers, of whom she said she was very anxious

---

42. HPL to F. Lee Baldwin, 13 January 1934 (ms., JHL).
43. HPL to Lillian D. Clark, 19–23 August 1925 (ms., JHL).

to get rid—but when I began to see some of the other anthropological types in the hallway my cynicism began to mount. Friends who came to see me—better versed in Brooklyn ways than I, for my metropolitan residence had been confined to the quiet section of Flatbush—were quicker than I to see and tell me what a wretched hole I had crawled into; but by that time I was all settled, and with my desperate finances the idea of a removal was quite impossible. I had only moved twice before in all my life, and was encamped amongst all my effects—for such is my ingrained domesticity that I could not live anywhere without my own household objects around me—the furniture my childhood knew, the books my ancestors read, and the pictures my mother and grandmother and aunt painted. The presence of all these things at the edge of Red Hook was really almost humorous, (although Dr. Love across the street was no doubt equally surrounded by his cherished hereditary things) and visitors not infrequently commented on the virtual transition from one world to another implied in the simple act of stepping within my door. Outside—Red Hook. Inside—Providence, R.I.! For it has always been Providence wherever I have been, and must always remain so. That is the valuable lesson I extracted from my asinine metropolitan experiment—a lesson which will teach me not to separate the spiritual from the geographical Providence again. But at the outset I was deluded. Comically enough, I even persuaded a friend—George Kirk, formerly of Cleveland—to take the room above mine, and for several months we had the mild amusement of telegraphing on the steam-pipes—for one quickly falls into boorish ways in a boorish milieu. Kirk has no sense of neatness, . . . so held out uncomplainingly till May; when, having fewer non-portable chattels than I, he betook himself to gay Manhattan. But laden as I was, I stuck; hence came to know that squalid world as few white men have ever known it. The sounds in the hall! The faces glimpsed on the stairs! The mice in the partitions! The fleeting touches of intangible horror from spheres and cycles outside time . . . . once a *Syrian* had the room next to mine and played eldritch and whining monotones on a strange bagpipe which made me dream ghoulish and incredible things of crypts under Bagdad and limitless corridors of Eblis beneath the moon-cursed ruins of Istakhar. I never *saw* this man, and my privilege to imagine him in any shape I chose lent glamour to his weird pneumatic cacophonies. In my vision he always wore a turban and long robe of pale figured silk, and had a right eye plucked out because it had looked upon something in a tomb at night which no eye may look upon and live. In truth, I never saw with actual sight the majority of my fellow-lodgers. I only *heard* them loathsomely— and sometimes glimpsed faces of sinister decadence in the hall. There was an old Turk under me, who used to get letters with outr, stamps from the Levant. Alexander D. Messayeh—Messayeh—what a name from the Arabian Nights! I suppose the praenomen implied a Greek strain—those Near-East spawn are hopelessly mongrelised, and belong for the most part to the Orthodox Greek Church. And what scraps of old papers with Arabic lettering did one find about the house! . . . The keynote of the whole setting—house, neighbourhood, and shop, was that of loathsome

ting—house, neighbourhood, and shop, was that of loathsome and insidious decay; masked just enough by the reliques of former splendour and
beauty to add terror and mystery and the fascination of crawling motion to
a deadness and dinginess otherwise static and prosaic. I conceived the idea
that the great brownstone house was a malignly sentient thing—a dead,
vampire creature which sucked something out of those within it and im-
planted in them the seeds of some horrible and immaterial psychic growth.
Every closed door seemed to hide some brooding crime—or blasphemy
too deep to form a crime in the crude and superficial calendar of earth. I
never quite learned the exact topography of that rambling and enormous
house. How to get to my room, and to Kirk's room when he was there,
and to the landlady's quarters to pay my rent or ask in vain for heat until I
bought an oil stove of my own—these things I knew, but there were wings
and corridors I never traversed; doors to rear and abutting halls and stair-
ways that I never saw opened. I know there were rooms above ground
without windows, and was at liberty to guess what might lie below ground.
There lay a pall of darkness and secrecy upon that house—it subtly dis-
couraged from first to last one's inclination to speak aloud, and at times
one felt a faint miasmal tangibility in the circumambient air. The great high
rooms had something of the mausolean in their crumbling stateliness, and
in the halls at night one always had to be sure the great, white flamboyant
Corinthian pilasters never moved just the least bit. Something unwholesome—something furtive—something vast lying subterrenely in obnoxious
slumber—that was the soul of 169 Clinton St. at the edge of Red Hook,
and in my great northwest corner room "The Horror" was written.[44]

Aside from the literary and geographic influences mentioned, the most
intimately personal was Lovecraft's well-known aversion to cold weather.
But whereas Dr. Muñoz created an artificially frigid habitat in which to survive (he needs refrigeration because he is, in fact, dead), Lovecraft required
very warm temperatures not only for comfort but for his very health. And
just as Lovecraft could barely navigate a pen across paper if the temperature
fell below 75°, Dr. Muñoz's last message, written as the temperature in his
apartment continued to rise, was reduced to a barely legible scrawl.

. . . yesterday was a day after my own heart—90° in the shade. Haven't felt so well since I was in New Orleans a year ago. I may not have
mentioned that I have a sort of tropical physique—have never been too
hot (don't know what the term means!) in my life, never feel really good
under 80°, can't control my muscles well enough to write legibly under
about 75°, & can't do anything but hibernate in winter. I crumple all up,
physically & mentally, in the cold, & have actually lost consciousness at
+14°. I have to stay indoors any winter day when the outside thermome-
ter reads less than +20°. The only 2 months that I have ever felt really

---

44. HPL to Bernard Austin Dwyer, 26 March 1927 (*SL* 2.114–18).

vigorous—uninterruptedly, that is—were those I spent in Florida—May & June 1931. I ought to live in the subtropics, but am so attached to the scenery & traditions of my native region that I can't break away. As a result, I feel really up to par only about 10 days each year. [45]

Lovecraft virtually hibernated in winter, and even in warmer months relied upon an oil heater, or the gas range, to provide heat. The free steam heat at his last residence allowed him to live comfortably without great expense.

"Cool Air" reworks a familiar theme, explored previously in "Herbert West—Reanimator" and, to a lesser degree, "The Horror at Red Hook." Nor was "Cool Air" Lovecraft's last word on revivification of the dead, for he revisited it at length in *The Case of Charles Dexter Ward.* He was always rather fond of "Cool Air," but it was not received with much favor. *Weird Tales* rejected the story, probably around April 1926, for much the same reason as "In the Vault"—excessive gruesomeness. It is not certain, but it is likely that "Cool Air" was among three stories that Lovecraft submitted to *Ghost Stories* in late August, all rejected.[46] Lovecraft next submitted "Cool Air" with seven other stories to *Tales of Magic & Mystery.* The stories were steadily returned until "after rejecting seven of my tales, [the magazine] finally accepted 'Cool Air'. I shall be glad to see the promised reward, due next month."[47] The story "only brought me $18.00. I haven't counted the words, but fancy this rate is only half or ¾ as much as the normal W.T. rate."[48] In fact, the publishers did not even send Lovecraft a copy of the magazine, and he had to buy his own.

—David E. Schultz and S. T. Joshi

---

45. HPL to Robert Bloch, 9 June 1933, *H. P. Lovecraft: Letters to Robert Bloch* (West Warwick, RI: Necronomicon Press, 1993), p. 18.

46. *Ghost Stories* was published by Constructive Publishing Co. from July 1926 to March 1930; Good Story Magazine Co. from April 1930 to December 1931/January 1932. It was a companion magazine to *True Story* and *True Detective Stories,* and employed a confession format. HPL submitted "In the Vault" and "Cool Air," and possibly "The Nameless City." "Pickman's Model" (written c. September 1926), has a somewhat "colloquial" tone not previously found in his fiction (there is a slight leaning toward such in "Cool Air") and it may have been written with *Ghost Stories* in mind, although it does not appear that HPL ever submitted the story there.

47. HPL to August Derleth, [6 January 1928] (ms., SHSW).

48. "Cool Air" has roughly 3,440 words, and so the rate was 0.5¢ a word, well below what *Weird Tales* was paying HPL. HPL later claimed to correspondents that he receive $17.00 or $17.50, but he undoubtedly received $18.00 as he told August Derleth at the time the story was published.

From the Pest Zone:
The New York Stories

The John Mawney House at 135 Benefit Street in Providence, known as "The Shunned House."

The Shunned House

I.

From even the greatest of horrors irony is seldom absent. Sometimes it enters directly into the composition of the events, while sometimes it relates only to their fortuitous position among persons and places. The latter sort is splendidly exemplified by a case in the ancient city of Providence, where in the late forties Edgar Allan Poe used to sojourn often during his unsuccessful wooing of the gifted poetess, Mrs. Whitman.[1] Poe generally stopped at the Mansion House in Benefit Street—the renamed Golden Ball Inn[2] whose roof has sheltered Washington, Jefferson, and Lafayette—and his favourite walk led northward along the same street to Mrs. Whitman's home and the neighbouring hillside churchyard of St. John's,[3] whose hidden expanse of eighteenth-century gravestones had for him a peculiar fascination.

Now the irony is this. In this walk, so many times repeated, the world's greatest master of the terrible and the bizarre was obliged to pass a particular house on the eastern side of the street; a dingy, antiquated structure perched on the abruptly rising side-hill,[4] with a great unkempt yard dating from a time when the region was partly open country. It does not appear that he ever wrote or spoke of it, nor is there any evidence that he even noticed it. And yet that house, to the two persons in possession of certain information, equals or outranks in horror the wildest phantasy of the genius who so often passed it unknowingly, and stands starkly leering as a symbol of all that is unutterably hideous.

The house was—and for that matter still is—of a kind to attract the attention of the curious. Originally a farm or semi-farm building, it followed the average New England colonial lines of the middle eighteenth century—the prosperous peaked-roof[5] sort, with two stories and dormerless attic, and with the Georgian doorway and interior panelling dictated by the progress of taste at that time. It faced south, with one gable end buried to the lower windows in the eastward rising hill, and the other exposed to the foundations toward the street. Its construction, over a century and a half ago, had followed the grading and straightening of the road in that especial vicinity; for Benefit Street—at first called Back Street—was laid out as a lane winding amongst the graveyards of the first settlers, and straightened only when the removal of the bodies to the North Burial Ground[6] made it decently possible to cut through the old family plots.

At the start, the western wall had lain some twenty feet up a pre-cipitous lawn from the roadway; but a widening of the street at about the time of the Revolution sheared off most of the intervening space, exposing the foundations so that a brick basement wall had to be made, giving the deep cellar a street frontage with door and two windows above ground, close to the new line of public travel. When the sidewalk was laid out a century ago the last of the intervening space was re-moved; and Poe in his walks must have seen only sheer ascent of dull grey brick flush with the sidewalk and surmounted at a height of ten
10   feet by the antique shingled bulk of the house proper.

The farm-like grounds extended back very deeply up the hill, al-most to Wheaton Street. The space south of the house, abutting on Benefit Street, was of course greatly above the existing sidewalk level, forming a terrace bounded by a high bank wall of damp, mossy stone pierced by a steep flight of narrow steps which led inward between canyon-like surfaces to the upper region of mangy lawn, rheumy brick walls, and neglected gardens whose dismantled cement urns, rusted kettles fallen from tripods of knotty sticks, and similar paraphernalia set off the weather-beaten front door with its broken fanlight, rotting Ionic
20   pilasters,[7] and wormy triangular pediment.

What I heard in my youth about the shunned house was merely that people died there in alarmingly great numbers. That, I was told, was why the original owners had moved out some twenty years after building the place. It was plainly unhealthy, perhaps because of the dampness and fungous growth in the cellar, the general sickish smell, the draughts of the hallways, or the quality of the well and pump water. These things were bad enough, and these were all that gained belief among the persons whom I knew. Only the notebooks of my anti-quarian uncle, Dr. Elihu Whipple,[8] revealed to me at length the darker,
30   vaguer surmises which formed an undercurrent of folklore among old-time servants and humble folk; surmises which never travelled far, and which were largely forgotten when Providence grew to be a metropolis with a shifting modern population.

The fact is, that the house was never regarded by the solid part of the community as in any real sense "haunted". There were no wide-spread tales of rattling chains, cold currents of air, extinguished lights, or faces at the window.[9] Extremists sometimes said the house was "unlucky", but that is as far as even they went. What was really beyond dispute is that a frightful proportion of persons died there; or more ac-
40   curately, *had* died there, since after some peculiar happenings over sixty years ago the building had become deserted through the sheer impossi-bility of renting it.[10] These persons were not all cut off suddenly by any

one cause; rather did it seem that their vitality was insidiously sapped,
so that each one died the sooner from whatever tendency to weakness
he may have naturally had. And those who did not die displayed in
varying degree a type of anaemia or consumption,[11] and sometimes a
decline of the mental faculties, which spoke ill for the salubriousness[12]
of the building. Neighbouring houses, it must be added, seemed entirely free from the noxious quality.

This much I knew before my insistent questioning led my uncle to
shew me the notes which finally embarked us both on our hideous in-
10   vestigation. In my childhood the shunned house was vacant, with barren, gnarled, and terrible old trees, long, queerly pale grass, and
nightmarishly misshapen weeds in the high terraced yard where birds
never lingered. We boys used to overrun the place, and I can still recall
my youthful terror not only at the morbid strangeness of this sinister
vegetation, but at the eldritch atmosphere and odour of the dilapidated
house, whose unlocked front door was often entered in quest of shud-
ders. The small-paned windows were largely broken, and a nameless air
of desolation hung round the precarious panelling, shaky interior shut-
ters, peeling wall-paper, falling plaster, rickety staircases, and such
20   fragments of battered furniture as still remained. The dust and cobwebs
added their touch of the fearful; and brave indeed was the boy who
would voluntarily ascend the ladder to the attic, a vast raftered length
lighted only by small blinking windows[13] in the gable ends, and filled
with a massed wreckage of chests, chairs, and spinning-wheels which
infinite years of deposit had shrouded and festooned into monstrous
and hellish shapes.

But after all, the attic was not the most terrible part of the house. It
was the dank, humid cellar which somehow exerted the strongest repulsion on us, even though it was wholly above ground on the street side,
30   with only a thin door and window-pierced brick wall to separate it from
the busy sidewalk. We scarcely knew whether to haunt it in spectral fascination, or to shun it for the sake of our souls and our sanity. For one
thing, the bad odour of the house was strongest there; and for another
thing, we did not like the white fungous growths which occasionally
sprang up in rainy summer weather from the hard earth floor. Those
fungi, grotesquely like the vegetation in the yard outside, were truly horrible in their outlines; detestable parodies of toadstools and Indian
pipes,[14] whose like we had never seen in any other situation. They rotted
quickly, and at one stage became slightly phosphorescent; so that noctur-
40   nal passers-by sometimes spoke of witch-fires glowing behind the broken
panes of the foetor-spreading windows.

We never—even in our wildest Hallowe'en moods—visited this cellar by night, but in some of our daytime visits could detect the phosphorescence, especially when the day was dark and wet. There was also a subtler thing we often thought we detected—a very strange thing which was, however, merely suggestive at most. I refer to a sort of cloudy whitish pattern on the dirt floor—a vague, shifting deposit of mould or nitre[15] which we sometimes thought we could trace amidst the sparse fungous growths near the huge fireplace of the basement kitchen. Once in a while it struck us that this patch bore an uncanny
10   resemblance to a doubled-up human figure, though generally no such kinship existed, and often there was no whitish deposit whatever.[16] On a certain rainy afternoon when this illusion seemed phenomenally strong, and when, in addition, I had fancied I glimpsed a kind of thin, yellowish, shimmering exhalation rising from the nitrous pattern toward the yawning fireplace, I spoke to my uncle about the matter. He smiled at this odd conceit, but it seemed that his smile was tinged with reminiscence. Later I heard that a similar notion entered into some of the wild ancient tales of the common folk—a notion likewise alluding to ghoulish, wolfish shapes taken by smoke from the great chimney,
20   and queer contours assumed by certain of the sinuous tree-roots that thrust their way into the cellar through the loose foundation-stones.[17]

II.

Not till my adult years did my uncle set before me the notes and data which he had collected concerning the shunned house. Dr. Whipple was a sane, conservative physician of the old school,[18] and for all his interest in the place was not eager to encourage young thoughts toward the abnormal. His own view, postulating simply a building and location of markedly unsanitary qualities, had nothing to do with abnormality; but he realised that the very picturesqueness which aroused
30   his own interest would in a boy's fanciful mind take on all manner of gruesome imaginative associations.

The doctor was a bachelor; a white-haired, clean-shaven, old-fashioned gentleman, and a local historian of note, who had often broken a lance with such controversial guardians of tradition as Sidney S. Rider and Thomas W. Bicknell.[19] He lived with one manservant in a Georgian homestead with knocker and iron-railed steps, balanced eerily on a steep ascent of North Court Street[20] beside the ancient brick court and colony house[21] where his grandfather—a cousin of that celebrated privateersman, Capt. Whipple,[22] who burnt His Majesty's armed
40   schooner *Gaspee* in 1772[23]—had voted in the legislature on May 4, 1776, for the independence of the Rhode-Island Colony. Around him

in the damp, low-ceiled library with the musty white panelling, heavy carved overmantel,[24] and small-paned, vine-shaded windows, were the relics and records of his ancient family, among which were many dubious allusions to the shunned house in Benefit Street. That pest spot lies not far distant—for Benefit runs ledgewise just above the court-house along the precipitous hill up which the first settlement climbed.

When, in the end, my insistent pestering and maturing years evoked from my uncle the hoarded lore I sought, there lay before me a strange enough chronicle. Long-winded, statistical, and drearily genea-
10   logical as some of the matter was, there ran through it a continuous thread of brooding, tenacious horror and preternatural malevolence which impressed me even more than it had impressed the good doctor. Separate events fitted together uncannily, and seemingly irrelevant details held mines of hideous possibilities. A new and burning curiosity grew in me, compared to which my boyish curiosity was feeble and inchoate.[25] The first revelation led to an exhaustive research, and finally to that shuddering quest which proved so disastrous to myself and mine. For at last my uncle insisted on joining the search I had commenced, and after a certain night in that house he did not come away
20   with me. I am lonely without that gentle soul whose long years were filled only with honour, virtue, good taste, benevolence, and learning. I have reared a marble urn to his memory in St. John's churchyard—the place that Poe loved—the hidden grove of giant willows on the hill, where tombs and headstones huddle quietly between the hoary bulk of the church and the houses and bank walls of Benefit Street.

The history of the house, opening amidst a maze of dates, revealed no trace of the sinister either about its construction or about the prosperous and honourable family who built it. Yet from the first a taint of calamity, soon increased to boding significance, was apparent. My un-
30   cle's carefully compiled record began with the building of the structure in 1763,[26] and followed the theme with an unusual amount of detail. The shunned house, it seems, was first inhabited by William Harris and his wife Rhoby Dexter, with their children, Elkanah, born in 1755, Abigail, born in 1757, William, Jr., born in 1759, and Ruth, born in 1761. Harris was a substantial merchant and seaman in the West India trade, connected with the firm of Obadiah Brown and his nephews.[27] After Brown's death in 1761,[28] the new firm of Nicholas Brown & Co. made him master of the brig *Prudence*, Providence-built, of 120 tons, thus enabling him to erect the new homestead he had desired ever
40   since his marriage.

The site he had chosen—a recently straightened part of the new and fashionable Back Street, which ran along the side of the hill above crowded Cheapside[29]—was all that could be wished, and the building did justice to the location. It was the best that moderate means could afford, and Harris hastened to move in before the birth of a fifth child which the family expected. That child, a boy, came in December; but was still-born. Nor was any child to be born alive in that house for a century and a half.

The next April sickness occurred among the children, and Abigail and Ruth died before the month was over. Dr. Job Ives diagnosed the trouble as some infantile fever, though others declared it was more of a
10 mere wasting-away or decline. It seemed, in any event, to be contagious; for Hannah Bowen, one of the two servants, died of it in the following June. Eli Liddeason, the other servant, constantly complained of weakness; and would have returned to his father's farm in Rehoboth[30] but for a sudden attachment for Mehitabel Pierce, who was hired to succeed Hannah. He died the next year—a sad year indeed, since it marked the death of William Harris himself, enfeebled as he was by the climate of Martinique,[31] where his occupation had kept him for considerable periods during the preceding decade.

The widowed Rhoby Harris never recovered from the shock of her
20 husband's death, and the passing of her first-born Elkanah two years later was the final blow to her reason. In 1768 she fell victim to a mild form of insanity, and was thereafter confined to the upper part of the house;[32] her elder maiden sister, Mercy Dexter, having moved in to take charge of the family. Mercy was a plain, raw-boned woman of great strength; but her health visibly declined from the time of her advent. She was greatly devoted to her unfortunate sister, and had an especial affection for her only surviving nephew William, who from a sturdy infant had become a sickly, spindling lad. In this year the servant Mehitabel died, and the other servant, Preserved Smith, left without coherent
30 explanation—or at least, with only some wild tales and a complaint that he disliked the smell of the place. For a time Mercy could secure no more help, since the seven deaths and case of madness, all occurring within five years' space, had begun to set in motion the body of fireside rumour which later became so bizarre. Ultimately, however, she obtained new servants from out of town; Ann White, a morose woman from the part of North Kingstown now set off as the township of Exeter,[33] and a capable Boston man named Zenas Low.

It was Ann White who first gave definite shape to the sinister idle talk. Mercy should have known better than to hire anyone from the
40 Nooseneck Hill country,[34] for that remote bit of backwoods was then, as now, a seat of the most uncomfortable superstitions. As lately as 1892 an Exeter community exhumed a dead body and ceremoniously burnt its

heart in order to prevent certain alleged visitations injurious to the public health and peace, and one may imagine the point of view of the same section in 1768.[35] Ann's tongue was perniciously active, and within a few months Mercy discharged her, filling her place with a faithful and amiable Amazon[36] from Newport, Maria Robbins.

Meanwhile poor Rhoby Harris, in her madness, gave voice to dreams and imaginings of the most hideous sort. At times her screams became insupportable, and for long periods she would utter shrieking horrors which necessitated her son's temporary residence with his cousin, Peleg Harris, in Presbyterian-Lane[37] near the new college building.[38] The boy would seem to improve after these visits, and had Mercy been as wise as she was well-meaning, she would have let him live permanently with Peleg. Just what Mrs. Harris cried out in her fits of violence, tradition hesitates to say; or rather, presents such extravagant accounts that they nullify themselves through sheer absurdity. Certainly it sounds absurd to hear that a woman educated only in the rudiments of French often shouted for hours in a coarse and idiomatic form of that language, or that the same person, alone and guarded, complained wildly of a staring thing which bit and chewed at her. In 1772 the servant Zenas died, and when Mrs. Harris heard of it she laughed with a shocking delight utterly foreign to her. The next year she herself died, and was laid to rest in the North Burial Ground beside her husband.

Upon the outbreak of trouble with Great Britain in 1775, William Harris, despite his scant sixteen years and feeble constitution, managed to enlist in the Army of Observation[39] under General Greene;[40] and from that time on enjoyed a steady rise in health and prestige. In 1780, as a Captain in Rhode Island forces in New Jersey under Colonel Angell,[41] he met and married Phebe Hetfield of Elizabethtown,[42] whom he brought to Providence upon his honourable discharge in the following year.

The young soldier's return was not a thing of unmitigated happiness. The house, it is true, was still in good condition; and the street had been widened and changed in name from Back Street to Benefit Street. But Mercy Dexter's once robust frame had undergone a sad and curious decay, so that she was now a stooped and pathetic figure with hollow voice and disconcerting pallor—qualities shared to a singular degree by the one remaining servant Maria. In the autumn of 1782 Phebe Harris gave birth to a still-born daughter, and on the fifteenth of the next May Mercy Dexter took leave of a useful, austere, and virtuous life.

William Harris, at last thoroughly convinced of the radically unhealthful nature of his abode, now took steps toward quitting and

closing it forever. Securing temporary quarters for himself and his wife at the newly opened Golden Ball Inn, he arranged for the building of a new and finer house in Westminster Street, in the growing part of the town across the Great Bridge.[43] There, in 1785, his son Dutee[44] was born; and there the family dwelt till the encroachments of commerce drove them back across the river and over the hill to Angell Street, in the newer East Side residence district, where the late Archer Harris built his sumptuous but hideous French-roofed mansion in 1876.[45] William and Phebe both succumbed to the yellow fever epidemic of
10   1797,[46] but Dutee was brought up by his cousin Rathbone Harris,[47] Peleg's son.

Rathbone was a practical man, and rented the Benefit Street house despite William's wish to keep it vacant. He considered it an obligation to his ward to make the most of all the boy's property, nor did he concern himself with the deaths and illnesses which caused so many changes of tenants, or the steadily growing aversion with which the house was generally regarded. It is likely that he felt only vexation when, in 1804, the town council ordered him to fumigate the place with sulphur, tar, and gum camphor[48] on account of the much-discussed
20   deaths of four persons, presumably caused by the then diminishing fever epidemic. They said the place had a febrile[49] smell.

Dutee himself thought little of the house, for he grew up to be a privateersman,[50] and served with distinction on the *Vigilant*[51] under Capt. Cahoone[52] in the War of 1812. He returned unharmed, married in 1814, and became a father on that memorable night of September 23, 1815, when a great gale[53] drove the waters of the bay over half the town, and floated a tall sloop well up Westminster Street so that its masts almost tapped the Harris windows in symbolic affirmation that the new boy, Welcome, was a seaman's son.
30   Welcome did not survive his father, but lived to perish gloriously at Fredericksburg[54] in 1862. Neither he nor his son Archer knew of the shunned house as other than a nuisance almost impossible to rent— perhaps on account of the mustiness and sickly odour of unkempt old age. Indeed, it never was rented after a series of deaths culminating in 1861, which the excitement of the war tended to throw into obscurity. Carrington Harris, last of the male line, knew it only as a deserted and somewhat picturesque centre of legend until I told him my experience. He had meant to tear it down and build an apartment house on the site, but after my account decide to let it stand, install plumbing, and rent it.
40   Nor has he yet had any difficulty in obtaining tenants. The horror has gone.

III.

It may well be imagined how powerfully I was affected by the annals of the Harrises. In this continuous record there seemed to me to brood a persistent evil beyond anything in Nature as I had known it; an evil clearly connected with the house and not with the family. This impression was confirmed by my uncle's less systematic array of miscellaneous data—legends transcribed from servant gossip, cuttings from the papers,[55] copies of death-certificates by fellow-physicians, and the like. All of this material I cannot hope to give, for my uncle was a tireless anti-
10   quarian and very deeply interested in the shunned house; but I may refer to several dominant points which earn notice by their recurrence through many reports from diverse sources. For example, the servant gossip was practically unanimous in attributing to the fungous and malodorous *cellar* of the house a vast supremacy in evil influence. There had been servants—Ann White especially—who would not use the cellar kitchen, and at least three well-defined legends bore upon the queer quasi-human or diabolic outlines assumed by tree-roots and patches of mould in that region. These latter narratives interested me profoundly, on account of what I had seen in my boyhood, but I felt that most of the significance
20   had in each case been largely obscured by additions from the common stock of local ghost lore.

Ann White, with her Exeter superstition, had promulgated the most extravagant and at the same time most consistent tale; alleging that there must lie buried beneath the house one of those vampires[56]— the dead who retain their bodily form and live on the blood or breath of the living—whose hideous legions send their preying shapes or spirits abroad by night. To destroy a vampire one must, the grandmothers say, exhume it and burn its heart, or at least drive a stake through that organ; and Ann's dogged insistence on a search under the cellar had
30   been prominent in bringing about her discharge.

Her tales, however, commanded a wide audience, and were the more readily accepted because the house indeed stood on land once used for burial purposes. To me their interest depended less on this circumstance than on the peculiarly appropriate way in which they dovetailed with certain other things—the complaint of the departing servant Preserved Smith, who had preceded Ann and never heard of her, that something "sucked his breath" at night; the death-certificates of fever victims of 1804, issued by Dr. Chad Hopkins,[57] and shewing the four deceased persons all unaccountably lacking in blood; and the obscure
40   passages of poor Rhoby Harris's ravings, where she complained of the sharp teeth of a glassy-eyed, half-visible presence.

Free from unwarranted superstition though I am, these things produced in me an odd sensation, which was intensified by a pair of widely
separated newspaper cuttings relating to deaths in the shunned
house—one from the *Providence Gazette and Country-Journal*[58] of April 12,
1815, and the other from the *Daily Transcript and Chronicle*[59] of October
27, 1845—each of which detailed an appallingly grisly circumstance
whose duplication was remarkable. It seems that in both instances the
dying person, in 1815 a gentle old lady named Stafford and in 1845 a
school-teacher of middle age named Eleazar Durfee,[60] became trans-
10   figured in a horrible way; glaring glassily and attempting to bite the
throat of the attending physician. Even more puzzling, though, was the
final case which put an end to the renting of the house—a series of
anaemia deaths preceded by progressive madnesses wherein the patient
would craftily attempt the lives of his relatives by incisions in the neck
or wrist.

This was in 1860 and 1861, when my uncle had just begun his
medical practice; and before leaving for the front he heard much of it
from his elder professional colleagues. The really inexplicable thing was
the way in which the victims—ignorant people, for the ill-smelling and
20   widely shunned house could now be rented to no others—would babble maledictions in French, a language they could not possibly have
studied to any extent. It made one think of poor Rhoby Harris nearly a
century before, and so moved my uncle that he commenced collecting
historical data on the house after listening, some time subsequent to his
return from the war, to the first-hand account of Drs. Chase and
Whitmarsh. Indeed, I could see that my uncle had thought deeply on
the subject, and that he was glad of my own interest—an open-minded
and sympathetic interest which enabled him to discuss with me matters
at which others would merely have laughed. His fancy had not gone so
30   far as mine, but he felt that the place was rare in its imaginative poten-
tialities, and worthy of note as an inspiration in the field of the grotesque and macabre.

For my part, I was disposed to take the whole subject with profound seriousness, and began at once not only to review the evidence,
but to accumulate as much more as I could. I talked with the elderly
Archer Harris, then owner of the house, many times before his death
in 1916; and obtained from him and his still surviving maiden sister
Alice an authentic corroboration of all the family data my uncle had
collected. When, however, I asked them what connexion with France
40   or its language the house could have, they confessed themselves as
frankly baffled and ignorant as I. Archer knew nothing, and all that
Miss Harris could say was that an old allusion her grandfather, Dutee

Harris, had heard of might have shed a little light. The old seaman, who had survived his son Welcome's death in battle by two years, had not himself known the legend; but recalled that his earliest nurse, the ancient Maria Robbins, seemed darkly aware of something that might have lent a weird significance to the French ravings of Rhoby Harris, which she had so often heard during the last days of that hapless woman. Maria had been at the shunned house from 1769 till the removal of the family in 1783, and had seen Mercy Dexter die. Once she hinted to the child Dutee of a somewhat peculiar circumstance in

10   Mercy's last moments, but he had soon forgotten all about it save that it was something peculiar. The granddaughter, moreover, recalled even this much with difficulty. She and her brother were not so much interested in the house as was Archer's son Carrington, the present owner, with whom I talked after my experience.

Having exhausted the Harris family of all the information it could furnish, I turned my attention to early town records and deeds with a zeal more penetrating than that which my uncle had occasionally shewn in the same work. What I wished was a comprehensive history of the site from its very settlement in 1636—or even before, if any Narragansett Indian[61]

20   legend could be unearthed to supply the data. I found, at the start, that the land had been part of the long strip of home lot granted originally to John Throckmorton;[62] one of many similar strips beginning at the Town Street[63] beside the river and extending up over the hill to a line roughly corresponding with the modern Hope Street. The Throckmorton lot had later, of course, been much subdivided; and I became very assiduous in tracing that section through which Back or Benefit Street was later run. It had, a rumour indeed said, been the Throckmorton graveyard; but as I examined the records more carefully, I found that the graves had all been transferred at an early date to the North Burial Ground on the Pawtucket

30   West Road.[64]

Then suddenly I came—by a rare piece of chance, since it was not in the main body of records and might easily have been missed—upon something which aroused my keenest eagerness, fitting in as it did with several of the queerest phases of the affair.[65] It was the record of a lease, in 1697, of a small tract of ground to an Etienne Roulet and wife. At last the French element had appeared—that, and another deeper element of horror which the name conjured up from the darkest recesses of my weird and heterogeneous reading—and I feverishly studied the platting of the locality as it had been before the cutting through

40   and partial straightening of Back Street between 1747 and 1758. I found what I had half expected, that where the shunned house now stood the Roulets had laid out their graveyard behind a one-story and

attic cottage, and that no record of any transfer of graves existed. The
document, indeed, ended in much confusion; and I was forced to ran-
sack both the Rhode Island Historical Society[66] and Shepley Library[67]
before I could find a local door which the name Etienne Roulet would
unlock. In the end I did find something; something of such vague but
monstrous import that I set about at once to examine the cellar of the
shunned house itself with a new and excited minuteness.

The Roulets, it seemed, had come in 1696 from East Greenwich,[68]
down the west shore of Narragansett Bay. They were Huguenots[69]
10   from Caude,[70] and had encountered much opposition before the
Providence selectmen allowed them to settle in the town. Unpopularity
had dogged them in East Greenwich, whither they had come in 1686,
after the revocation of the Edict of Nantes,[71] and rumour said that the
cause of dislike extended beyond mere racial and national prejudice, or
the land disputes which involved other French settlers with the English
in rivalries which not even Governor Andros[72] could quell. But their
ardent Protestantism—too ardent, some whispered—and their evident
distress when virtually driven from the village down the bay, had
moved the sympathy of the town fathers. Here the strangers had been
20   granted a haven; and the swarthy Etienne Roulet, less apt at agriculture
than at reading queer books and drawing queer diagrams, was given a
clerical post in the warehouse at Pardon Tillinghast's[73] wharf, far south
in Town Street. There had, however, been a riot of some sort later
on—perhaps forty years later, after old Roulet's death—and no one
seemed to hear of the family after that.

For a century and more, it appeared, the Roulets had been well
remembered and frequently discussed as vivid incidents in the quiet life
of a New England seaport. Etienne's son Paul, a surly fellow whose er-
ratic conduct had probably provoked the riot which wiped out the
30   family, was particularly a source of speculation; and though Providence
never shared the witchcraft panics of her Puritan neighbours, it was
freely intimated by old wives that his prayers were neither uttered at the
proper time nor directed toward the proper object. All this had undoubtedly formed the basis of the legend known by old Maria Robbins.
What relation it had to the French ravings of Rhoby Harris and other
inhabitants of the shunned house, imagination or future discovery
alone could determine. I wondered how many of those who had known
the legends realised that additional link with the terrible which my wide
reading had given me; that ominous item in the annals of morbid hor-
40   ror which tells of the creature *Jacques Roulet, of Caude,* who in 1598 was
condemned to death as a daemoniac but afterward saved from the
stake by the Paris parliament and shut in a madhouse. He had been

found covered with blood and shreds of flesh in a wood, shortly after the killing and rending of a boy by a pair of wolves.[74] One wolf was seen to lope away unhurt. Surely a pretty hearthside tale, with a queer significance as to name and place; but I decided that the Providence gossips could not have generally known of it. Had they known, the co-incidence of names would have brought some drastic and frightened action—indeed, might not its limited whispering have precipitated the final riot which erased the Roulets from the town?

I now visited the accursed place with increased frequency; studying
10 the unwholesome vegetation of the garden, examining all the walls of the building, and poring over every inch of the earthen cellar floor. Finally, with Carrington Harris's permission, I fitted a key to the disused door opening from the cellar directly upon Benefit Street, preferring to have a more immediate access to the outside world than the dark stairs, ground floor hall, and front door could give. There, where morbidity lurked most thickly, I searched and poked during long afternoons when the sunlight filtered in through the cobwebbed above-ground windows, and a sense of security glowed from the unlocked door which placed me only a few feet from the placid sidewalk outside. Nothing new re-
20 warded my efforts—only the same depressing mustiness and faint suggestions of noxious odours and nitrous outlines on the floor—and I fancy that many pedestrians must have watched me curiously through the broken panes.

At length, upon a suggestion of my uncle's, I decided to try the spot nocturnally; and one stormy midnight ran the beams of an electric torch[75] over the mouldy floor with its uncanny shapes and distorted, half-phosphorescent fungi. The place had dispirited me curiously that evening, and I was almost prepared when I saw—or thought I saw—amidst the whitish deposits a particularly sharp definition of the "hud-
30 dled form" I had suspected from boyhood. Its clearness was astonishing and unprecedented—and as I watched I seemed to see again the thin, yellowish, shimmering exhalation which had startled me on that rainy afternoon so many years before.

Above the anthropomorphic[76] patch of mould by the fireplace it rose; a subtle, sickish, almost luminous vapour which as it hung trembling in the dampness seemed to develop vague and shocking suggestions of form, gradually trailing off into nebulous decay and passing up into the blackness of the great chimney with a foetor in its wake. It was truly horrible, and the more so to me because of what I knew of the
40 spot. Refusing to flee, I watched it fade—and as I watched I felt that it was in turn watching me greedily with eyes more imaginable than visible. When I told my uncle about it he was greatly aroused; and after a tense

hour of reflection, arrived at a definite and drastic decision. Weighing in his mind the importance of the matter, and the significance of our relation to it, he insisted that we both test—and if possible destroy—the horror of the house by a joint night or nights of aggressive vigil in that musty and fungus-cursed cellar.

IV.

On Wednesday, June 25, 1919, after a proper notification of Carrington Harris which did not include surmises as to what we expected to find, my uncle and I conveyed to the shunned house two camp
10   chairs[77] and a folding camp cot, together with some scientific mechanism of greater weight and intricacy. These we placed in the cellar during the day, screening the windows with paper and planning to return in the evening for our first vigil. We had locked the door from the cellar to the ground floor; and having a key to the outside cellar door, we were prepared to leave our expensive and delicate apparatus—which we had obtained secretly and at great cost—as many days as our vigils might need to be protracted. It was our design to sit up together till very late, and then watch singly till dawn in two-hour stretches, myself first and then my companion; the inactive member resting on the cot.
20   The natural leadership with which my uncle procured the instruments from the laboratories of Brown University and the Cranston Street Armoury,[78] and instinctively assumed direction of our venture, was a marvellous commentary on the potential vitality and resilience of a man of eighty-one. Elihu Whipple had lived according to the hygienic laws he had preached as a physician, and but for what happened later would be here in full vigour today. Only two persons suspect what did happen—Carrington Harris and myself. I had to tell Harris because he owned the house and deserved to know what had gone out of it. Then too, we had spoken to him in advance of our quest; and I felt after my
30   uncle's going that he would understand and assist me in some vitally necessary public explanations. He turned very pale, but agreed to help me, and decided that it would now be safe to rent the house.

To declare that we were not nervous on that rainy night of watching would be an exaggeration both gross and ridiculous. We were not, as I have said, in any sense childishly superstitious, but scientific study and reflection had taught us that the known universe of three dimensions embraces the merest fraction of the whole cosmos of substance and energy.[79] In this case an overwhelming preponderance of evidence from numerous authentic sources pointed to the tenacious existence of
40   certain forces of great power and, so far as the human point of view is concerned, exceptional malignancy. To say that we actually believed in

vampires or werewolves would be a carelessly inclusive statement. Rather must it be said that we were not prepared to deny the possibility of certain unfamiliar and unclassified modifications of vital force and attenuated matter; existing very infrequently in three-dimensional space because of its more intimate connexion with other spatial units, yet close enough to the boundary of our own to furnish us occasional manifestations which we, for lack of a proper vantage-point, may never hope to understand.

    In short, it seemed to my uncle and me that an incontrovertible ar-
10 ray of facts pointed to some lingering influence in the shunned house; traceable to one or another of the ill-favoured French settlers of two centuries before, and still operative through rare and unknown laws of atomic and electronic motion. That the family of Roulet had possessed an abnormal affinity for outer circles of entity—dark spheres which for normal folk hold only repulsion and terror—their recorded history seemed to prove. Had not, then, the riots of those bygone seventeen-thirties set moving certain kinetic patterns in the morbid brain of one or more of them—notably the sinister Paul Roulet—which obscurely survived the bodies murdered and buried by the mob, and continued to
20 function in some multiple-dimensioned space along the original lines of force determined by a frantic hatred of the encroaching community?

    Such a thing was surely not a physical or biochemical impossibility in the light of a newer science which includes the theories of relativity and intra-atomic action.[80] One might easily imagine an alien nucleus of substance or energy, formless or otherwise, kept alive by imperceptible or immaterial subtractions from the life-force or bodily tissues and fluids of other and more palpably living things into which it penetrates and with whose fabric it sometimes completely merges itself. It might be actively hostile, or it might be dictated merely by blind motives of
30 self-preservation. In any case such a monster must of necessity be in our scheme of things an anomaly and an intruder, whose extirpation forms a primary duty with every man not an enemy to the world's life, health, and sanity.

    What baffled us was our utter ignorance of the aspect in which we might encounter the thing. No sane person had even seen it, and few had ever felt it definitely. It might be pure energy—a form ethereal and outside the realm of substance—or it might be partly material; some unknown and equivocal mass of plasticity, capable of changing at will to nebulous approximations of the solid, liquid, gaseous, or tenuously
40 unparticled states. The anthropomorphic patch of mould on the floor, the form of the yellowish vapour, and the curvature of the tree-roots in some of the old tales, all argued at least a remote and reminiscent con-

nexion with the human shape; but how representative or permanent that similarity might be, none could say with any kind of certainty.

We had devised two weapons to fight it; a large and specially fitted Crookes tube[81] operated by powerful storage batteries and provided with peculiar screens and reflectors, in case it proved intangible and opposable only by vigorously destructive ether radiations,[82] and a pair of military flame-throwers[83] of the sort used in the world-war, in case it proved partly material and susceptible of mechanical destruction—for like the superstitious Exeter rustics, we were prepared to burn the
10   thing's heart out if heart existed to burn. All this aggressive mechanism we set in the cellar in positions carefully arranged with reference to the cot and chairs, and to the spot before the fireplace where the mould had taken strange shapes. That suggestive patch, by the way, was only faintly visible when we placed our furniture and instruments, and when we returned that evening for the actual vigil. For a moment I half doubted that I had ever seen it in the more definitely limned form—but then I thought of the legends.

Our cellar vigil began at 10 p.m., daylight saving time,[84] and as it continued we found no promise of pertinent developments. A weak, fil-
20   tered glow from the rain-harassed street-lamps outside, and a feeble phosphorescence from the detestable fungi within, shewed the dripping stone of the walls, from which all traces of whitewash had vanished; the dank, foetid, and mildew-tainted hard earth floor with its obscene fungi; the rotting remains of what had been stools, chairs, and tables, and other more shapeless furniture; the heavy planks and massive beams of the ground floor overhead; the decrepit plank door leading to bins and chambers beneath other parts of the house; the crumbling stone staircase with ruined wooden hand-rail; and the crude and cavernous fireplace of blackened brick where rusted iron fragments revealed the past presence
30   of hooks, andirons, spit, crane, and a door to the Dutch oven[85]—these things, and our austere cot and camp chairs, and the heavy and intricate destructive machinery we had brought.

We had, as in my own former explorations, left the door to the street unlocked; so that a direct and practical path of escape might lie open in case of manifestations beyond our power to deal with. It was our idea that our continued nocturnal presence would call forth whatever malign entity lurked there; and that being prepared, we could dispose of the thing with one or the other of our provided means as soon as we had recognised and observed it sufficiently. How long it might
40   require to evoke and extinguish the thing, we had no notion. It occurred to us, too, that our venture was far from safe; for in what strength the thing might appear no one could tell. But we deemed the game worth

the hazard, and embarked on it alone and unhesitatingly; conscious that the seeking of outside aid would only expose us to ridicule and perhaps defeat our entire purpose. Such was our frame of mind as we talked— far into the night, till my uncle's growing drowsiness made me remind him to lie down for his two-hour sleep.

Something like fear chilled me as I sat there in the small hours alone—I say alone, for one who sits by a sleeper is indeed alone; per- haps more alone than he can realise. My uncle breathed heavily, his deep inhalations and exhalations accompanied by the rain outside, and punctuated by another nerve-racking sound of distant dripping water within—for the house was repulsively damp even in dry weather, and in this storm positively swamp-like. I studied the loose, antique ma- sonry of the walls in the fungus-light and the feeble rays which stole in from the street through the screened windows; and once, when the noisome atmosphere of the place seemed about to sicken me, I opened the door and looked up and down the street, feasting my eyes on fa- miliar sights and my nostrils on the wholesome air. Still nothing oc- curred to reward my watching; and I yawned repeatedly, fatigue getting the better of apprehension.

Then the stirring of my uncle in his sleep attracted my notice. He had turned restlessly on the cot several times during the latter half of the first hour, but now he was breathing with unusual irregularity, occa- sionally heaving a sigh which held more than a few of the qualities of a choking moan. I turned my electric flashlight on him and found his face averted, so rising and crossing to the other side of the cot, I again flashed the light to see if he seemed in any pain. What I saw unnerved me most surprisingly, considering its relative triviality. It must have been merely the association of any odd circumstance with the sinister nature of our location and mission, for surely the circumstance was not in itself frightful or unnatural. It was merely that my uncle's facial ex- pression, disturbed no doubt by the strange dreams which our situation prompted, betrayed considerable agitation, and seemed not at all char- acteristic of him. His habitual expression was one of kindly and well- bred calm, whereas now a variety of emotions seemed struggling within him. I think, on the whole, that it was the *variety* which chiefly disturbed me. My uncle, as he gasped and tossed in increasing perturbation and with eyes that had now started open, seemed not one but many men, and suggested a curious quality of alienage from himself.

All at once he commenced to mutter, and I did not like the look of his mouth and teeth as he spoke. The words were at first indistinguish- able, and then—with a tremendous start—I recognised something about them which filled me with icy fear till I recalled the breadth of my uncle's

education and the interminable translations he had made from anthropological and antiquarian articles in the *Revue des Deux Mondes*.[86] For the
venerable Elihu Whipple was muttering *in French,* and the few phrases I
could distinguish seemed connected with the darkest myths he had ever
adapted from the famous Paris magazine.

Suddenly a perspiration broke out on the sleeper's forehead, and
he leaped abruptly up, half awake. The jumble of French changed to a
cry in English, and the hoarse voice shouted excitedly, "My breath, my
breath!" Then the awakening became complete, and with a subsidence
10 of facial expression to the normal state my uncle seized my hand and
began to relate a dream whose nucleus of significance I could only
surmise with a kind of awe.

He had, he said, floated off from a very ordinary series of dream-
pictures into a scene whose strangeness was related to nothing he had
ever read. It was of this world, and yet not of it—a shadowy geometrical
confusion[87] in which could be seen elements of familiar things in most
unfamiliar and perturbing combinations. There was a suggestion of
queerly disordered pictures superimposed one upon another; an arrangement in which the essentials of time as well as of space seemed
20 dissolved and mixed in the most illogical fashion. In this kaleidoscopic
vortex of phantasmal images were occasional snapshots, if one might
use the term, of singular clearness but unaccountable heterogeneity.

Once my uncle thought he lay in a carelessly dug open pit, with a
crowd of angry faces framed by straggling locks and three-cornered
hats frowning down on him. Again he seemed to be in the interior of a
house—an old house, apparently—but the details and inhabitants were
constantly changing, and he could never be certain of the faces or the
furniture, or even of the room itself, since doors and windows seemed
in just as great a state of flux as the more presumably mobile objects. It
30 was queer—damnably queer—and my uncle spoke almost sheepishly,
as if half expecting not to be believed, when he declared that of the
strange faces many had unmistakably borne the features of the Harris
family. And all the while there was a personal sensation of choking, as
if some pervasive presence had spread itself through his body and
sought to possess itself of his vial processes. I shuddered at the thought
of those vital processes, worn as they were by eighty-one years of continuous functioning, in conflict with unknown forces of which the
youngest and strongest system might well be afraid; but in another
moment reflected that dreams are only dreams,[88] and that these un-
40 comfortable visions could be, at most, no more than my uncle's reaction to the investigations and expectations which had lately filled our
minds to the exclusion of all else.

Conversation, also, soon tended to dispel my sense of strangeness; and in time I yielded and took my turn at slumber. My uncle seemed now very wakeful, and welcomed his period of watching even though the nightmare had aroused him far ahead of his allotted two hours. Sleep seized me quickly, and I was at once haunted with dreams of the most disturbing kind. I felt, in my visions, a cosmic and abysmal loneness; with hostility surging from all sides upon some prison where I lay confined. I seemed bound and gagged, and taunted by the echoing yells of distant multitudes who thirsted for my blood. My uncle's face came to me with

10   less pleasant associations than in waking hours, and I recall many futile struggles and attempts to scream. It was not a pleasant sleep, and for a second I was not sorry for the echoing shriek which clove through the barriers of dream and flung me to a sharp and startled awakeness in which every actual object before my eyes stood out with more than natural clearness and reality.

V.

I had been lying with my face away from my uncle's chair, so that in this sudden flash of awakening I saw only the door to the street, the more northerly window, and the wall and floor and ceiling toward the

20   north of the room, all photographed with morbid vividness on my brain in a light brighter than the glow of the fungi or the rays from the street outside. It was not a strong or even a fairly strong light; certainly not nearly strong enough to read an average book by. But it cast a shadow of myself and the cot on the floor, and had a yellowish, penetrating force that hinted at things more potent than luminosity. This I perceived with unhealthy sharpness despite the fact that two of my other senses were violently assailed. For on my ears rang the reverberations of that shocking scream, while my nostrils revolted at the stench which filled the place. My mind, as alert as my senses, recognised the gravely unusual; and al-

30   most automatically I leaped up and turned about to grasp the destructive instruments which we had left trained on the mouldy spot before the fireplace. As I turned, I dreaded what I was to see; for the scream had been in my uncle's voice, and I knew not against what menace I should have to defend him and myself.

Yet after all, the sight was worse than I had dreaded. There are horrors beyond horrors, and this was one of those nuclei of all dreamable hideousness which the cosmos saves to blast an accursed and unhappy few. Out of the fungus-ridden earth steamed up a vaporous corpse-light,[89] yellow and diseased, which bubbled and lapped to a

40   gigantic height in vague outlines half-human and half-monstrous, through which I could see the chimney and fireplace beyond. It was all

eyes—wolfish and mocking—and the rugose[90] insect-like head dissolved at the top to a thin stream of mist which curled putridly about and finally vanished up the chimney. I say that I saw this thing, but it is only in conscious retrospection that I ever definitely traced its damnable approach to form. At the time it was to me only a seething, dimly phosphorescent cloud of fungous loathsomeness, enveloping and dissolving to an abhorrent plasticity the one object to which all my attention was focussed. That object was my uncle—the venerable Elihu Whipple—who with blackening and decaying features leered and gib-
10   bered at me, and reached out dripping claws to rend me in the fury which this horror had brought.

It was a sense of routine which kept me from going mad. I had drilled myself in preparation for the crucial moment, and blind training saved me. Recognising the bubbling evil as no substance reachable by matter or material chemistry, and therefore ignoring the flame-thrower which loomed on my left, I threw on the current of the Crookes tube apparatus, and focussed toward that scene of immortal blasphemousness the strongest ether radiations which man's art can arouse from the spaces and fluids of Nature. There was a bluish haze and a frenzied
20   sputtering, and the yellowish phosphorescence grew dimmer to my eyes. But I saw the dimness was only that of contrast, and that the waves from the machine had no effect whatever.

Then, in the midst of that daemoniac spectacle, I saw a fresh horror which brought cries to my lips and sent me fumbling and staggering toward that unlocked door to the quiet street, careless of what abnormal terrors I loosed upon the world,[91] or what thoughts or judgments of men I brought down upon my head. In that dim blend of blue and yellow the form of my uncle had commenced a nauseous liquefaction whose essence eludes all description, and in which there played across
30   his vanishing face such changes of identity as only madness can conceive. He was at once a devil and a multitude, a charnel-house and a pageant. Lit by the mixed and uncertain beams, that gelatinous face assumed a dozen—a score—a hundred—aspects; grinning, as it sank to the ground on a body that melted like tallow, in the caricatured likeness of legions strange and yet not strange.

I saw the features of the Harris line, masculine and feminine, adult and infantile, and other features old and young, coarse and refined, familiar and unfamiliar. For a second there flashed a degraded counterfeit of a miniature of poor mad Rhoby Harris that I had seen in the School
40   of Design Museum,[92] and another time I thought I caught the raw-boned image of Mercy Dexter as I recalled her from a painting in Carrington Harris's house. It was frightful beyond conception; toward the last, when

a curious blend of servant and baby visages flickered close to the fungous floor where a pool of greenish grease was spreading, it seemed as though the shifting features fought against themselves, and strove to form contours like those of my uncle's kindly face. I like to think that he existed at that moment, and that he tried to bid me farewell. It seems to me I hiccoughed a farewell from my own parched throat as I lurched out into the street; a thin stream of grease following me through the door to the rain-drenched sidewalk.

The rest is shadowy and monstrous. There was no one in the soaking street, and in all the world there was no one I dared tell. I walked aimlessly south past College Hill and the Athenaeum,[93] down Hopkins Street,[94] and over the bridge to the business section where tall buildings seemed to guard me as the modern material things guard the world from ancient and unwholesome wonder. Then grey dawn unfolded wetly from the east, silhouetting the archaic hill and its venerable steeples, and beckoning me to the place where my terrible work was still unfinished. And in the end I went, wet, hatless, and dazed in the morning light, and entered that awful door in Benefit Street which I had left ajar, and which still swung cryptically in full sight of the early householders to whom I dared not speak.

The grease was gone, for the mouldy floor was porous. And in front of the fireplace was no vestige of the giant doubled-up form in nitre. I looked at the cot, the chairs, the instruments, my neglected hat, and the yellowed straw hat of my uncle. Dazedness was uppermost, and I could scarcely recall what was dream and what was reality. Then thought trickled back, and I knew that I had witnessed things more horrible than I had dreamed. Sitting down, I tried to conjecture as nearly as sanity would let me just what had happened, and how I might end the horror, if indeed it had been real. Matter it seemed not to be, nor ether, nor anything else conceivable by mortal mind. What, then, but some exotic *emanation;* some vampirish vapour such as Exeter rustics tell of as lurking over certain churchyards? This I felt was the clue, and again I looked at the floor before the fireplace where the mould and nitre had taken strange forms. In ten minutes my mind was made up, and taking my hat I set out for home, where I bathed, ate, and gave by telephone an order for a pickaxe, a spade, a military gas-mask, and six carboys[95] of sulphuric acid, all to be delivered the next morning at the cellar door of the shunned house in Benefit Street. After that I tried to sleep; and failing, passed the hours in reading and in the composition of inane verses[96] to counteract my mood.

At 11 a.m. the next day I commenced digging. It was sunny weather, and I was glad of that. I was still alone, for as much as I feared

the unknown horror I sought, there was more fear in the thought of
telling anybody. Later I told Harris only through sheer necessity, and
because he had heard odd tales from old people which disposed him
ever so little toward belief. As I turned up the stinking black earth in
front of the fireplace, my spade causing a viscous yellow ichor to ooze
from the white fungi which it severed, I trembled at the dubious
thoughts of what I might uncover. Some secrets of inner earth are not
good for mankind, and this seemed to me one of them.

My hand shook perceptibly, but still I delved; after a while standing
10   in the large hole I had made. With the deepening of the hole, which was
about six feet square, the evil smell increased; and I lost all doubt of my
imminent contact with the hellish thing whose emanations had cursed
the house for over a century and a half. I wondered what it would look
like—what its form and substance would be, and how big it might have
waxed through long ages of life-sucking. At length I climbed out of the
hole and dispersed the heaped-up dirt, then arranging the great carboys
of acid around and near two sides, so that when necessary I might empty
them all down the aperture in quick succession. After that I dumped
earth only along the other two sides; working more slowly and donning
20   my gas-mask as the smell grew. I was nearly unnerved at my proximity to
a nameless thing at the bottom of a pit.

Suddenly my spade struck something softer than earth. I shuddered, and made a motion as if to climb out of the hole, which was
now as deep as my neck. Then courage returned, and I scraped away
more dirt in the light of the electric torch I had provided. The surface I
uncovered was fishy and glassy—a kind of semi-putrid congealed jelly
with suggestions of translucency. I scraped further, and saw that it had
form. There was a rift where a part of the substance was folded over.
The exposed area was huge and roughly cylindrical; like a mammoth
30   soft blue-white stovepipe doubled in two, its largest part some two feet
in diameter. Still more I scraped, and then abruptly I leaped out of the
hole and away from the filthy thing; frantically unstopping and tilting
the heavy carboys, and precipitating their corrosive contents one after
another down that charnel gulf and upon the unthinkable abnormality
whose titan *elbow* I had seen.[97]

The blinding maelstrom of greenish-yellow vapour which surged
tempestuously up from that hole as the floods of acid descended, will
never leave my memory. All along the hill people tell of the yellow day,
when virulent and horrible fumes arose from the factory waste dumped
40   in the Providence River, but I know how mistaken they are as to the
source.[98] They tell, too, of the hideous roar[99] which at the same time
came from some disordered water-pipe or gas main underground—but

again I could correct them if I dared. It was unspeakably shocking, and I do not see how I lived through it. I did faint after emptying the fourth carboy, which I had to handle after the fumes had begun to penetrate my mask; but when I recovered I saw that the hold was emitting no fresh vapours.

The two remaining carboys I emptied down without particular result, and after a time I felt it safe to shovel the earth back into the pit. It was twilight before I was done, but fear had gone out of the place. The dampness was less foetid, and all the strange fungi had withered to a kind of harmless greyish powder which blew ash-like along the floor. One of earth's nethermost terrors had perished forever; and if there be a hell, it had received at last the daemon soul of an unhallowed thing. And as I patted down the last spadeful of mould, I shed the first of the many tears with which I have paid unaffected tribute to my beloved uncle's memory.

The next spring no more pale grass and strange weeds came up in the shunned house's terraced garden, and shortly afterward Carrington Harris rented the place. It is still spectral, but its strangeness fascinates me, and I shall find mixed with my relief a queer regret when it is torn down to make way for a tawdry shop or vulgar apartment building. The barren old trees in the yard have begun to bear small, sweet apples, and last year the birds nested in their gnarled boughs.

The Horror at Red Hook[1]

"There are sacraments of evil as well as of good about us, and
we live and move to my belief in an unknown world, a place where
there are caves and shadows and dwellers in twilight. It is possible
that man may sometimes return on the track of evolution,[2] and it
is my belief that an awful lore is not yet dead."

—*Arthur Machen.*[3]

I.

Not many weeks ago, on a street corner in the village of Pascoag, Rhode
10 Island,[4] a tall, heavily built, and wholesome-looking pedestrian furnished
much speculation by a singular lapse of behaviour. He had, it appears,
been descending the hill by the road from Chepachet;[5] and encountering
the compact section, had turned to his left into the main thoroughfare
where several modest business blocks convey a touch of the urban. At
this point, without visible provocation, he committed his astonishing
lapse; staring queerly for a second at the tallest of the buildings before
him, and then, with a series of terrified, hysterical shrieks, breaking into a
frantic run which ended in a stumble and fall at the next crossing. Picked
up and dusted off by ready hands, he was found to be conscious, organi-
20 cally unhurt, and evidently cured of his sudden nervous attack. He muttered some shamefaced explanations involving a strain he had
undergone, and with downcast glance turned back up the Chepachet
road, trudging out of sight without once looking behind him. It was a
strange incident to befall so large, robust, normal-featured, and capable-
looking a man, and the strangeness was not lessened by the remarks of a
bystander who had recognised him as the boarder of a well-known
dairyman on the outskirts of Chepachet.[6]

He was, it developed, a New York police detective named Thomas
F. Malone, now on a long leave of absence under medical treatment
30 after some disproportionately arduous work on a gruesome local case
which accident had made dramatic. There had been a collapse of several old brick buildings during a raid in which he had shared, and
something about the wholesale loss of life, both of prisoners and of his
companions, had peculiarly appalled him. As a result, he had acquired
an acute and anomalous[7] horror of any buildings even remotely sug-
gesting the ones which had fallen in, so that in the end mental specialists forbade him the sight of such things for an indefinite period. A
police surgeon with relatives in Chepachet had put forward that quaint
hamlet[8] of wooden colonial houses as an ideal spot for the psychological

The "dance hall" church in Red Hook (no longer extant).

convalescence; and thither[9] the sufferer had gone, promising never to
venture among the brick-lined streets of larger villages till duly advised
by the Woonsocket[10] specialist with whom he was put in touch. This
walk to Pascoag for magazines had been a mistake,[11] and the patient
had paid in fright, bruises, and humiliation for his disobedience.

    So much the gossips of Chepachet and Pascoag knew; and so
much, also, the most learned specialists believed. But Malone had at
first told the specialists much more, ceasing only when he saw that utter incredulity was his portion.[12] Thereafter he held his peace, protest-
10 ing not at all when it was generally agreed that the collapse of certain
squalid brick houses in the Red Hook[13] section of Brooklyn, and the
consequent death of many brave officers, had unseated his nervous
equilibrium. He had worked too hard,[14] all said, in trying to clean up
those nests of disorder and violence; certain features were shocking
enough, in all conscience, and the unexpected tragedy was the last
straw. This was a simple explanation which everyone could understand,
and because Malone was not a simple person he perceived that he had
better let it suffice. To hint to unimaginative people of a horror beyond
all human conception—a horror of houses and blocks and cities lep-
20 rous[15] and cancerous[16] with evil dragged from elder worlds—would be
merely to invite a padded cell instead of restful rustication,[17] and
Malone was a man of sense despite his mysticism. He had the Celt's far
vision of weird and hidden things, but the logician's quick eye for the
outwardly unconvincing; an amalgam which had led him far afield in
the forty-two years of his life, and set him in strange places for a Dublin University[18] man born in a Georgian villa near Phoenix Park.[19]

    And now, as he reviewed the things he had seen and felt and ap-
prehended, Malone was content to keep unshared the secret of what
could reduce a dauntless fighter to a quivering neurotic; what could
30 make old brick slums and seas of dark, subtle faces a thing of nightmare and eldritch[20] portent. It would not be the first time his sensa-
tions had been forced to bide uninterpreted—for was not his very act
of plunging into the polyglot[21] abyss of New York's underworld a freak
beyond sensible explanation? What could he tell the prosaic of the antique witcheries and grotesque marvels discernible to sensitive eyes
amidst the poison cauldron where all the varied dregs of unwholesome
ages mix the venom and perpetuate their obscene terrors? He had seen
the hellish green flame of secret wonder[22] in this blatant, evasive welter
of outward greed and inward blasphemy, and had smiled gently when
40 all the New-Yorkers he knew scoffed at his experiment in police work.
They had been very witty and cynical, deriding his fantastic pursuit of
unknowable mysteries[23] and assuring him that in these days New York

held nothing but cheapness and vulgarity.[24] One of them had wagered him a heavy sum that he could not—despite many poignant things to his credit in the *Dublin Review*[25]—even write a truly interesting story of New York low life; and now, looking back, he perceived that cosmic irony had justified the prophet's words while secretly confuting their flippant meaning. The horror, as glimpsed at last, could not make a story—for like the book cited by Poe's German authority, *"er lasst sich nicht lesen*—it does not permit itself to be read."[26]

II.

To Malone the sense of latent mystery in existence was always present. In youth he had felt the hidden beauty and ecstasy of things, and had been a poet; but poverty and sorrow and exile had turned his gaze in darker directions, and he had thrilled at the imputations of evil in the world around.[27] Daily life had for him come to be a phantasmagoria[28] of macabre shadow-studies; now glittering and leering with concealed rottenness as in Beardsley's[29] best manner, now hinting terrors behind the commonest shapes and objects as in the subtler and less obvious work of Gustave Doré.[30] He would often regard it as merciful that most persons of high intelligence jeer at the inmost mysteries;[31] for, he argued, if superior minds were ever placed in fullest contact with the secrets preserved by ancient and lowly cults, the resultant abnormalities would soon not only wreck the world, but threaten the very integrity of the universe.[32] All this reflection was no doubt morbid, but keen logic and a deep sense of humour ably offset it. Malone was satisfied to let his notions remain as half-spied and forbidden visions to be lightly played with; and hysteria came only when duty flung him into a hell of revelation too sudden and insidious to escape.

He had for some time been detailed to the Butler Street[33] station in Brooklyn when the Red Hook matter came to his notice. Red Hook is a maze of hybrid squalor near the ancient waterfront opposite Governor's Island,[34] with dirty highways climbing the hill from wharves to that higher ground where the decayed lengths of Clinton and Court Streets[35] lead off toward the Borough Hall.[36] Its houses are mostly of brick, dating from the first quarter to the middle of the nineteenth century, and some of the obscurer alleys and byways have that alluring antique flavour which conventional reading leads us to call "Dickensian".[37] The population is a hopeless tangle and enigma; Syrian, Spanish, Italian, and negro elements impinging upon one another, and fragments of Scandinavian and American belts lying not far distant. It is a babel of sound and filth, and sends out strange cries to answer the lapping of oily waves at its grimy piers and the monstrous organ litanies of the harbour whis-

tles.[38] Here long ago a brighter picture dwelt, with clear-eyed mariners on the lower streets and homes of taste and substance where the larger houses line the hill. One can trace the relics of this former happiness in the trim shapes of the buildings, the occasional graceful churches, and the evidences of original art and background in bits of detail here and there—a worn flight of steps, a battered doorway, a wormy pair of decorative columns or pilasters, or a fragment of once green space with bent and rusted iron railing.[39] The houses are generally in solid blocks, and now and then a many-windowed cupola arises to tell of days when
10   the households of captains and ship-owners watched the sea.[40]

From this tangle of material and spiritual putrescence the blasphemies of an hundred dialects assail the sky. Hordes of prowlers reel shouting and singing along the lanes and thoroughfares, occasional furtive hands suddenly extinguish lights and pull down curtains, and swarthy, sin-pitted faces disappear from windows when visitors pick their way through. Policemen despair of order or reform, and seek rather to erect barriers protecting the outside world from the contagion. The clang of the patrol is answered by a kind of spectral silence, and such prisoners as are taken are never communicative. Visible of-
20   fences are as varied as the local dialects, and run the gamut from the smuggling of rum and prohibited aliens through diverse stages of lawlessness and obscure vice to murder and mutilation in their most abhorrent guises. That these visible affairs are not more frequent is not to the neighbourhood's credit, unless the power of concealment be an art demanding credit. More people enter Red Hook than leave it—or at least, than leave it by the landward side—and those who are not loquacious[41] are the likeliest to leave.

Malone found in this state of things a faint stench of secrets more terrible than any of the sins denounced by citizens and bemoaned by
30   priests and philanthropists. He was conscious, as one who united imagination with scientific knowledge, that modern people under lawless conditions tend uncannily to repeat the darkest instinctive patterns of primitive half-ape savagery in their daily life and ritual observances; and he had often viewed with an anthropologist's shudder the chanting, cursing processions of blear-eyed and pockmarked young men which wound their way along in the dark small hours of morning. One saw groups of these youths incessantly; sometimes in leering vigils on street corners, sometimes in doorways playing eerily on cheap instruments of music,[42] sometimes in stupefied dozes or indecent dialogues around
40   cafeteria tables near Borough Hall, and sometimes in whispering converse around dingy taxicabs drawn up at the high stoops of crumbling and closely shuttered old houses. They chilled and fascinated him more

than he dared confess to his associates on the force, for he seemed to
see in them some monstrous thread of secret continuity; some fiendish,
cryptical, and ancient pattern utterly beyond and below the sordid mass
of facts and habits and haunts listed with such conscientious technical
care by the police. They must be, he felt inwardly, the heirs of some
shocking and primordial tradition; the sharers of debased and broken
scraps from cults and ceremonies older than mankind.[43] Their coher-
ence and definiteness suggested it, and it shewed in the singular suspi-
cion of order which lurked beneath their squalid disorder. He had not
10   read in vain such treatises as Miss Murray's *Witch-Cult in Western
Europe*,[44] and knew that up to recent years there had certainly survived
among peasants and furtive folk a frightful and clandestine system of
assemblies and orgies descended from dark religions antedating the Ar-
yan world, and appearing in popular legends as Black Masses[45] and
Witches' Sabbaths.[46] That these hellish vestiges of old Turanian-
Asiatic[47] magic and fertility-cults were even now wholly dead he could
not for a moment suppose, and he frequently wondered how much
older and how much blacker than the very worst of the muttered tales
some of them might really be.

20   III.

It was the case of Robert Suydam[48] which took Malone to the
heart of things in Red Hook. Suydam was a lettered recluse of ancient
Dutch family, possessed óriginally of barely independent means, and
inhabiting the spacious but ill-preserved mansion which his grandfather
had built in Flatbush[49] when the village was little more than a pleasant
group of colonial cottages surrounding the steepled and ivy-clad Reformed Church[50] with its iron-railed yard of Netherlandish gravestones.
In his lonely house, set back from Martense Street[51] amidst a yard of
venerable trees, Suydam had read and brooded for some six decades
30   except for a period a generation before, when he had sailed for the old
world and remained there out of sight for eight years.[52] He could afford
no servants, and would admit but few visitors to his absolute solitude;
eschewing close friendships and receiving his rare acquaintances in one
of the three ground-floor rooms which he kept in order—a vast, high-
ceiled library whose walls were solidly packed with tattered books of
ponderous, archaic, and vaguely repellent aspect. The growth of the
town and its final absorption in the Brooklyn district had meant nothing to Suydam, and he had come to mean less and less to the town.
Elderly people still pointed him out on the streets, but to most of the
40   recent population he was merely a queer, corpulent old fellow whose
unkempt white hair, stubbly beard, shiny black clothes, and gold-

headed cane earned him an amused glance and nothing more. Malone did not know him by sight till duty called him to the case, but had heard of him indirectly as a really profound authority on mediaeval superstition, and had once idly meant to look up an out-of-print pamphlet of his on the Kabbalah[53] and the Faustus legend,[54] which a friend had quoted from memory.

Suydam became a "case" when his distant and only relatives sought court pronouncements on his sanity.[55] Their action seemed sudden to the outside world, but was really undertaken only after pro-
10   longed observation and sorrowful debate. It was based on certain odd changes in his speech and habits; wild references to impending wonders, and unaccountable hauntings of disreputable Brooklyn neighbourhoods. He had been growing shabbier and shabbier with the years, and now prowled about like a veritable mendicant;[56] seen occasionally by humiliated friends in subway stations, or loitering on the benches around Borough Hall in conversation with groups of swarthy, evil-looking strangers. When he spoke it was to babble of unlimited powers almost within his grasp, and to repeat with knowing leers such mystical words or names as "Sephiroth", "Ashmodai", and "Samaël".[57] The
20   court action revealed that he was using up his income and wasting his principal in the purchase of curious tomes imported from London and Paris, and in the maintenance of a squalid basement flat in the Red Hook district where he spent nearly every night, receiving odd delegations of mixed rowdies and foreigners, and apparently conducting some kind of ceremonial service behind the green blinds of secretive windows. Detectives assigned to follow him reported strange cries and chants and prancing of feet filtering out from these nocturnal rites, and shuddered at their peculiar ecstasy and abandon despite the commonness of weird orgies in that sodden section. When, however, the matter
30   came to a hearing, Suydam managed to preserve his liberty. Before the judge his manner grew urbane and reasonable, and he freely admitted the queerness of demeanour and extravagant cast of language into which he had fallen through excessive devotion to study and research. He was, he said, engaged in the investigation of certain details of European tradition which required the closest contact with foreign groups and their songs and folk dances.[58] The notion that any low secret society was preying upon him, as hinted by his relatives, was obviously absurd; and shewed how sadly limited was their understanding of him and his work. Triumphing with his calm explanations, he was suffered to
40   depart unhindered; and the paid detectives of the Suydams, Corlears, and Van Brunts[59] were withdrawn in resigned disgust.

It was here that an alliance of Federal inspectors and police, Malone with them, entered the case. The law had watched the Suydam action with interest, and had in many instances been called upon to aid the private detectives. In this work it developed that Suydam's new associates were among the blackest and most vicious criminals of Red Hook's devious lanes, and that at least a third of them were known and repeated offenders in the matter of thievery, disorder, and the importation of illegal immigrants. Indeed, it would not have been too much to say that the old scholar's particular circle coincided almost perfectly with the worst

10 of the organised cliques which smuggled ashore certain nameless and unclassified Asian dregs wisely turned back by Ellis Island.[60] In the teeming rookeries of Parker Place[61]—since renamed—where Suydam had his basement flat, there had grown up a very unusual colony of unclassified slant-eyed folk who used the Arabic alphabet but were eloquently repudiated by the great mass of Syrians in and around Atlantic Avenue.[62] They could all have been deported for lack of credentials, but legalism is slow-moving, and one does not disturb Red Hook unless publicity forces one to.

These creatures attended a tumbledown stone church, used

20 Wednesdays as a dance-hall, which reared its Gothic buttresses near the vilest part of the waterfront. It was nominally Catholic; but priests throughout Brooklyn denied the place all standing and authenticity, and policemen agreed with them when they listened to the noises it emitted at night.[63] Malone used to fancy he heard terrible cracked bass notes from a hidden organ[64] far underground when the church stood empty and unlighted, whilst all observers dreaded the shrieking and drumming which accompanied the visible services. Suydam, when questioned, said he thought the ritual was some remnant of Nestorian Christianity[65] tinctured with the Shamanism of Thibet.[66] Most of the people, he con-

30 jectured, were of Mongoloid[67] stock, originating somewhere in or near Kurdistan[68]—and Malone could not help recalling that Kurdistan is the land of Yezidis,[69] last survivors of the Persian devil-worshippers. However this may have been, the stir of the Suydam investigation made it certain that these unauthorised newcomers were flooding Red Hook in increasing numbers; entering through some marine conspiracy unreached by revenue officers and harbour police, overrunning Parker Place and rapidly spreading up the hill, and welcomed with curious fraternalism by the other assorted denizens of the region. Their squat figures and characteristic squinting physiognomies, grotesquely com-

40 bined with flashy American clothing,[70] appeared more and more numerously among the loafers and nomad gangsters of the Borough Hall section; till at length it was deemed necessary to compute their num-

bers, ascertain their sources and occupations, and find if possible a way to round them up and deliver them to the proper immigration authorities. To this task Malone was assigned by agreement of Federal and city forces, and as he commenced his canvass of Red Hook he felt poised upon the brink of nameless terrors, with the shabby, unkempt figure of Robert Suydam as arch-fiend and adversary.

IV.

Police methods are varied and ingenious. Malone, through unostentatious rambles, carefully casual conversations, well-timed offers of
10   hip-pocket liquor,[71] and judicious dialogues with frightened prisoners, learned many isolated facts about the movement whose aspect had become so menacing.[72] The newcomers were indeed Kurds, but of a dialect obscure and puzzling to exact philology. Such of them as worked lived mostly as dock-hands and unlicenced pedlars, though frequently serving in Greek restaurants and tending corner news stands. Most of them, however, had no visible means of support; and were obviously connected with underworld pursuits, of which smuggling and "bootlegging" were the least indescribable. They had come in steamships, apparently tramp freighters,[73] and had been unloaded by stealth on
20   moonless nights in rowboats which stole under a certain wharf and followed a hidden canal to a secret subterranean pool beneath a house. This wharf, canal, and house Malone could not locate, for the memories of his informants were exceedingly confused, while their speech was to a great extent beyond even the ablest interpreters; nor could he gain any real data on the reasons for their systematic importation. They were reticent about the exact spot from which they had come, and were never sufficiently off guard to reveal the agencies which had sought them out and directed their course. Indeed, they developed something like acute fright when asked the reasons for their presence. Gangsters
30   of other breeds were equally taciturn, and the most that could be gathered was that some god or great priesthood had promised them unheard-of powers and supernatural glories and rulerships in a strange land.[74]

The attendance of both newcomers and old gangsters at Suydam's closely guarded nocturnal meetings was very regular, and the police soon learned that the erstwhile[75] recluse had leased additional flats to accommodate such guests as knew his password; at last occupying three entire houses and permanently harbouring many of his queer companions. He spent but little time now at his Flatbush home, appar-
40   ently going and coming only to obtain and return books; and his face and manner had attained an appalling pitch of wildness. Malone twice

interviewed him, but was each time brusquely repulsed. He knew nothing, he said, of any mysterious plots or movements; and had no idea how the Kurds could have entered or what they wanted. His business was to study undisturbed the folklore of all the immigrants of the district; a business with which policemen had no legitimate concern. Malone mentioned his admiration for Suydam's old brochure on the Kabbalah and other myths, but the old man's softening was only momentary. He sensed an intrusion, and rebuffed his visitor in no uncertain way; till Malone withdrew disgusted, and turned to other channels
10   of information.

What Malone would have unearthed could he have worked continuously on the case, we shall never know. As it was, a stupid conflict between city and Federal authority suspended the investigations for several months, during which the detective was busy with other assignments. But at no time did he lose interest, or fail to stand amazed at what began to happen to Robert Suydam. Just at the time when a wave of kidnappings and disappearances spread its excitement over New York, the unkempt scholar embarked upon a metamorphosis as startling as it was absurd. One day he was seen near Borough Hall with
20   clean-shaved face, well-trimmed hair, and tastefully immaculate attire, and on every day thereafter some obscure improvement was noticed in him. He maintained his new fastidiousness without interruption, added to it an unwonted sparkle of eye and crispness of speech, and began little by little to shed the corpulence which had so long deformed him. Now frequently taken for less than his age, he acquired an elasticity of step and buoyancy of demeanour to match the new tradition, and shewed a curious darkening of the hair which somehow did not suggest dye. As the months passed, he commenced to dress less and less conservatively, and finally astonished his new friends by renovating and
30   redecorating his Flatbush mansion, which he threw open in a series of receptions, summoning all the acquaints he could remember, and extending a special welcome to the fully forgiven relatives who had so lately sought his restraint. Some attended through curiosity, others through duty; but all were suddenly charmed by the dawning grace and urbanity of the former hermit. He had, he asserted, accomplished most of his allotted work; and having just inherited some property from a half-forgotten European friend, was about to spend his remaining years in a brighter second youth which ease, care, and diet had made possible to him. Less and less was he seen at Red Hook, and more and more did
40   he move in the society to which he was born. Policemen noted a tendency of the gangsters to congregate at the old stone church and

dance-hall instead of at the basement flat in Parker Place, though the
latter and its recent annexes still overflowed with noxious life.

Then two incidents occurred—wide enough apart, but both of in-
tense interest in the case as Malone envisaged it. One was a quiet announcement in the *Eagle*[76] of Robert Suydam's engagement to Miss
Cornelia Gerritsen[77] of Bayside,[78] a young woman of excellent position,[79] and distantly related to the elderly bridegroom-elect; whilst the
other was a raid on the dance-hall church by city police, after a report
that the face of a kidnapped child had been seen for a second at one of
10   the basement windows. Malone had participated in this raid, and studied the place with much care when inside. Nothing was found—in fact,
the building was entirely deserted when visited—but the sensitive Celt
was vaguely disturbed by many things about the interior. There were
crudely painted panels he did not like[80]—panels which depicted sacred
faces with peculiarly worldly and sardonic expressions, and which occasionally took liberties that even a layman's sense of decorum could
scarcely countenance.[81] Then, too, he did not relish the Greek inscrip-
tion on the wall above the pulpit; an ancient incantation which he had
once stumbled upon in Dublin college days, and which read, literally
20   translated,

> "O friend and companion of night, thou who rejoicest in the baying
> of dogs and spilt blood, who wanderest in the midst of shades among
> the tombs, who longest for blood and bringest terror to mortals, Gorgo,
> Mormo, thousand-faced moon, look favourably on our sacrifices!"[82]

When he read this he shuddered, and thought vaguely of the cracked
bass organ notes he fancied he had heard beneath the church on certain
nights. He shuddered again at the rust around the rim of a metal basin
which stood on the altar, and paused nervously when his nostrils
seemed to detect a curious and ghastly stench from somewhere in the
30   neighbourhood. That organ memory haunted him, and he explored the
basement with particular assiduity before he left. The place was very
hateful to him; yet after all, were the blasphemous panels and inscriptions more than mere crudities perpetrated by the ignorant?

By the time of Suydam's wedding the kidnapping epidemic had become a popular newspaper scandal. Most of the victims were young
children of the lowest classes, but the increasing number of disappearances had worked up a sentiment of the strongest fury. Journals clam-
oured for action from the police, and once more the Butler Street
station sent its men over Red Hook for clues, discoveries, and criminals.
40   Malone was glad to be on the trail again, and took pride in a raid on one
of Suydam's Parker Place houses. There, indeed, no stolen child was

found, despite the tales of screams and the red sash picked up in the areaway; but the paintings and rough inscriptions on the peeling walls of most of the rooms, and the primitive chemical laboratory in the attic, all helped to convince the detective that he was on the track of something tremendous. The paintings were appalling—hideous monsters of every shape and size, and parodies on human outlines which cannot be described.[83] The writing was in red, and varied from Arabic to Greek, Roman, and Hebrew letters. Malone could not read much of it, but what he did decipher was portentous and cabbalistic enough. One frequently
10   repeated motto was in a sort of Hebraised Hellenistic Greek,[84] and suggested the most terrible daemon-evocations of the Alexandrian decadence:[85]

"HEL * HELOYM * SOTHER * EMMANVEL * SABAOTH * AGLA * TETRAGRAMMATON * AGYROS * OTHEOS * ISCHYROS * ATHANATOS * IEHOVA * VA * ADONAI * SADAY * HOMOVSION * MESSIAS * ESCHEREHEYE."[86]

Circles and pentagrams loomed on every hand, and told indubitably of the strange beliefs and aspirations of those who dwelt so squalidly here. In the cellar, however, the strangest thing was found—a pile of genuine
20   gold ingots covered carelessly with a piece of burlap, and bearing upon their shining surfaces the same weird hieroglyphics which also adorned the walls. During the raid the police encountered only a passive resistance from the squinting Orientals that swarmed from every door. Finding nothing relevant, they had to leave all as it was; but the precinct captain wrote Suydam a note advising him to look closely to the character of his tenants and protégés in view of the growing public clamour.

V.

Then came the June wedding and the great sensation. Flatbush was
30   gay for the hour about high noon, and pennanted motors thronged the streets near the old Dutch church where an awning stretched from door to highway. No local event ever surpassed the Suydam-Gerritsen nuptials in tone and scale, and the party which escorted bride and groom to the Cunard Pier[87] was, if not exactly the smartest, at least a solid page from the Social Register.[88] At five o'clock adieux were waved, and the ponderous liner edged away from the long pier, slowly turned its nose seaward, discarded its tug, and headed for the widening water spaces that led to old world wonders. By night the outer harbour was cleared, and late passengers watched the stars twinkling above an
40   unpolluted ocean.

Whether the tramp steamer[89] or the scream was first to gain attention, no one can say. Probably they were simultaneous, but it is of no
use to calculate. The scream came from the Suydam stateroom, and the
sailor who broke down the door could perhaps have told frightful things
if he had not forthwith gone completely mad—as it is, he shrieked more
loudly than the first victims, and thereafter ran simpering about the vessel till caught and put in irons. The ship's doctor who entered the stateroom and turned on the lights a moment later did not go mad, but told
nobody what he saw till afterward, when he corresponded with Malone
10   in Chepachet. It was murder—strangulation—but one need not say that
the claw-mark on Mrs. Suydam's throat could not have come from her
husband's or any other human hand, or that upon the white wall there
flickered for an instant in hateful red a legend which, later copied from
memory, seems to have been nothing less than the fearsome Chaldee
letters[90] of the word "LILITH".[91] One need not mention these things
because they vanished so quickly—as for Suydam, one could at least bar
others from the room until one knew what to think oneself. The doctor
has distinctly assured Malone that he did not see *IT.* The open porthole,
just before he turned on the lights, was clouded for a second with a
20   certain phosphorescence, and for a moment there seemed to echo in the
night outside the suggestion of a faint and hellish tittering; but no real
outline met the eye. As proof the doctor points to his continued sanity.

Then the tramp steamer claimed all attention. A boat put off, and a
horde of swart, insolent ruffians in officers' dress swarmed aboard the
temporarily halted Cunarder. They wanted Suydam or his body—they
had known of his trip, and for certain reasons were sure he would die.
The captain's deck was almost a pandemonium; for at the instant, between the doctor's report from the stateroom and the demands of the
men from the tramp, not even the wisest and gravest seaman could
30   think what to do. Suddenly the leader of the visiting mariners, an Arab
with a hatefully negroid mouth, pulled forth a dirty, crumpled paper
and handed it to the captain. It was signed by Robert Suydam, and bore
the following odd message:

> "In case of sudden or unexplained accident or death on my part, please
> deliver me or my body unquestioningly into the hands of the bearer and
> his associates. Everything, for me, and perhaps for you, depends on ab-
> solute compliance. Explanations can come later—do not fail me now.
> ROBERT SUYDAM."

Captain and doctor looked at each other, and the latter whispered
40   something to the former. Finally they nodded rather helplessly and led
the way to the Suydam stateroom. The doctor directed the captain's

glance away as he unlocked the door and admitted the strange seamen, nor did he breathe easily till they filed out with their burden after an unaccountably long period of preparation. It was wrapped in bedding from the berths, and the doctor was glad that the outlines were not very revealing. Somehow the men got the thing over the side and away to their tramp steamer without uncovering it. The Cunarder started again, and the doctor and a ship's undertaker sought out the Suydam stateroom to perform what last services they could. Once more the physician was forced to reticence and even to mendacity, for a hellish thing had hap-
10   pened. When the undertaker asked him why he had drained off all of Mrs. Suydam's blood, he neglected to affirm that he had not done so; nor did he point to the vacant bottle-spaces on the rack, or to the odour in the sink which shewed the hasty disposition of the bottles' original contents. The pockets of those men—if men they were—had bulged damnably when they left the ship. Two hours later, and the world knew by radio all that it ought to know of the horrible affair.

VI.

        That same June evening, without having heard a word from the sea, Malone was desperately busy among the alleys of Red Hook. A sudden
20   stir seemed to permeate the place, and as if apprised by "grapevine telegraph" of something singular,[92] the denizens clustered expectantly around the dance-hall church and the houses in Parker Place. Three children had just disappeared—blue-eyed Norwegians from the streets toward Gowanus[93]—and there were rumours of a mob forming among the sturdy Vikings of that section. Malone had for weeks been urging his colleagues to attempt a general cleanup; and at last, moved by conditions more obvious to their common sense than the conjectures of a Dublin dreamer, they had agreed upon a final stroke. The unrest and menace of this evening had been the deciding factor, and just about midnight a
30   raiding party recruited from three stations descended upon Parker Place and its environs. Doors were battered in, stragglers arrested, and candlelighted rooms forced to disgorge unbelievable throngs of mixed foreigners in figured robes, mitres,[94] and other inexplicable devices. Much was lost in the melee, for objects were thrown hastily down unexpected shafts, and betraying odours deadened by the sudden kindling of pungent incense. But spattered blood was everywhere, and Malone shuddered whenever he saw a brazier or altar from which the smoke was still rising.
        He wanted to be in several places at once, and decided on Suydam's basement flat only after a messenger had reported the complete
40   emptiness of the dilapidated dance-hall church. The flat, he thought,

must hold some clue to a cult of which the occult scholar had so obviously become the centre and leader; and it was with real expectancy
that he ransacked the musty rooms, noted their vaguely charnel odour,
and examined the curious books, instruments, gold ingots, and glass-
stoppered bottles scattered carelessly here and there. Once a lean,
black-and-white cat edged between his feet and tripped him, overturn-
ing at the same time a beaker half full of a red liquid. The shock was
severe, and to this day Malone is not certain of what he saw; but in
dreams he still pictures that cat as it scuttled away with certain mon-
10   strous alterations and peculiarities.[95] Then came the locked cellar door,
and the search for something to break it down. A heavy stool stood
near, and its tough seat was more than enough for the antique panels.
A crack formed and enlarged, and the whole door gave way—but from
the *other* side; whence poured a howling tumult of ice-cold wind with all
the stenches of the bottomless pit, and whence reached a sucking force
not of earth or heaven, which, coiling sentiently about the paralysed
detective, dragged him through the aperture and down unmeasured
spaces filled with whispers and wails, and gusts of mocking laughter.

Of course it was a dream.[96] All the specialists have told him so, and
20   he has nothing to prove the contrary. Indeed, he would rather have it
thus; for then the sight of old brick slums and dark foreign faces would
not eat so deeply into his soul. But at the time it was all horribly real,
and nothing can ever efface the memory of those nighted crypts, those
titan arcades, and those half-formed shapes of hell that strode giganti-
cally in silence holding half-eaten things whose still surviving portions
screamed for mercy or laughed with madness. Odours of incense and
corruption joined in sickening concert, and the black air was alive with
the cloudy, semi-visible bulk of shapeless elemental things with eyes.
Somewhere dark sticky water was lapping at onyx piers, and once the
30   shivery tinkle of raucous little bells pealed out to greet the insane titter
of a naked phosphorescent thing which swam into sight, scrambled
ashore, and climbed up to squat leeringly on a carved golden pedestal
in the background.

Avenues of limitless night seemed to radiate in every direction, till
one might fancy that here lay the root of a contagion destined to sicken
and swallow cities, and engulf nations in the foetor of hybrid pestilence.
Here cosmic sin had entered, and festered by unhallowed rites had
commenced the grinning march of death that was to rot us all to fungous abnormalities too hideous for the grave's holding. Satan here held
40   his Babylonish court, and in the blood of stainless childhood the leprous limbs of phosphorescent Lilith were laved. Incubi[97] and succubae[98] howled praise to Hecate,[99] and headless moon-calves bleated to

the Magna Mater.[100] Goats leaped to the sound of thin accursed flutes, and Ægipans[101] chased endlessly after misshapen fauns over rocks twisted like swollen toads. Moloch and Ashtaroth[102] were not absent; for in this quintessence of all damnation the bounds of consciousness were let down, and man's fancy lay open to vistas of every realm of horror and every forbidden dimension that evil had power to mould. The world and Nature were helpless against such assaults from un-sealed wells of night, nor could any sign or prayer check the Walpurgis-riot[103] of horror which had come when a sage with the hateful key had
10   stumbled on a horde with the locked and brimming coffer of transmit-ted daemon-lore.

Suddenly a ray of physical light shot through these phantasms, and Malone heard the sound of oars amidst the blasphemies of things that should be dead. A boat with a lantern in its prow darted into sight, made fast to an iron ring in the slimy stone pier, and vomited forth several dark men bearing a long burden swathed in bedding. They took it to the naked phosphorescent thing on the carved golden pedestal, and the thing tittered and pawed at the bedding. Then they unswathed it, and propped upright before the pedestal the gangrenous corpse of a
20   corpulent old man with stubbly beard and unkept white air. The phos-phorescent thing tittered again, and the men produced bottles from their pockets and anointed its feet with red, whilst they afterward gave the bottles to the thing to drink from.

All at once, from an arcaded avenue leading endlessly away, there came the daemoniac rattle and wheeze of a blasphemous organ, choking and rumbling out the mockeries of hell in a cracked, sardonic bass. In an instant every moving entity was electrified; and forming at once into a ceremonial procession, the nightmare horde slithered away in quest of the sound—goat, satyr,[104] and Ægipan, incubus, succuba, and lemur,[105]
30   twisted toad and shapeless elemental,[106] dog-faced howler[107] and silent stutterer in darkness—all led by the abominable naked phosphorescent thing that had squatted on the carved golden throne, and that now strode insolently bearing in its arms the glassy-eyed corpse of the cor-pulent old man. The strange dark men danced in the rear, and the whole column skipped and leaped with Dionysiac[108] fury. Malone staggered after them a few steps, delirious and hazy, and doubtful of his place in this or any world. Then he turned, faltered, and sank down on the cold damp stone, gasping and shivering as the daemon organ croaked on, and the howling and drumming and tinkling of the mad procession grew
40   fainter and fainter.

Vaguely he was conscious of chanted horrors and shocking croak-ings afar off. Now and then a wail or whine of ceremonial devotion would float to him through the black arcade, whilst eventually there rose the dreadful Greek incantation whose text he had read above the pulpit of that dance-hall church.

"O friend and companion of night, though who rejoicest in the baying of dogs (*here a hideous howl burst forth*) and spilt blood (*here nameless sounds vied with morbid shriekings*), who wanderest in the midst of shades among the tombs (*here a whistling sigh occurred*), who longest for blood and bringest terror to mortals (*short, sharp cries from myriad throats*), Gorgo (*repeated as response*), Mormo (*repeated with ecstasy*), thousand-faced moon (*sighs and flute notes*), look favourably on our sacrifices!"

As the chant closed, a general shout went up, and hissing sounds nearly drowned the croaking of the cracked bass organ. Then a gasp as from many throats, and a babel of barked and bleated words—"Lilith, Great Lilith, behold the Bridegroom!" More cries, a clamour of rioting, and the sharp, clicking footfalls of a running figure. The footfalls approached, and Malone raised himself to his elbow to look.

The luminosity of the crypt, lately diminished, had now slightly increased; and in that devil-light there appeared the fleeing form of that which should not flee or feel or breathe—the glassy-eyed, gangrenous corpse of the corpulent old man, now needing no support, but animated by some infernal sorcery of the rite just closed. After it raced the naked, tittering, phosphorescent thing that belonged on the carven pedestal, and still farther behind panted the dark men, and all the dread crew of sentient loathsomenesses. The corpse was gaining on its pursuers, and seemed bent on a definite object, straining with every rotting muscle toward the carved golden pedestal, whose necromantic importance was evidently so great. Another moment and it had reached its goal, whilst the trailing throng laboured on with more frantic speed. But they were too late, for in one final spurt of strength which ripped tendon from tendon and sent its noisome bulk floundering to the floor in a state of jellyish dissolution, the staring corpse which had been Robert Suydam achieved its object and its triumph. The push had been tremendous, but the force had held out; and as the pusher collapsed to a muddy blotch of corruption the pedestal he had pushed tottered, tipped, and finally careened from its onyx base into the thick waters below, sending up a parting gleam of carven gold as it sank heavily to undreamable gulfs of lower Tartarus.[109] In that instant, too, the whole scene of horror faded to nothingness before Malone's eyes; and he fainted amidst a thunderous crash which seemed to blot out all the evil universe.

VII.

Malone's dream, experienced in full before he knew of Suydam's death and transfer at sea, was curiously supplemented by some odd realities of the case; though that is no reason why anyone should believe it. The three old houses in Parker Place, doubtless long rotten with decay in its most insidious form, collapsed without visible cause while half the raiders and most of the prisoners were inside; and of both the greater number were instantly killed. Only in the basements and cellars was there much saving of life, and Malone was lucky to have been deep
10 below the house of Robert Suydam. For he really was there, as no one is disposed to deny. They found him unconscious by the edge of a night-black pool, with a grotesquely horrible jumble of decay and bone, identifiable through dental work[110] as the body of Suydam, a few feet away. The case was plain, for it was hither that the smugglers' underground canal led; and the men who took Suydam from the ship had brought him home. They themselves were never found, or at least never identified; and the ship's doctor is not yet satisfied with the simple certitudes of the police.

Suydam was evidently a leader in extensive man-smuggling opera-
20 tions, for the canal to his house was but one of several subterranean channels and tunnels in the neighbourhood.[111] There was a tunnel from this house to a crypt beneath the dance-hall church; a crypt accessible from the church only through a narrow secret passage in the north wall, and in whose chambers some singular and terrible things were discovered. The croaking organ was there, as well as a vast arched chapel with wooden benches and a strangely figured altar. The walls were lined with small cells, in seventeen of which—hideous to relate—solitary prisoners in a state of complete idiocy were found chained, including four mothers with infants of disturbingly strange appearance.[112] These infants died
30 soon after exposure to the light; a circumstance which the doctors thought rather merciful. Nobody but Malone, among those who inspected them, remembered the sombre question of old Delrio: *"An sint unquam daemones incubi et succubae, et an ex tali congressu proles nasci queat?"*[113]

Before the canals were filled up they were thoroughly dredged, and yielded forth a sensational array of sawed and split bones of all sizes.[114] The kidnapping epidemic, very clearly, had been traced home; though only two of the surviving prisoners could by any legal thread be connected with it. These men are now in prison, since they failed of conviction as accessories in the actual murders. The carved golden pedestal
40 or throne so often mentioned by Malone as of primary occult importance was never brought to light, though at one place under the Suydam house the canal was observed to sink into a well too deep for

dredging.[115] It was choked up at the mouth and cemented over when
the cellars of the new houses were made, but Malone often speculates
on what lies beneath. The police, satisfied that they had shattered a
dangerous gang of maniacs and man-smugglers, turned over the Federal authorities the unconvicted Kurds, who before their deportation
were conclusively found to belong to the Yezidi clan of devil-
worshippers. The tramp ship and its crew remain an elusive mystery,
though cynical detectives are once more ready to combat its smuggling
and rum-running ventures. Malone thinks these detectives shew a sadly
10   limited perspective in their lack of wonder at the myriad unexplainable
details, and the suggestive obscurity of the whole case; though he is just
as critical of the newspapers, which saw only a morbid sensation and
gloated over a minor sadist cult which they might have proclaimed a
horror from the universe's very heart. But he is content to rest silent in
Chepachet, calming his nervous system and praying that time may
gradually transfer his terrible experience from the realm of present reality to that of picturesque and semi-mythical remoteness.

Robert Suydam sleeps beside his bride in Greenwood Cemetery.[116]
No funeral was held over the strangely released bones, and relatives are
20   grateful for the swift oblivion which overtook the case as a whole. The
scholar's connexion with the Red Hook horrors, indeed, was never
emblazoned by legal proof; since his death forestalled the inquiry he
would otherwise have faced. His own end is not much mentioned, and
the Suydams hope that posterity may recall him only as a gentle recluse
who dabbled in harmless magic and folklore.

As for Red Hook—it is always the same. Suydam came and went; a
terror gathered and faded; but the evil spirit of darkness and squalor
broods on amongst the mongrels in the old brick houses, and prowling
bands still parade on unknown errands past windows where lights and
30   twisted faces unaccountably appear and disappear. Age-old horror is a
hydra[117] with a thousand heads, and the cults of darkness are rooted in
blasphemies deeper than the well of Democritus.[118] The soul of the
beast is omnipresent and triumphant, and Red Hook's legions of blear-
eyed, pockmarked youths still chant and curse and howl as they file
from abyss to abyss, none knows whence or whither, pushed on by
blind laws of biology which they may never understand. As of old,
more people enter Red Hook than leave it on the landward side, and
there are already rumours of new canals running underground to certain centres of traffic in liquor and less mentionable things.
40   The dance-hall church is now mostly a dance-hall, and queer faces
have appeared at night at the windows. Lately a policeman expressed
the belief that the filled-up crypt has been dug out again, and for no

simply explainable purpose. Who are we to combat poisons older than history and mankind? Apes danced in Asia to those horrors, and the cancer lurks secure and spreading where furtiveness hides in rows of decaying brick.

Malone does not shudder without cause—for only the other day an officer overheard a swarthy squinting hag teaching a small child some whispered patois in the shadow of an areaway. He listened, and thought it very strange when he heard her repeat over and over again,

10

"O friend and companion of night, thou who rejoicest in the baying of dogs and spilt blood, who wanderest in the midst of shades among the tombs, who longest for blood and bringest terror to mortals, Gorgo, Mormo, thousand-faced moon, look favourably on our sacrifices!"

93 Perry Street and its courtyard.

He

I saw him on a sleepless night when I was walking desperately to save
my soul and my vision. My coming to New York had been a mistake;
for whereas I had looked for poignant wonder and inspiration in the
teeming labyrinths of ancient streets that twist endlessly from forgotten
courts and squares and waterfronts to courts and squares and waterfronts equally forgotten, and in the Cyclopean[1] modern towers and
pinnacles that rise blackly Babylonian under waning moons, I had
found instead only a sense of horror and oppression which threatened
to master, paralyse, and annihilate me.

The disillusion had been gradual. Coming for the first time upon
the town, I had seen it in the sunset from a bridge, majestic above its
waters, its incredible peaks and pyramids rising flower-like and delicate
from pools of violet mist to play with the flaming golden clouds and
the first stars of evening.[2] Then it had lighted up window by window[3]
above the shimmering tides where lanterns nodded and glided and deep
horns bayed weird harmonies,[4] and itself become a starry firmament of
dream, redolent of faery music, and one with the marvels of Carcassonne[5] and Samarcand[6] and El Dorado[7] and all glorious and half-
fabulous cities. Shortly afterward I was taken through those antique
ways so dear to my fancy—narrow, curving alleys and passages where
rows of red Georgian brick blinked with small-paned dormers above
pillared doorways that had looked on gilded sedans and panelled
coaches[8]—and in the first flush of realisation of these long-wished
things I thought I had indeed achieved such treasures as would make
me in time a poet.

But success and happiness were not to be. Garish daylight shewed
only squalor and alienage and the noxious elephantiasis[9] of climbing,
spreading stone where the moon had hinted of loveliness and elder
magic; and the throngs of people that seethed through the flume-like
streets were squat, swarthy strangers[10] with hardened faces and narrow
eyes, shrewd strangers without dreams and without kinship to the
scenes about them, who could never mean aught to a blue-eyed man of
the old folk, with the love of fair green lanes and white New England
village steeples in his heart.

So instead of the poems I had hoped for, there came only a shuddering blankness and ineffable loneliness; and I saw at last a fearful
truth which no one had ever dared to breathe before—the unwhisper-
able secret of secrets—the fact that this city of stone and stridor[11] is
not a sentient perpetuation of Old New York as London is of Old

London and Paris of Old Paris, but that it is in fact quite dead, its sprawling body imperfectly embalmed and infested with queer animate things which have nothing to do with it as it was in life. Upon making this discovery I ceased to sleep comfortably; though something of re-signed tranquillity came back as I gradually formed the habit of keeping off the streets by day and venturing abroad only at night, when dark-ness calls forth what little of the past still hovers wraith-like about, and old white doorways remember the stalwart forms that once passed through them. With this mode of relief I even wrote a few poems, and

10   still refrained from going home to my people lest I seem to crawl back ignobly in defeat.

Then, on a sleepless night's walk, I met the man. It was in a gro-tesque hidden courtyard of the Greenwich section,[12] for there in my ig-norance I had settled, having heard of the place as the natural home of poets and artists. The archaic lanes and houses and unexpected bits of square and court had indeed delighted me, and when I found the poets and artists to be loud-voiced pretenders whose quaintness is tinsel and whose lives are a denial of all that pure beauty which is poetry and art, I stayed on for love of these venerable things.[13] I fancied them as they

20   were in their prime, when Greenwich was a placid village not yet en-gulfed by the town; and in the hours before dawn, when all the revellers had slunk away, I used to wander alone among their cryptical windings and brood upon the curious arcana[14] which generations must have de-posited there. This kept my soul alive, and gave me a few of those dreams and visions for which the poet far within me cried out.

The man came upon me at about two one cloudy August morning, as I was threading a series of detached courtyards; now accessible only through the unlighted hallways of intervening buildings, but once forming parts of a continuous network of picturesque alleys. I had

30   heard of them by vague rumour, and realised that they could not be upon any map of today; but the fact that they were forgotten only en-deared them to me, so that I had sought them with twice my usual ea-gerness.[15] Now that I had found them, my eagerness was again redoubled; for something in their arrangement dimly hinted that they might be only a few of many such, with dark, dumb counterparts wedged obscurely betwixt high blank walls and deserted rear tene-ments, or lurking lamplessly behind archways, unbetrayed by hordes of the foreign-speaking or guarded by furtive and uncommunicative artists whose practices do not invite publicity or the light of day.

40   He spoke to me without invitation, noting my mood and glances as I studied certain knockered doorways above iron-railed steps, the pallid glow of traceried transoms feebly lighting my face. His own face was in

shadow, and he wore a wide-brimmed hat which somehow blended perfectly with the out-of-date cloak he affected; but I was subtly disquieted even before he addressed me. His form was very slight, thin almost to cadaverousness; and his voice proved phenomenally soft and hollow, through not particularly deep.[16] He had, he said, noticed me several times at my wanderings; and inferred that I resembled him in loving the vestiges of former years. Would I not like the guidance of one long practiced in these explorations, and possessed of local information profoundly deeper than any which an obvious newcomer could
10   possibly have gained?

As he spoke, I caught a glimpse of his face in the yellow beam from a solitary attic window. It was a noble, even a handsome, elderly countenance; and bore the marks of a lineage and refinement unusual for the age and place. Yet some quality about it disturbed me almost as much as its features pleased me—perhaps it was too white, or too expressionless, or too much out of keeping with the locality, to make me feel easy or comfortable. Nevertheless I followed him; for in those dreary days my quest for antique beauty and mystery was all that I had to keep my soul alive, and I reckoned it a rare favour of Fate to fall in
20   with one whose kindred seekings seemed to have penetrated so much farther than mine.

Something in the night constrained the cloaked man to silence, and for a long hour he led me forward without needless words; making only the briefest of comments concerning ancient names and dates and changes, and directing my progress very largely by gestures as we squeezed through interstices, tiptoed through corridors, clambered over brick walls, and once crawled on hands and knees through a low, arched passage of stone whose immense length and tortuous twistings effaced at last every hint of geographical location I had managed to
30   preserve.[17] The things we saw were very old and marvellous, or at least they seemed so in the few straggling rays of light by which I viewed them, and I shall never forget the tottering Ionic columns[18] and fluted pilasters[19] and urn-headed iron fence-posts and flaring-lintelled windows[20] and decorative fanlights[21] that appeared to grow quainter and stranger the deeper we advanced into this inexhaustible maze of unknown antiquity.

We met no person, and as time passed the lighted windows became fewer and fewer. The street-lights we first encountered had been of oil, and of the ancient lozenge pattern. Later I noticed some with candles;
40   and at last, after traversing a horrible unlighted court where my guide had to lead with his gloved hand through total blackness to a narrow wooden gate in a high wall, we came upon a fragment of alley lit only by

lanterns in front of every seventh house—unbelievably colonial tin lanterns with conical tops and holes punched in the sides. This alley led
steeply uphill—more steeply than I thought possible in this part of New
York—and the upper end was blocked squarely by the ivy-clad wall of a
private estate,[22] beyond which I could see a pale cupola,[23] and the tops
of trees waving against a vague lightness in the sky. In this wall was a
small, low-arched gate of nail-studded black oak, which the man proceeded to unlock with a ponderous key. Leading me within, he steered a
course in utter blackness over what seemed to be a gravel path, and fi-
10   nally up a flight of stone steps to the door of the house, which he unlocked and opened for me.

We entered, and as we did so I grew faint from a reek of infinite
mustiness which welled out to meet us, and which must have been the
fruit of unwholesome centuries of decay. My host appeared not to notice this, and in courtesy I kept silent as he piloted me up a curving
stairway, across a hall, and into a room whose door I heard him lock
behind us. Then I saw him pull the curtains of the three small-paned
windows that barely shewed themselves against the lightening sky; after
which he crossed to the mantel, struck flint and steel, lighted two can-
20   dles of a candelabrum of twelve sconces, and made a gesture enjoining
soft-toned speech.

In this feeble radiance I saw that we were in a spacious, well-
furnished, and panelled library dating from the first quarter of the
eighteenth century, with splendid doorway pediments,[24] a delightful
Doric cornice,[25] and a magnificently carved overmantel[26] with scroll-
and-urn top. Above the crowded bookshelves at intervals along the
walls were well-wrought family portraits; all tarnished to an enigmatical
dimness, and bearing an unmistakable likeness to the man who now
motioned me to a chair beside the graceful Chippendale[27] table. Before
30   seating himself across the table from me, my host paused for a moment
as if in embarrassment; then, tardily removing his gloves, wide-
brimmed hat, and cloak, stood theatrically revealed in full mid-
Georgian[28] costume from queued[29] hair and neck ruffles to knee-
breeches, silk hose, and the buckled shoes[30] I had not previously noticed. Now slowly sinking into a lyre-back chair, he commenced to eye
me intently.

Without his hat he took on an aspect of extreme age which was
scarcely visible before, and I wondered if this unperceived mark of singular longevity were not one of the sources of my original disquiet.
40   When he spoke at length, his soft, hollow, and carefully muffled voice
not infrequently quavered; and now and then I had great difficulty in

following him as I listened with a thrill of amazement and half-disavowed alarm which grew each instant.

"You behold, Sir," my host began, "a man of very eccentrical habits, for whose costume no apology need be offered to one with your wit and inclinations. Reflecting upon better times, I have not scrupled to ascertain their ways and adopt their dress and manners; an indulgence which offends none if practiced without ostentation. It hath been my good-fortune to retain the rural seat of my ancestors, swallowed though it was by two towns, first Greenwich, which built up hither after 1800,
10 then New-York, which joined on near 1830. There were many reasons for the close keeping of this place in my family, and I have not been remiss in discharging such obligations. The squire who succeeded to it in 1768 studied sartain[31] arts and made sartain discoveries, all connected with influences residing in this particular plot of ground, and eminently desarving[32] of the strongest guarding. Some curious effects of these arts and discoveries I now purpose[33] to shew you, under the strictest secrecy; and I believe I may rely on my judgment of men enough to have no distrust of either your interest or your fidelity."

He paused, but I could only nod my head. I have said that I was
20 alarmed, yet to my soul nothing was more deadly than the material daylight world of New York, and whether this man were a harmless eccentric or a wielder of dangerous arts I had no choice save to follow him and slake my sense of wonder on whatever he might have to offer. So I listened.

"To—my ancestor—" he softly continued, "there appeared to reside some very remarkable qualities in the will of mankind; qualities having a little-suspected dominance not only over the acts of one's self and of others, but over every variety of force and substance in Nature, and over many elements and dimensions deemed more univarsal than
30 Nature herself. May I say that he flouted the sanctity of things as great as space and time, and that he put to strange uses the rites of sartain half-breed red Indians once encamped upon this hill?[34] These Indians shewed choler[35] when the place was built, and were plaguy[36] pestilent in asking to visit the grounds at the full of the moon. For years they stole over the wall each month when they could, and by stealth performed sartain acts. Then, in '68, the new squire catched[37] them at their doings, and stood still at what he saw. Thereafter he bargained with them and exchanged the free access of his grounds for the exact inwardness of what they did; larning[38] that their grandfathers got part of their cus-
40 tom[39] from red ancestors and part from an old Dutchman in the time of the States-General.[40] And pox on him, I'm afeared[41] the squire must have sarved them monstrous bad rum—whether or not by intent—for

a week after he larnt the secret he was the only man living that knew it. You, sir, are the first outsider to be told there is a secret, and split me if I'd have risked tampering that much with—the powers—had ye not been so hot after bygone things."

I shuddered as the man grew colloquial—and with familiar speech of another day. He went on.

"But you must know, Sir, that what—the squire—got from those mongrel salvages[42] was but a small part of the larning he came to have. He had not been at Oxford for nothing, nor talked to no account with
10   an ancient chymist[43] and astrologer in Paris. He was, in fine,[44] made sensible that all the world is but the smoke of our intellects; past the bidding of the vulgar, but by the wise to be puffed out and drawn in like any cloud of prime Virginia tobacco.[45] What we want, we may make about us; and what we don't want, we may sweep away. I won't say that all this is wholly true in body, but 'tis sufficient true to furnish a very pretty spectacle now and then. You, I conceive, would be tickled by a better sight of sartain other years than your fancy affords you; so be pleased to hold back any fright at what I design to shew. Come to the window and be quiet."[46]
20   My host now took my hand to draw me to one of the two windows on the long side of the malodorous room, and at the first touch of his ungloved fingers I turned cold. His flesh, though dry and firm, was the quality of ice; and I almost shrank away from his pulling. But again I thought of the emptiness and horror of reality, and boldly prepared to follow whithersoever I might be led. Once at the window, the man drew apart the yellow silk curtains and directed my stare into the blackness outside.[47] For a moment I saw nothing save a myriad of tiny dancing lights, far, far before me. Then, as if in response to an insidious motion of my host's hand, a flash of heat-lightning played over the
30   scene, and I looked out upon a sea of luxuriant foliage—foliage unpolluted, and not the sea of roofs to be expected by any normal mind. On my right the Hudson glittered wickedly, and in the distance ahead I saw the unhealthy shimmer of a vast salt marsh constellated with nervous fireflies. The flash died, and an evil smile illumined the waxy face of the aged necromancer.

"That was before my time—before the new squire's time. Pray let us try again."

I was faint, even fainter than the hateful modernity of that accursed city had made me.
40   "Good God!" I whispered, "can you do that for *any time?*" And as he nodded, and bared the black stumps of what had once been yellow fangs, I clutched at the curtains to prevent myself from falling. But he

steadied me with that terrible, ice-cold claw, and once more made his
insidious gesture.

Again the lightning flashed—but this time upon a scene not wholly
strange. It was Greenwich, the Greenwich that used to be, with here and
there a roof or row of houses as we see it now, yet with lovely green
lanes and fields and bits of grassy common. The marsh still glittered beyond, but in the farther distance I saw the steeples of what was then all of
New York; Trinity and St. Paul's and the Brick Church[48] dominating
their sisters, and a faint haze of wood smoke hovering over the whole. I
10   breathed hard, but not so much from the sight itself as from the possibilities my imagination terrifiedly conjured up.

"Can you—dare you—go *far?*" I spoke with awe, and I think he
shared it for a second, but the evil grin returned.

"Far? What I have seen would blast ye to a mad statue of stone!
Back, back—forward, *forward*—look, ye puling lack-wit!"[49]

And as he snarled the phrase under his breath he gestured anew;
bringing to the sky a flash more blinding than either which had come
before. For full three seconds I could glimpse that pandaemoniac sight,
and in those seconds I saw a vista which will ever afterward torment
20   me in dreams. I saw the heavens verminous with strange flying things,[50]
and beneath them a hellish black city of giant stone terraces with impi-
ous pyramids flung savagely to the moon, and devil-lights burning from
unnumbered windows. And swarming loathsomely on aërial galleries I
saw the yellow, squint-eyed people of that city, robed horribly in orange
and red, and dancing insanely to the pounding of fevered kettle-drums,
and the clatter of obscene crotala,[51] and the maniacal moaning of
muted horns whose ceaseless dirges rose and fell undulantly like the
waves of an unhallowed ocean of bitumen.[52]

I saw this vista, I say, and heard as with the mind's ear the blas-
30   phemous domdaniel[53] of cacophony which companioned it. It was the
shrieking fulfilment of all the horror which that corpse-city had ever
stirred in my soul, and forgetting every injunction to silence I screamed
and screamed and screamed as my nerves gave way and the walls quiv-
ered about me.

Then, as the flash subsided, I saw that my host was trembling too;
a look of shocking fear half blotting from his face the serpent distor-
tion of rage which my screams had excited. He tottered, clutched at the
curtains as I had done before, and wriggled his head wildly, like a
hunted animal. God knows he had cause, for as the echoes of my
40   screaming died away there came another sound so hellishly suggestive
that only numbed emotion kept me sane and conscious. It was the
steady, stealthy creaking of the stairs beyond the locked door, as with

the ascent of a barefoot or skin-shod horde; and at the last the cautious, purposeful rattling of the brass latch that glowed in the feeble candlelight. The old man clawed and spat at me through the mouldy air, and barked things in his throat as he swayed with the yellow curtain he clutched.

"The full moon—damn ye—ye . . . ye yelping dog—ye called 'em, and they've come for me! Moccasined feet—dead men—Gad sink ye, ye red devils, but I poisoned no rum o' yours—han't I kept your pox-rotted magic safe?—ye swilled yourselves sick, curse ye, and ye must
10   needs blame the squire—let go, you! Unhand that latch—I've naught for ye here—"

At this point three slow and very deliberate raps shook the panels of the door, and a white foam gathered at the mouth of the frantic magician. His fright, turning to steely despair, left room for a resurgence of his rage against me; and he staggered a step toward the table on whose edge I was steadying myself. The curtains, still clutched in his right hand as his left clawed out at me, grew taut and finally crashed down from their lofty fastenings; admitting to the room a flood of that full moonlight which the brightening of the sky had presaged. In those
20   greenish beams the candles paled, and a new semblance of decay spread over the musk-reeking room with its wormy panelling, sagging floor, battered mantel, rickety furniture, and ragged draperies. It spread over the old man, too, whether from the same source or because of his fear and vehemence, and I saw him shrivel and blacken as he lurched near and strove to rend me with vulturine[54] talons. Only his eyes stayed whole, and they glared with a propulsive, dilated incandescence which grew as the face around them charred and dwindled.

The rapping was now repeated with greater insistence, and this time bore a hint of metal. The black thing facing me had become only a
30   head with eyes, impotently trying to wriggle across the sinking floor in my direction, and occasionally emitting feeble little spits of immortal malice. Now swift and splintering blows assailed the sickly panels, and I saw the gleam of a tomahawk as it cleft the rending wood. I did not move, for I could not; but watched dazedly as the door fell in pieces to admit a colossal, shapeless influx of inky substance starred with shining, malevolent eyes.[55] It poured thickly, like a flood of oil bursting a rotten bulkhead, overturned a chair as it spread, and finally flowed under the table and across the room to where the blackened head with the eyes still glared at me. Around that head it closed, totally swallowing it up,
40   and in another moment it had begun to recede; bearing away its invisible burden without touching me, and flowing again out of that black

doorway and down the unseen stairs, which creaked as before, though in reverse order.

Then the floor gave way at last, and I slid gaspingly down into the nighted chamber below, choking with cobwebs and half swooning with terror. The green moon, shining through broken windows, shewed me the hall door half open; and as I rose from the plaster-strown floor and twisted myself free from the sagged ceilings, I saw sweep past it an awful torrent of blackness, with scores of baleful eyes glowing in it. It was seeking the door to the cellar, and when it found it, it vanished therein.

10   I now felt the floor of this lower room giving as that of the upper chamber had done, and once a crashing above had been followed by the fall past the west window of something which must have been the cupola. Now liberated for an instant from the wreckage, I rushed through the hall to the front door; and finding myself unable to open it, seized a chair and broke a window, climbing frenziedly out upon the unkempt lawn where moonlight danced over yard-high grass and weeds. The wall was high, and all the gates were locked; but moving a pile of boxes in a corner I managed to gain the top and cling to the great stone urn set there.[56]

20   About me in my exhaustion I could see only strange walls and windows and old gambrel roofs. The steep street of my approach was nowhere visible, and the little I did see succumbed rapidly to a mist that rolled in from the river despite the glaring moonlight. Suddenly the urn to which I clung began to tremble, as if sharing my own lethal dizziness; and in another instant my body was plunging downward to I knew not what fate.

The man who found me said that I must have crawled a long way despite my broken bones, for a trail of blood stretched off as far as he dared look. The gathering rain soon effaced this link with the scene of
30   my ordeal, and reports could state no more than that I had appeared from a place unknown, at the entrance of a little black court off Perry Street.

I never sought to return to those tenebrous labyrinths, nor would I direct any sane man thither if I could. Of who or what that ancient creature was, I have no idea; but I repeat that the city is dead and full of unsuspected horrors. Whither *he* has gone, I do not know; but I have gone home to the pure New England lanes up which fragrant sea-winds sweep at evening.[57]

*The Stephen Randal tomb in the North Burial Ground, Providence,
similar to the receiving tomb of "In the Vault."*

In the Vault

Dedicated to C. W. Smith,[1]
from whose suggestion the central situation is taken.

There is nothing more absurd, as I view it, than that conventional association of the homely and the wholesome which seems to pervade the
psychology of the multitude. Mention a bucolic Yankee setting, a bun-
gling and thick-fibred village undertaker, and a careless mishap in a
tomb, and no average reader can be brought to expect more than a
hearty albeit grotesque phase of comedy. God knows, though, that the
10 prosy tale which George Birch's death permits me to tell has in it aspects beside which some of our darkest tragedies are light.

Birch acquired a limitation[2] and changed his business in 1881, yet
never discussed the case when he could avoid it. Neither did his old
physician Dr. Davis,[3] who died years ago. It was generally stated that the
affliction and shock were results of an unlucky slip whereby Birch had
locked himself for nine hours in the receiving tomb of Peck Valley
Cemetery, escaping only by crude and disastrous mechanical means; but
while this much was undoubtedly true, there were other and blacker
things which the man used to whisper to me in his drunken delirium
20 toward the last. He confided in me because I was his doctor, and because he probably felt the need of confiding in someone else after Davis
died. He was a bachelor, wholly without relatives.

Birch, before 1881, had been the village undertaker of Peck Valley;
and was a very calloused and primitive specimen even as such speci-
mens go. The practices I heard attributed to him would be unbelievable
today, at least in a city; and even Peck Valley would have shuddered a
bit had it known the easy ethics of its mortuary artist in such debatable
matters as the ownership of costly "laying out" apparel invisible beneath the casket's lid, and the degree of dignity to be maintained in
30 posing and adapting the unseen members of lifeless tenants to contain-
ers not always calculated with sublimest accuracy. Most distinctly Birch
was lax, insensitive, and professionally undesirable; yet I still think he
was not an evil man. He was merely crass of fibre and function—
thoughtless, careless, and liquorish, as his easily avoidable accident
proves, and without that modicum of imagination which holds the
average citizen within certain limits fixed by taste.

Just where to begin Birch's story I can hardly decide, since I am no
practiced teller of tales. I suppose one should start in the cold December of 1880, when the ground froze and the cemetery delvers found
40 they could dig no more graves till spring. Fortunately the village was

small and the death rate low, so that it was possible to give all of
Birch's inanimate charges a temporary haven in the single antiquated
receiving tomb. The undertaker grew doubly lethargic in the bitter
weather, and seemed to outdo even himself in carelessness. Never did
he knock together flimsier and ungainlier caskets, or disregard more
flagrantly the needs of the rusty lock on the tomb door[4] which he
slammed open and shut with such nonchalant abandon.

At last the spring thaw came, and graves were laboriously prepared
for the nine silent harvests of the grim reaper which waited in the
10 tomb. Birch, though dreading the bother of removal and interment, began his task of transference one disagreeable April morning, but ceased
before noon because of a heavy rain that seemed to irritate his horse,
after having laid but one mortal tenement[5] to his permanent rest. That
was Darius Peck, the nonagenarian, whose grave was not far from the
tomb. Birch decided that he would begin the next day with little old
Matthew Fenner,[6] whose grave was also near by; but actually postponed the matter for three days, not getting to work till Good Friday,
the 15th.[7] Being without superstition, he did not heed the day at all;
though ever afterward he refused to do anything of importance on that
20 fateful sixth day of the week. Certainly, the events of that evening
greatly changed George Birch.

On the afternoon of Friday, April 15th, then, Birch set out for the
tomb with horse and wagon to transfer the body of Matthew Fenner.
That he was not perfectly sober, he subsequently admitted; though he
had not then taken to the wholesale drinking by which he later tried to
forget certain things. He was just dizzy and careless enough to annoy
his sensitive horse, which as he drew it viciously up at the tomb
neighed and pawed and tossed its head, much as on that former occasion when the rain had vexed it. The day was clear, but a high wind had
30 sprung up; and Birch was glad to get to shelter as he unlocked the iron
door and entered the side-hill[8] vault. Another might not have relished
the damp, odorous chamber with the eight carelessly placed coffins;
but Birch in those days was insensitive, and was concerned only in getting the right coffin for the right grave. He had not forgotten the criti-
cism aroused when Hannah Bixby's[9] relatives, wishing to transport her
body to the cemetery in the city whither they had moved, found the
casket of Judge Capwell beneath her headstone.

The light was dim, but Birch's sight was good, and he did not get
Asaph Saywer's coffin by mistake, although it was very similar. He had,
40 indeed, made that coffin for Matthew Fenner; but had cast it aside at
last as too awkward and flimsy, in a fit of curious sentimentality
aroused by recalling how kindly and generous the little old man had

been to him during his bankruptcy five years before. He gave old Matt the very best his skill could produce, but was thrifty enough to save the rejected specimen, and to use it when Asaph Sawyer[10] died of a malignant fever. Sawyer was not a lovable man, and many stories were told of his almost inhuman vindictiveness and tenacious memory for wrongs real or fancied. To him Birch had felt no compunction in assigning the carelessly made coffin which he now pushed out of the way in his quest for the Fenner casket.

It was just as he had recognised old Matt's coffin that the door
10 slammed to in the wind, leaving him in a dusk even deeper than before. The narrow transom admitted only the feeblest of rays, and the overhead ventilation funnel virtually none at all; so that he was reduced to a profane fumbling as he made his halting way among the long boxes toward the latch. In this funereal twilight he rattled the rusty handles, pushed at the iron panels, and wondered why the massive portal had grown so suddenly recalcitrant. In this twilight, too, he began to realise the truth and to shout loudly as if his horse outside could do more than neigh an unsympathetic reply. For the long-neglected latch was obviously broken, leaving the careless undertaker trapped in the vault, a
20 victim of his own oversight.

The thing must have happened at about three-thirty in the afternoon. Birch, being by temperament phlegmatic[11] and practical, did not shout long; but proceeded to grope about for some tools which he recalled seeing in a corner of the tomb. It is doubtful whether he was touched at all by the horror and exquisite weirdness of his position, but the bald fact of imprisonment so far from the daily paths of men was enough to exasperate him thoroughly. His day's work was sadly interrupted, and unless chance presently brought some rambler hither, he might have to remain all night or longer. The pile of tools soon
30 reached, and a hammer and chisel selected, Birch returned over the coffins to the door. The air had begun to be exceedingly unwholesome; but to this detail he paid no attention as he toiled, half by feeling, at the heavy and corroded metal of the latch. He would have given much for a lantern or bit of candle; but lacking these, bungled semi-sightlessly as best he might.

When he perceived that the latch was hopelessly unyielding, at least to such meagre tools and under such tenebrous[12] conditions as these, Birch glanced about for other possible points of escape. The vault had been dug from a hillside, so that the narrow ventilation funnel in the
40 top ran through several feet of earth, making this direction utterly useless to consider. Over the door, however, the high, slit-like transom in the brick facade gave promise of possible enlargement to a diligent

worker; hence upon this his eyes long rested as he racked his brains for means to reach it. There was nothing like a ladder in the tomb, and the coffin niches on the sides and rear—which Birch seldom took the trouble to use—afforded no ascent to the space above the door. Only the coffins themselves remained as potential stepping-stones, and as he considered these he speculated on the best mode of arranging them. Three coffin-heights, he reckoned, would permit him to reach the transom; but he could do better with four. The boxes were fairly even, and could be piled up like blocks; so he began to compute how he might

10 most stably use the eight to rear a scalable platform four deep. As he planned, he could not but wish that the units of his contemplated staircase had been more securely made. Whether he had imagination enough to wish they were empty, is strongly to be doubted.

Finally he decided to lay a base of three parallel with the wall, to place upon this two layers of two each, and upon these a single box to serve as the platform. This arrangement could be ascended with a minimum of awkwardness, and would furnish the desired height. Better still, though, he would utilise only two boxes of the base to support the superstructure, leaving one free to be piled on top in case the actual feat

20 of escape required an even greater altitude. And so the prisoner toiled in the twilight, heaving the unresponsive remnants of mortality with little ceremony as his miniature Tower of Babel[13] rose course by course. Several of the coffins began to split under the stress of handling, and he planned to save the stoutly built casket of little Matthew Fenner for the top, in order that his feet might have as certain a surface as possible. In the semi-gloom he trusted mostly to touch to select the right one, and indeed came upon it almost by accident, since it tumbled into his hands as if through some odd volition after he had unwittingly placed it beside another on the third layer.

30 The tower at length finished, and his aching arms rested by a pause during which he sat on the bottom step of his grim device, Birch cautiously ascended with his tools and stood abreast of the narrow transom. The borders of the space were entirely of brick, and there seemed little doubt but that he could shortly chisel away enough to allow his body to pass. As his hammer blows began to fall, the horse outside whinnied in a tone which may have been encouraging and may have been mocking. In either case it would have been appropriate; for the unexpected tenacity of the easy-looking brickwork was surely a sardonic commentary on the vanity of mortal hopes,[14] and the source of a

40 task whose performance deserved every possible stimulus.

Dusk fell and found Birch still toiling. He worked largely by feeling now, since newly gathered clouds hid the moon; and though progress

was still slow, he felt heartened at the extent of his encroachments on the top and bottom of the aperture. He could, he was sure, get out by midnight—though it is characteristic of him that this thought was untinged with eerie implications. Undisturbed by oppressive reflections on the time, the place, and the company beneath his feet, he philosophically chipped away the stony brickwork; cursing when a fragment hit him in the face, and laughing when one struck the increasingly excited horse that pawed near the cypress tree. In time the hole grew so large that he ventured to try his body in it now and then, shifting about
10 so that the coffins beneath him rocked and creaked. He would not, he found, have to pile another on his platform to make the proper height; for the hole was on exactly the right level to use as soon as its size might permit.

It must have been midnight at least when Birch decided he could get through the transom. Tired and perspiring despite many rests, he descended to the floor and sat a while on the bottom box to gather strength for the final wriggle and leap to the ground outside. The hungry horse was neighing repeatedly and almost uncannily, and he vaguely wished it would stop. He was curiously unelated over his impending
20 escape, and almost dreaded the exertion, for his form had the indolent stoutness of early middle age. As he remounted the splitting coffins he felt his weight very poignantly; especially when, upon reaching the topmost one, he heard that aggravated crackle which bespeaks the wholesale rending of wood. He had, it seems, planned in vain when choosing the stoutest coffin for the platform; for no sooner was his full bulk again upon it than the rotting lid gave way, jouncing him two feet down on a surface which even he did not care to imagine. Maddened by the sound, or by the stench which billowed forth even to the open air, the waiting horse gave a scream[15] that was too frantic for a neigh,
30 and plunged madly off through the night, the wagon rattling crazily behind it.[16]

Birch, in his ghastly situation, was now too low for an easy scramble out of the enlarged transom; but gathered his energies for a determined try. Clutching the edges of the aperture, he sought to pull himself up, when he noticed a queer retardation in the form of an apparent drag on both his ankles. In another moment he knew fear for the first time that night; for struggle as he would, he could not shake clear of the unknown grasp which held his feet in relentless captivity. Horrible pains, as of savage wounds, shot through his calves; and in his
40 mind was a vortex of fright mixed with an unquenchable materialism that suggested splinters, loose nails, or some other attribute of a breaking wooden box. Perhaps he screamed. At any rate he kicked and

squirmed frantically and automatically whilst his consciousness was almost eclipsed in a half-swoon.

Instinct guided him in his wriggle through the transom, and in the
crawl which followed his jarring thud on the damp ground. He could
not walk, it appeared, and the emerging moon must have witnessed a
horrible sight as he dragged his bleeding ankles toward the cemetery
lodge; his fingers clawing the black mould in brainless haste, and his
body responding with that maddening slowness from which one suffers
when chased by the phantoms of nightmare. There was evidently, how-
10   ever, no pursuer; for he was alone and alive when Armington, the lodge-
keeper, answered his feeble clawing at the door.

Armington helped Birch to the outside of a spare bed and sent his
little son Edwin for Dr. Davis. The afflicted man was fully conscious,
but would say nothing of any consequence; merely muttering such
things as "oh, my ankles!", "let go!", or "shut in the tomb". Then the
doctor came with his medicine-case and asked crisp questions, and removed the patient's outer clothing, shoes, and socks. The wounds—for
both ankles were frightfully lacerated about the Achilles' tendons—
seemed to puzzle the old physician greatly, and finally almost to
20   frighten him. His questioning grew more than medically tense, and his
hands shook as he dressed the mangled members; binding them as if he
wished to get the wounds out of sight as quickly as possible.

For an impersonal doctor, Davis' ominous and awestruck cross-
examination became very strange indeed as he sought to drain from the
weakened undertaker every least detail of his horrible experience. He
was oddly anxious to know if Birch were sure—absolutely sure—of the
identity of that top coffin in the pile; how he had chosen it, how he had
been certain of it as the Fenner coffin in the dusk, and how he had dis-
tinguished it from the inferior duplicate coffin of vicious Asaph Saw-
30   yer. Would the firm Fenner casket have caved in so readily? Davis, an
old-time village practitioner, had of course seen both at the respective
funerals, as indeed he had attended both Fenner and Sawyer in their
last illnesses. He had even wondered, at Sawyer's funeral, how the vin-
dictive farmer had managed to lie straight in a box so closely akin to
that of the diminutive Fenner.

After a full two hours Dr. Davis left, urging Birch to insist at all
times that his wounds were caused entirely by loose nails and splintering wood. What else, he added, could ever in any case be proved or believed? But it would be well to say as little as could be said, and to let
40   no other doctor treat the wounds. Birch heeded this advice all the rest
of his life till he told me his story; and when I saw the scars—ancient
and whitened as they then were—I agreed that he was wise in so doing.

He always remained lame, for the great tendons had been severed; but I think the greatest lameness was in his soul. His thinking processes, once so phlegmatic and logical, had become ineffaceably scarred; and it was pitiful to note his response to certain chance allusions such as "Friday", "tomb", "coffin", and words of less obvious concatenation. His frightened horse had gone home, but his frightened wits never quite did that. He changed his business, but something always preyed upon him. It may have been just fear, and it may have been fear mixed with a queer belated sort of remorse for bygone crudities. His drinking,
10   of course, only aggravated what it was meant to alleviate.

When Dr. Davis left Birch that night he had taken a lantern and gone to the old receiving tomb. The moon was shining on the scattered brick fragments and marred facade, and the latch of the great door yielded readily to a touch from the outside. Steeled by old ordeals in dissecting rooms, the doctor entered and looked about, stifling the nausea of mind and body that everything in sight and smell induced. He cried aloud once, and a little later gave a gasp that was more terrible than a cry. Then he fled back to the lodge and broke all the rules of his calling by rousing and shaking his patient, and hurling at him a succes-
20   sion of shuddering whispers that seared into the bewildered ears like the hissing of vitriol.

"It was Asaph's coffin, Birch, just as I thought! I knew his teeth, with the front ones missing on the upper jaw—never, for God's sake, shew those wounds! The body was pretty badly gone, but if I ever saw vindictiveness on any face—or former face. . . . You know what a fiend he was for revenge—how he ruined old Raymond thirty years after their boundary suit, and how he stepped on the puppy that snapped at him a year ago last August. . . . He was the devil incarnate, Birch, and I believe his eye-for-an-eye fury could beat old Father Death himself.
30   God, what a rage! I'd hate to have it aimed at me!

"Why did you do it, Birch? He was a scoundrel, and I don't blame you for giving him a cast-aside coffin, but you always did go too damned far! Well enough to skimp on the thing some way, but you knew what a little man old Fenner was.

"I'll never get the picture out of my head as long as I live. You kicked hard, for Asaph's coffin was on the floor. His head was broken in, and everything was tumbled about. I've seen sights before, but there was one thing too much here. An eye for an eye! Great heavens, Birch, but you got what you deserved. The skull turned my stomach, but the other
40   was worse—*those ankles cut neatly off to fit Matt Fenner's cast-aside coffin!*"

317 West 14th Street, and a former location of George Kirk's Chelsea Book Shop.

Cool Air

You ask me to explain why I am afraid of a draught[1] of cool air; why I shiver more than others upon entering a cold room, and seem nauseated and repelled when the chill of evening creeps through the heat of a mild autumn day. There are those who say I respond to cold as others do to a bad odour, and I am the last to deny the impression. What I will do is to relate the most horrible circumstance I ever encountered, and leave it to you to judge whether or not this forms a suitable explanation of my peculiarity.

10   It is a mistake to fancy that horror is associated inextricably with darkness, silence, and solitude. I found it in the glare of mid-afternoon, in the clangour of a metropolis, and in the teeming midst of a shabby and commonplace rooming-house with a prosaic landlady and two stalwart men by my side. In the spring of 1923 I had secured some dreary and unprofitable magazine work in the city of New York;[2] and being unable to pay any substantial rent, began drifting from one cheap boarding establishment to another in search of a room which might combine the qualities of decent cleanliness, endurable furnishings, and very reasonable price.[3] It soon developed that I had only a choice be-
20   tween different evils, but after a time I came upon a house in West Fourteenth Street which disgusted me much less than the others I had sampled.[4]

The place was a four-story mansion of brownstone, dating apparently from the late forties, and fitted with woodwork and marble whose stained and sullied splendour argued a descent from high levels of tasteful opulence. In the rooms, large and lofty, and decorated with impossible paper and ridiculously ornate stucco cornices, there lingered a depressing mustiness and hint of obscure cookery;[5] but the floors were clean, the linen tolerably regular, and the hot water not too often cold
30   or turned off, so that I came to regard it as at least a bearable place to hibernate till one might really live again.[6] The landlady, a slatternly, almost bearded Spanish woman named Herrero,[7] did not annoy me with gossip or with criticisms of the late-burning electric light in my third-floor front hall room; and my fellow-lodgers were as quiet and uncommunicative as one might desire, being mostly Spaniard a little above the coarsest and crudest grade. Only the din of street cars in the thoroughfare below proved a serious annoyance.

I had been there about three weeks when the first odd incident occurred. One evening at about eight I heard a spattering on the floor and
40   became suddenly aware that I had been smelling the pungent odour of

ammonia for some time. Looking about, I saw that the ceiling was wet and dripping; the soaking apparently proceeding from a corner on the side toward the street. Anxious to stop the matter at its source, I hastened to the basement to tell the landlady; and was assured by her that the trouble would quickly be set right.

"Doctair Muñoz," she cried as she rushed upstairs ahead of me, "he have speel hees chemicals. He ees too seek for doctair heemself— seecker and seecker all the time—but he weel not have no othair for help. He ees vairy queer in hees seeckness—all day he take funnee-
10 smelling baths, and he cannot get excite or warm. All hees own house-work he do—hees leetle room are full of bottles and machines, and he do not work as doctair. But he was great once—my fathair in Barce-lona[8] have hear of heem—and only joost now he feex a arm of the plumber that get hurt of sudden. He nevair go out, only on roof, and my boy Esteban, he breeng heem hees food and laundry and mediceens and chemicals. My Gawd, the sal-ammoniac that man use for keep heem cool!"

Mrs. Herrero disappeared up the staircase to the fourth floor, and I returned to my room. The ammonia ceased to drip, and as I cleaned up
20 what had spilled and opened the window for air, I heard the landlady's heavy footsteps above me. Dr. Muñoz I had never heard, save for cer-tain sounds as of some gasoline-driven mechanism; since his step was soft and gentle. I wondered for a moment what the strange affliction of this man might be, and whether his obstinate refusal of outside aid were not the result of a rather baseless eccentricity. There is, I reflected tritely, an infinite deal of pathos in the state of an eminent person who has come down in the world.[9]

I might never have known Dr. Muñoz had it not been for the heart attack that suddenly seized me one forenoon as I sat writing in my
30 room. Physicians had told me of the danger of those spells, and I knew there was no time to be lost; so remembering what the landlady had said about the invalid's help of the injured workman, I dragged myself up-stairs and knocked feebly at the door above mine. My knock was an-swered in good English by a curious voice some distance to the right, asking my name and business; and these things being stated, there came an opening of the door next to the one I had sought.

A rush of cool air greeted me; and though the day was one of the hottest of late June, I shivered as I crossed the threshold into a large apartment whose rich and tasteful decoration surprised me in this nest of
40 squalor and seediness.[10] A folding couch[11] now filled its diurnal role of sofa, and the mahogany furniture, sumptuous hangings, old paintings, and mellow bookshelves all bespoke a gentleman's study rather than a

boarding-house bedroom. I now saw that the hall room above mine—the "leetle room" of bottles and machines which Mrs. Herrero had mentioned—was merely the laboratory of the doctor; and that his main living quarters lay in the spacious adjoining room whose convenient alcoves and large contiguous bathroom permitted him to hide all dressers and obtrusive utilitarian devices. Dr. Muñoz, most certainly, was a man of birth, cultivation, and discrimination.

The figure before me was short but exquisitely proportioned, and clad in somewhat formal dress of perfect cut and fit. A high-bred face of

10   masterful though not arrogant expression was adorned by a short iron-grey full beard,[12] and an old-fashioned pince-nez[13] shielded the full, dark eyes and surmounted an aquiline[14] nose which gave a Moorish[15] touch to a physiognomy otherwise dominantly Celtiberian.[16] Thick, well-trimmed hair that argued the punctual calls of a barber[17] was parted gracefully above a high forehead; and the whole picture was one of striking intelligence and superior blood and breeding.

Nevertheless, as I saw Dr. Muñoz in that blast of cool air, I felt a repugnance which nothing in his aspect could justify. Only his lividly inclined complexion and coldness of touch could have afforded a

20   physical basis for this feeling, and even these things should have been excusable considering the man's known invalidism. It might, too, have been the singular cold that alienated me; for such chilliness was abnormal on so hot a day, and the abnormal always excites aversion, distrust, and fear.

But repugnance was soon forgotten in admiration, for the strange physician's extreme skill at once became manifest despite the ice-coldness and shakiness of his bloodless-looking hands. He clearly understood my needs at a glance, and ministered to them with a master's deftness; the while reassuring me in finely modulated though oddly

30   hollow and timbreless voice[18] that he was the bitterest of sworn enemies to death, and had sunk his fortune and lost all his friends in a lifetime of bizarre experiment devoted to its bafflement and extirpation.[19] Something of the benevolent fanatic seemed to reside in him, and he rambled on almost garrulously as he sounded my chest and mixed a suitable draught of drugs fetched from the smaller laboratory room. Evidently he found the society of a well-born man a rare novelty in this dingy environment, and was moved to unaccustomed speech as memories of better days surged over him.

His voice, if queer, was at least soothing; and I could not even per-

40   ceive that he breathed as the fluent sentences rolled urbanely out. He sought to distract my mind from my own seizure by speaking of his theories and experiments; and I remember his tactfully consoling me

about my weak heart by insisting that will and consciousness are stronger than organic life itself, so that if a bodily frame be but originally healthy and carefully preserved, it may through a scientific enhancement of these qualities retain a kind of nervous animation despite the most serious impairments, defects, or even absences in the battery of specific organs. He might, he half jestingly said, some day teach me to live—or at least to possess some kind of conscious existence—without any heart at all![20] For his part, he was afflicted with a complication of maladies requiring a very exact regimen which included constant

10 cold. Any marked rise in temperature might, if prolonged, affect him fatally;[21] and the frigidity of his habitation—some 55 or 56 degrees Fahrenheit—was maintained by an absorption system of ammonia cooling, the gasoline engine of whose pumps I had often heard in my own room below.[22]

Relieved of my seizure in a marvellously short while, I left the shivery place a disciple and devotee of the gifted recluse. After that I paid him frequent overcoated calls; listening while he told of secret researches and almost ghastly results, and trembling a bit when I examined the unconventional and astonishingly ancient volumes on his shelves. I

20 was eventually, I may add, almost cured of my disease for all time by his skilful ministrations. It seems that he did not scorn the incantations of the mediaevalists,[23] since he believed these cryptic formulae to contain rare psychological stimuli which might conceivably have singular effects on the substance of a nervous system from which organic pulsations had fled. I was touched by his account of the aged Dr. Torres of Valencia,[24] who had shared his earlier experiments with him through the great illness of eighteen years before, whence his present disorders proceeded. No sooner had the venerable practitioner saved his colleague than he himself succumbed to the grim enemy he had fought. Perhaps the strain

30 had been too great; for Dr. Muñoz made it whisperingly clear—though not in detail—that the methods of healing had been most extraordinary, involving scenes and processes not welcomed by elderly and conservative Galens.[25]

As the weeks passed, I observed with regret that my new friend was indeed slowly but unmistakably losing ground physically, as Mrs. Herrero had suggested. The livid aspect of his countenance was intensified, his voice became more hollow and indistinct, his muscular motions were less perfectly coördinated, and his mind and will displayed less resilience and initiative. Of this sad change he seemed by no means

40 unaware, and little by little his expression and conversation both took on a gruesome irony which restored in me something of the subtle repulsion I had originally felt.

He developed strange caprices, acquiring a fondness of exotic spices and Egyptian incense till his room smelled like the vault of a sepulchred Pharaoh in the Valley of Kings.[26] At the same time his demands for cold air increased, and with my aid he amplified the ammonia piping of his room and modified the pumps and feed of his refrigerating machine till he could keep the temperature as low as 34° or 40°, and finally even 28°; the bathroom and laboratory, of course, being less chilled, in order that water might not freeze, and that chemical processes might not be impeded. The tenant adjoining him com-
10 plained of the icy air from around the connecting door, so I helped him fit heavy hangings to obviate the difficulty. A kind of growing horror, of outré and morbid cast, seemed to possess him. He talked of death incessantly, but laughed hollowly when such things as burial or funeral arrangements were gently suggested.

All in all, he became a disconcerting and even gruesome companion; yet in my gratitude for his healing I could not well abandon him to the strangers around him, and was careful to dust his room and attend to his needs each day, muffled in a heavy ulster which I bought especially for he purpose. I likewise did much of his shopping, and gasped
20 in bafflement at some of the chemicals he ordered from druggists and laboratory supply houses.[27]

An increasing and unexplained atmosphere of panic seemed to rise around his apartment. The whole house, as I have said, had a musty odour; but the smell in his room was worse—and in spite of all the spices and incense, and the pungent chemicals of the now incessant baths which he insisted on taking unaided. I perceived that it must be connected with his ailment, and shuddered when I reflected on what that ailment might be. Mrs. Herrero crossed herself when she looked at him, and gave him up unreservedly to me; not even letting her son
30 Esteban continue to run errands for him. When I suggested other physicians, the sufferer would fly into as much of a rage as he seemed to dare to entertain. He evidently feared the physical effect of violent emotion, yet his will and driving force waxed rather than waned, and he refused to be confined to his bed. The lassitude of his earlier ill days gave place to a return of his fiery purpose, so that he seemed about to hurl defiance at the death-daemon even as that ancient enemy seized him. The pretence of eating, always curiously like a formality with him, he virtually abandoned; and mental power alone appeared to keep him from total collapse.
40 He acquired a habit of writing long documents of some sort, which he carefully sealed and filled with injunctions that I transmit after his death to certain persons whom he named—for the most part lettered

East Indians, but including a once celebrated French physician now generally thought dead, and about whom the most inconceivable things had been whispered. As it happened, I burned all these papers undelivered and unopened. His aspect and voice became utterly frightful, and his presence almost unbearable. One September day an unexpected glimpse of him induced an epileptic fit in a man who had come to repair his electric desk lamp; a fit for which he prescribed effectively whilst keeping himself well out of sight. That man, oddly enough, had been through the terrors of the Great War[28] without having incurred
10   any fright so thorough.

Then, in the middle of October, the horror of horrors came with stupefying suddenness. One night about eleven the pump of the refrigerating machine broke down, so that within three hours the process of ammonia cooling became impossible. Dr. Muñoz summoned me by thumping on the floor,[29] and I worked desperately to repair the injury while my host cursed in a tone whose lifeless, rattling hollowness surpassed description. My amateur efforts, however, proved of no use; and when I had brought in a mechanic from a neighbouring all-night garage we learned that nothing could be done till morning, when a new
20   piston would have to be obtained. The moribund hermit's rage and fear, swelling to grotesque proportions, seemed likely to shatter what remained of his failing physique; and once a spasm caused him to clap his hands to his eyes and rush into the bathroom. He groped his way out with face tightly bandaged, and I never saw his eyes again.

The frigidity of the apartment was now sensibly diminishing, and at about 5 a.m. the doctor retired to the bathroom, commanding me to keep him supplied with all the ice I could obtain at all-night drug stores and cafeterias. As I would return from my sometimes discouraging trips and lay my spoils before the closed bathroom door, I could hear a
30   restless splashing within, and a thick voice croaking out the order for "More—more!" At length a warm day broke, and the shops opened one by one. I asked Esteban either to help with the ice-fetching whilst I obtained the pump piston, or to order the piston while I continued with the ice; but instructed by his mother, he absolutely refused.

Finally I hired a seedy-looking loafer whom I encountered on the corner of Eighth Avenue to keep the patient supplied with ice from a little shop where I introduced him, and applied myself diligently to the task of finding a pump piston and engaging workmen competent to install it. The task seemed interminable, and I raged almost as violently
40   as the hermit when I saw the hours slipping by in a breathless, foodless round of vain telephoning, and a hectic quest from place to place, hither and thither by subway and surface car. About noon I encoun-

tered a suitable supply house far downtown, and at approximately 1:30 p.m. arrived at my boarding-place with the necessary paraphernalia and two sturdy and intelligent mechanics. I had done all I could, and hoped I was in time.

Black terror, however, had preceded me. The house was in utter turmoil, and above the chatter of awed voices I heard a man praying in a deep basso. Fiendish things were in the air, and lodgers told over the beads of their rosaries as they caught the odour from beneath the doctor's closed door. The lounger I had hired, it seems, had fled screaming and mad-eyed not long after his second delivery of ice; perhaps as a result of excessive curiosity.[30] He could not, of course, have locked the door behind him; yet it was now fastened, presumably from the inside. There was no sound within save a nameless sort of slow, thick dripping.

Briefly consulting with Mrs. Herrero and the workmen despite a fear that gnawed my inmost soul, I advised the breaking down of the door; but the landlady found a way to turn the key from the outside with some wire device. We had previously opened the doors of all the other rooms on that hall, and flung all the windows to the very top. Now, noses protected by handkerchiefs, we tremblingly invaded the accursed south room which blazed with the warm sun of early afternoon.

A kind of dark, slimy trail led from the open bathroom door to the hall door, and thence to the desk, where a terrible little pool had accumulated.[31] Something was scrawled there in pencil in an awful, blind hand on a piece of paper hideously smeared as though by the very claws that traced the hurried last words. Then the trail led to the couch and ended unutterably.

What was, or had been, on the couch I cannot and dare not say here. But this is what I shiveringly puzzled out on the stickily smeared paper before I drew a match and burned it to a crisp; what I puzzled out in terror as the landlady and two mechanics rushed frantically from that hellish place to babble their incoherent stories at the nearest police station. The nauseous words seemed well-nigh incredible in that yellow sunlight, with the clatter of cars and motor trucks ascending clamorously from crowded Fourteenth Street, yet I confess that I believed them then. Whether I believe them now I honestly do not know. There are things about which it is better not to speculate, and all that I can say is that I hate the smell of ammonia, and grow faint at a draught of unusually cool air.

"The end," ran the noisome scrawl, "is here. No more ice—the man looked and ran away. Warmer every minute, and the tissues can't last. I fancy you know—what I said about the will and the nerves and the preserved body after the organs ceased to work. It was good theory, but couldn't keep up indefinitely. There was a gradual deterioration I had not foreseen. Dr. Torres knew, but the shock killed him. He couldn't stand what he had to do—he had to get me in a strange, dark place when he minded my letter and nursed me back. And the organs never would work again. It had to be done my way—artificial preservation—*for you see I died that time eighteen years ago.*" [32]

Appendix

Preface to *The Shunned House*

The Shunned House is a wonderful story. It is so far removed in theme from our familiar world of radios and politicians and adding machines that it does not touch, at any point, the ancillary stream of modern writing. I can discern in it, hewre and there, faint analogies to contemporary "terror tales", to the work of Lord Dunsany and Arthur Machen and Algernon Blackwood, but in the main Mr. Lovecraft begins where other writers leave off. *The Shunned House* suggests, somehow, the startling and disturbing excursions of S. H. Hinton into the fourth dimension. Only a mathematician, an inspired mathematician, could write a story like this without an intimate realistic perception of the spheres that lie outside the field of ordinary experience. And Lovecraft is not a mathematician. Has he transcended the critical idealism of Kant by training his imagination to become independent of the space-limitations imposed by our normal forms of perception? I can only propound the question; I cannot answer it. Ben De Casseres says somewhere that there is a profound courage in certain forms of credulity, and I shall continue to believe that Lovecraft is occultly endowed until he convinces me that he isn't by writing a story that doesn't suggest new dimensions of space and time.

The Shunned House would probably be rejected by every editor in America. I question the advisability of commending it further! The fact that Mr. O'Brien has included one of Lovecraft's tales in his 1928 Roll of Honor may afford critical support to those who are wary of acclaiming work that is bizarre and vivid and new, but the discriminating reader will appraise the book for himself with a dash of Emersonian self-reliance, and faring valiantly through its pages of mystery and terror, will rejoice exceedingly.

FRANK BELKNAP LONG, JR.

Little Sketches About Town

[*New York Evening Post*, 29 August 1924, p. 9]

The city ought to establish a lost and found department to help recapture odd little streets and courts and alleys that have wandered away like strayed waifs and lost themselves in the bewildering mass of New York byways.

There would be plenty of digging and excavating and burrowing in labyrinths, and then would come a series of shower baths and general dry-cleanings. All the nameless wayfarers would be christened, and brushed and combined, until the city looked like an advertisement for the most sparkling, miraculous cleaner ever used on pots and pans in the history of housewives.

Take, for instance, one little alley just off Perry Street, past Bleecker. Everything about it is lost—name, country, identification of any sort. Its most prominent feature, an old oil lamp by a pair of crooked cellar steps, looks as if it came, after many years of shipwrecked isolation, from the Isle of Lost Ships, and feels more helplessly out of place than it can express.

One boarded house, with several layers of steps leading up to a heavy, frayed balcony, seems to have been left over from the past centuries, and the washbasket hanging neglected from the side wall appears utterly neglected. Behind a fence, clotheslines swing from house to house, fluttering fitfully with community apparel that may never be reclaimed by the rightful owners.

Some people have lived there for years, and are still at a loss for an address. If the old alley ever had a name, it has long ago retired into relentless obscurity, never to reappear in the annals of the New York directory.

Sometimes, to be sure, out of sheer necessity, the residents of Nameless alley supply the title of "Perry Court," in accordance with the memory of Oliver Hazard Perry, the hero of Lake Erie. Or some one adopts the rumor that the old place was called "Love Lane" in other, shadowy days.

No one ventures a definite solution of the mystery. But there is singing from an open window where bright flowers edge the sill, and the least tinge of corned beef and cabbage in the air. Everybody's happy—and what's in a name?

Notes

The Shunned House

1. Poe (1809–1849) courted Sarah Helen (Power) Whitman (1803–1878) during 1848–49. She lived at 88 Benefit Street, and a plaque on the house testifies that she was a "Friend of Edgar Allan Poe." HPL owned Whitman's *Poems* (Providence: Preston & Rounds, 2nd ed. 1894; *LL* 951) as well as Caroline Ticknor's *Poe's Helen* (New York: Scribner's, 1916; *LL* 886), an account of Poe's involvement with Whitman.

2. *Golden Ball Inn:* Built in 1784 by Frank Rice. It no longer survives.

3. HPL had long been fond of St. John's Churchyard—the burial-ground adjacent to St. John's Episcopal Church (1810). He invariably showed it to visitors, and Helen Sully engagingly writes that on one occasion he took her there at night and told her an extemporaneous horror story that so frightened her that she fled from the place ("Memories of Lovecraft: II," *Lovecraft Remembered,* ed. Peter Cannon [Sauk City, WI: Arkham House, 1998], pp. 277–78). In August 1936 HPL, R. H. Barlow, and Adolphe de Castro sat in the churchyard and wrote acrostic "sonnets" on the name *Edgar Allan Poe.*

4. *side-hill:* HPL to R. H. Barlow, [10? February 1934] (ms, JHL): ". . . did you ever hear the old New-England expression *side-hill* for *hillside?* In the ancient rural speech still to be found north of here, 'I live *to* Providence in a *haouse* on a *side-hill* nigh the *cullidge.*'"

5. *peaked-roof:* An architectural form prevalent in New England in the middle seventeenth century, preceding the gambrel roof and presenting a very sharp inverted V-shape at the roofline. The so-called Witch House (1642) in Salem is of this type, as is the house (c. 1660) upon which Hawthorne based *The House of the Seven Gables.* Cf. HPL's "An Account of a Trip to the Antient Fairbanks House, in Dedham . . ." (1929): "This oldest of all New-England houses . . . is built of massive timbers from Old England . . . in the early 1700's the peaked roofs of the wings (but not that of the original part) were made gambrel according to the universal fashion of that time" (ms., JHL).

6. *North Burial Ground:* An immense cemetery at the junction of North Main Street and Branch Avenue. It figures prominently in *The Case of Charles Dexter Ward* (1927).

7. *pilasters:* "A square or rectangular pillar; *spec.* such a pillar engaged in a wall, from which it projects with its capital and base a third, fourth, or other portion of its breadth" (*OED*).

8. *Elihu Whipple:* Whipple's surname is a clear allusion to HPL's maternal grandfather, Whipple Van Buren Phillips (1833–1904), named for Esther Whipple (1767–1848), HPL's maternal great-great-grandmother.

9. Cf. "Supernatural Horror in Literature" (1925–27): "The true weird tale has something more than secret murder, bloody bones, or a sheeted form clanking chains according to rule" (*D* 368). For a "face at the window" see "The Thing on the Doorstep" (*DH* 285).

10. In fact, the house never has been deserted from the time of its building to the present day.

11. *consumption:* An antiquated term for tuberculosis.

12. *salubriousness:* Noun form of *salubrious,* "Favourable or conducive to health" (*OED*).

13. Cf. "The Picture in the House" (1920): "the small-paned windows still stare shockingly, as if blinking through a lethal stupor which wards off madness by dulling the memory of unutterable things" (*DH* 316–17); and "He": "I was taken through those antique ways so dear to my fancy—narrow, curving alleys and passages where rows of red Georgian brick blinked with small-paned dormers above pillared doorways that had looked on gilded sedans and panelled coaches . . ." (p. 73).

14. *Indian pipes:* "An American name for *Monotropa uniflora,* a leafless plant with a solitary drooping flower, of a uniform pinkish-white throughout, parasitic on the roots of trees" (*OED*).

15. *nitre:* Saltpeter; a mineral of potassium nitrate, used in making gunpowder.

16. This image (and, accordingly, much of the supernatural premise of the entire story) appears to be derived from a brief anecdote, "The Green Picture," in Charles M. Skinner's *Myths and Legends of Our Own Land* (Philadelphia: J. B. Lippincott Co., 1896; *LL* 806), 1.76–77:

> In a cellar in Green Street, Schenectady, there appeared, some years ago, the silhouette of a human form, painted on the floor in mould. It was swept and scrubbed away, but presently it was there again, and month by month, after each removal, it returned: a mass of fluffy mould, always in the shape of a recumbent man. When it was found that the house stood on the site of the old Dutch burial ground, the gossips fitted this and that

together and concluded that the mould was planted by a spirit whose mortal part was put to rest a century and more ago, on the spot covered by the house, and that the spirit took this way of apprising people that they were trespassing on its grave. Others held that foul play had been done, and that a corpse, hastily and shallowly buried, was yielding itself back to the damp cellar in vegetable form, before its resolution into simpler elements. But a darker meaning was that it was the outline of a vampire that vainly strove to leave its grave, and could not because a virtuous spell had been worked about the place.

A vampire is a dead man who walks about seeking for those whose blood he can suck, for only by supplying new life to its cold limbs can he keep the privilege of moving about the earth. He fights his way from his coffin, and those who meet his gray and stiffened shape, with fishy eyes and blackened mouth, lurking by open windows, biding his time to steal in and drink up a human life, fly from him in terror and disgust. In northern Rhode Island those who die of consumption are believed to be victims of vampires who work by charm, draining the blood by slow draughts as they lie in their graves. To lay this monster he must be taken up and burned; at least, his heart must be; and he must be disinterred in the daytime when he is asleep and unaware. If he died with blood in his heart he has this power of nightly resurrection. As late as 1892 the ceremony of heart-burning was performed at Exeter, Rhode Island, to save the family of a dead woman that was threatened with the same disease that removed her, namely, consumption. But the Schenectady vampire has yielded up all his substance, and the green picture is no more.

HPL alludes to the Exeter incident later in the story (p. 38). See n. 34. Skinner's book also was a source for some folklore elements mentioned in "The Dunwich Horror" (1928).

17. This appears to be an allusion to a celebrated anecdote from Rhode Island history concerning Roger Williams, which HPL probably found in *A Fourteen Weeks' Course in Chemistry* (1867) by Joel Dorman Steele (1836–1866). (HPL did not own this volume, as far as is known, but since he owned several other textbooks by Steele he probably had read it.) Steele writes:

> The truth that matter passes from the animal back to the vegetable, and from the vegetable to the animal kingdom again, received a curious illustration not long since, as stated in the Hartford Press. For the purpose of erecting a suitable monument in memory of Roger Williams, the founder of Rhode Island, his private burying-ground was searched for the graves of himself and wife. It was found that everything had passed into oblivion. The shape of the coffins could only be traced by a black line of carbonaceous matter. The rusted hinges and nails, and a round wooden knot, alone remained in one grave; while a single lock of braided hair was found in the

other. Near the graves stood an apple-tree. This had sent down two main roots into the very presence of the coffined dead. The larger root, pushing its way to the precise spot occupied by the skull of Roger Williams, had made a turn as if passing around it, and followed the direction of the backbone to the hips. Here it divided into two branches, sending one along each leg to the heel, when both turned upward to the toes. One of these roots formed a slight crook at the knee, which made the whole bear a striking resemblance to the human form. There were the graves, but their occupants had disappeared; the bones even had vanished. There stood the thief—the guilty apple-tree—caught in the very act of robbery. The spoliation was complete. The organic matter—the flesh, the bones, of Roger Williams—had passed into an apple-tree. The elements had been absorbed by the roots, transmuted into woody fibre, which could now be burned as fuel, or carved into ornaments; had bloomed into fragrant blossoms, which had delighted the eye of passers-by, and scattered the sweetest perfume of spring; more than that—had been converted into luscious fruit, which, from year to year, had been gathered and eaten. How pertinent, then, is the question, "Who Ate Roger Williams?" (Joel Dorman Steele, *A Fourteen Weeks' Course in Chemistry* [New York: A. S. Barnes, 1867], pp. 259–60.)

HPL saw the tree root on several occasions at the museum of the Rhode Island Historical Society. A brief manuscript on this subject entitled "Who Ate Roger Williams?" (JHL), once thought to be by HPL, has been determined to be the work of Wilfred B. Talman.

18. Dr. Franklin Chase Clark (1847–1915), clearly the model for Whipple, had received an A.B. from Brown University (1869) and attended Harvard Medical School in 1869–70, where he apparently studied with Oliver Wendell Holmes; he then received his M.D. from the College of Physicians and Surgeons in New York in 1872.

19. Sidney Smith Rider (1833–1917) was a prolific editor and publisher as well as the author of a number of historical tracts about Rhode Island. Thomas W. Bicknell (1834–1925) is most noted for his five-volume *History of the State of Rhode Island and Providence Plantations* (1920), one of many historical works he wrote over a long career.

20. *North Court Street:* A small, two-block street off Benefit Street, virtually around the corner from the Shunned House.

21. The Old State House (built 1762), 150 Benefit Street. Rhode Island declared its independence from England in the Providence Colony House two months before the Declaration of Independence. Cf. *The Case of Charles Dexter Ward* (1927): "When the Colony House burned down, he [Joseph Curwen] subscribed handsomely to the lotteries by which the new brick

one—still standing at the head of its parade in the old main street—was built in 1761" (*MM* 123).

22. Captain Abraham Whipple (1733–1819) was appointed commodore of a fleet of two Rhode Island ships in defense of trade in 1775. He served throughout the early stages of the Revolutionary War, but was captured in 1779 at Charleston, South Carolina; when released, he was paroled and sent to Chester, Pennsylvania, for the rest of the war. HPL was descended from Whipple through his great-great-grandmother, Esther Whipple (see n. 8).

23. Whipple led a party of 50 men in burning the *Gaspée* on June 9, 1772; the ship had run aground on Namquit Point in Warwick, R.I. Some scholars believe that this daring exploit was the first overt act of the American Revolution. It is mentioned again in *The Case of Charles Dexter Ward* (*MM* 146).

24. *overmantel:* "A piece of ornamental cabinet-work, often including a mirror, placed over a mantelpiece" (*OED*). An overmantel plays a critical role in *The Case of Charles Dexter Ward* (see *MM* 154–57).

25. *inchoate:* "Just begun, incipient; in an initial or early stage; hence elementary, imperfect, undeveloped, immature" (*OED*).

26. The John Mawney House (built c. 1764) at 135 Benefit Street was one of the first houses built on Benefit Street after it opened in 1758. In 1790 the house stood virtually alone on the east side of the street.

27. Obadiah and James Brown established the first Brown commercial house, largely in shipping. After the death of James in 1739, Obediah went into business with James's four sons, John, Joseph, Nicholas, and Moses—the famous "four Brown brothers."

28. Actually, Obadiah died in 1762, whereupon the four brothers took over their uncle's business and renamed it Nicholas Brown & Co.

29. *Cheapside:* A shopping district in colonial Providence, on North Main Street between Market Square and Waterman Street.

30. *Rehoboth:* A small town in Massachusetts, just across the Rhode Island border; population in 1937: 2777. HPL and his boyhood friends would ride there on bicycles, and built the Great Meadow Country Clubhouse there around 1907.

31. *Martinique:* An island in the eastern Caribbean, controlled by France.

32. Nabby Gardner, wife of Nahum Gardner, was similarly confined to an upstairs bedroom in "The Colour out of Space" (*DH* 69–70). This com-

mon New England practice is the basis of one of the greatest weird tales in all literature, Charlotte Perkins Gilman's "The Yellow Wall Paper" (1892).

33. Exeter originally was part of North Kingstown but later became a separate community; it was incorporated in 1743.

34. *Nooseneck Hill country:* A region north of Exeter, around the village of Nooseneck (population in 1937: 402). The hill is 511 feet in altitude.

35. On this matter see Faye Ringel Hazel, "Some Strange New England Mortuary Practices: Lovecraft Was Right," *Lovecraft Studies* No. 29 (Fall 1993): 13–18, which discusses in detail the 1892 Exeter incident here described.

36. *Amazon:* Originally, a race of female warriors believed by the ancient Greeks to dwell in Scythia, and who supposedly removed the right breast in order that it not interfere with handling a bow (hence the popular derivation of the word, "lacking a breast"). In later usage, "A very strong, tall, or masculine woman" (*OED*).

37. *Presbyterian-Lane:* The original name for what is now College Street, where HPL lived from 1933 to 1937.

38. The original college building (King's College, later Brown University) was erected in 1770 and still stands as University Hall.

39. *Army of Observation:* On April 22, 1775, the Rhode Island Assembly approved the raising of 1500 men, under the command of General Nathanael Greene (see n. 40), to serve in an army in the event of a war with Great Britain. In May three regiments were formed, with Greene as brigadier in charge of them; they shortly joined other colonial regiments upon the outbreak of hostilities.

40. General Nathanael Greene (1742–1786) became a major general in April 1776, at the age of twenty-four. He was quartermaster-general at Valley Forge in 1778; he took command of the Southern Army in 1780, distinguishing himself in many battles in the South. HPL later visited his gravesite at Savannah, Georgia.

41. Israel Angell (1740–1832) became a colonel in 1777, serving in Rhode Island, New Jersey, and New York; on June 23, 1780 he led his troops in a victorious battle at Springfield, New Jersey.

42. *Elizabethtown:* The eighteenth-century name for Elizabeth, New Jersey. HPL's visits there in 1924 partially inspired the writing of "The Shunned House." He considered moving there in 1925 after his wife Sonia accepted

a job in the Midwest but decided to settle at 169 Clinton Street in Brooklyn Heights.

43. *Great Bridge:* The Great Bridge was an immense bridge—the widest covered bridge in the world before its recent removal—that spanned the Providence River, which separates the older East Side of the city from the newer West Side.

44. Cf. the name Dutee Tillinghast in *The Case of Charles Dexter Ward.*

45. This appears to be the Francis W. Carpenter house at 276 Angell Street (built in 1896, not 1876 as HPL states), an example of the French Rennaissance Revival (Carrère & Hastings, architects).

46. The yellow fever epidemic in August 1797 killed thirty-six people in Providence. There was another epidemic in 1800.

47. *Rathbone Harris:* Rathbone (or Rathbun) is an old family name in Rhode Island, and HPL was related to the line through his great-grandfather Jeremiah Phillips (1800–1848), who married Roby Rathbun.

48. *gum camphor:* A type of camphor obtained from the wood and bark of the camphor tree and used primarily as a stimulant in medicine or as an insect repellent.

49. *febrile:* Relating to fever.

50. *privateersman:* An officer or seaman of a privateer, "An armed vessel owned and officered by private persons, and holding a commission from the government, called 'letters of marque', authorizing the owners to use it against a hostile nation, and especially in the capture of merchant shipping" (*OED*).

51. The *Vigilant* was a schooner built in 1812 at Newport, RI. It saw its first action in the fall of 1813. The ill-fated freighter *Vigilant* and its crew are the subject of the concluding section of "The Call of Cthulhu."

52. Capt. John Cahoone commanded the U.S. revenue cutter *Vigilant* during its engagement with the British privateer *Dart* during the War of 1812.

53. *great gale:* An actual event that caused tremendous damage throughout the state.

54. The Battle of Fredericksburg (Virginia) took place on December 13, 1862. HPL visited the town in 1931.

55. Francis Wayland Thurston—narrator of "The Call of Cthulhu"—similarly finds newspaper clippings and other documentation among the papers of his uncle George Gammell Angell, from his investigation of the Cthulhu Cult.

56. *vampires:* The vampire enters horror literature no later than John William Polidori's "The Vampyre" (1819). Of Bram Stoker's *Dracula* (1897), HPL remarked in "Supernatural Horror in Literature" that it "has become almost the standard modern exploitation of the frightful vampire myth" (*SHL* 56).

57. Dr. Chad Hopkins apparently is fictitious, although Hopkins is, of course, a prominent name in colonial Rhode Island.

58. The newspaper—the first daily paper in Providence—began in 1762 and continued to 1825. In his youth HPL read the entire run of it at the Providence Public Library (*SL* 1.298).

59. A paper founded in 1841 as the *Daily Transcript;* in 1844 it became the *Daily Transcript and Chronicle;* in 1847 the *Daily Evening Transcript;* in 1848 the *Daily Evening Transcript and Free Soil Advocate.* It folded in 1849.

60. *Eleazar Durfee:* The Durfee family was a prominent one in Rhode Island; it is cited in *The Case of Charles Dexter Ward* (*DH* 126). Eleazar Smith is a character in that novel.

61. The Narragansett Indian tribe, for which the town of Narragansett, RI, was named, was dispersed by King Philip's War (1675–76).

62. John Throckmorton was one of the thirteen original proprietors of Providence. See Samuel Green Arndt, *History of the State of Rhode Island and Providence Plantations* (New York: D. Appleton and Co., 1859), 1.100.

63. *Town Street:* The original name for Main Street, one block south of Benefit Street.

64. *Pawtucket West Road:* The original name for Arlington Avenue.

65. In *The Case of Charles Dexter Ward,* Ward stumbles upon traces of Joseph Curwen in the historical record, although the references to Curwen had been deliberately effaced.

66. *Rhode Island Historical Society:* Located at the John Brown house (1786–88) at 52 Power Street.

67. *Shepley Library:* A private library founded in 1921 and located at 292 Benefit Street.

68. *East Greenwich:* A town 15 miles south of Providence, incorporated in 1677; population in 1937, 3666.

69. *Huguenots:* French Protestants.

70. *Caude:* An error by S. Baring-Gould (see n. 74 below) for the town of Cande, in northwest France, 20 miles west of Angers.

71. The Edict of Nantes (passed in 1598) had offered tolerance to French Protestants; its revocation in 1685 by King Louis XIV effectively forced Protestants to flee the country.

72. Edmund Andros (1637–1714) was Governor of the "Dominion of New England" (the region now occupied by Massachusetts, Maine, Rhode Island, Connecticut, and New Hampshire) in 1686; later his administration extended over New York and New Jersey. He was deposed in 1689 because of his interference with colonial rights.

73. Pardon Tillinghast (c. 1622–1718) was a leading businessman in colonial Providence. He constructed the first warehouse and built the first wharf on the Providence River.

74. This entire passage is taken directly from John Fiske's *Myths and Myth-Makers: Old Tales and Superstitions Interpreted by Comparative Mythology* (Boston: Houghton Mifflin, 1872; *LL* 317), an important book in the development of HPL's views on the anthropology of religion. Fiske writes:

> In the year 1598, "in a wild and unfrequented spot near Caude [*sic*], some countrymen came one day upon the corpse of a boy of fifteen, horribly mutilated and bespattered with blood. As the men approached, two wolves, which had been rending the body, bounded away into the thicket. The men gave chase immediately, following their bloody tracks till they lost them; when, suddenly crouching among the bushes, his teeth chattering with fear, they found a man half naked, with long hair and beard, and with his hands dyed in blood. His nails were long as claws, and were clotted with fresh gore and shreds of human flesh."
>
> This man, Jacques Roulet, was a poor, half-witted creature under the dominion of a cannibal appetite. He was employed in tearing to pieces the corpse of the boy when these countrymen came up. Whether there were any wolves in the case, except what the excited imaginations of the men may have conjured up, I will not presume to determine; but it is certain that Roulet supposed himself to be a wolf, and killed and ate several persons under the influence of the delusion. He was sentenced to death, but the parliament of Paris reversed the sentence, and charitably shut him up in a madhouse. (pp. 114–15)

The first paragraph of Fiske's text is a quotation from S. Baring-Gould's *Book of Werewolves* (1865); but HPL could not have derived his information on Roulet from that book, as he did not read it until 1934 (HPL to Clark Ashton Smith, [11 February 1934]; ms. in private hands). It does not appear to have troubled HPL that an apparent werewolf would be the ancestor of a vampire.

75. *torch:* HPL used the British "torch" and the American "flashlight" interchangeably in his work.

76. *anthropomorphic:* In the shape of a human being.

77. *camp chair:* "A form of folding chair" (*OED*).

78. At [375] Cranston Street, erected in 1907. It currently houses the Rhode Island National Guard.

79. Cf. "The Dreams in the Witch House" (1933): "He had been thinking too much about the vague regions which his formulae told him must lie beyond the three dimensions we know . . ." (*MM* 266).

80. HPL was forced to accept the theory of relativity (first propounded by Albert Einstein in 1905) in the spring of 1923, when observations of an eclipse established it beyond reasonable doubt (see *SL* 1.231); he alludes to it, however, in "Hypnos" (1922): "One man with Oriental eyes has said that all time and space are relative, and men have laughed" (*D* 165). "Intra-atomic action" refers to the quantum theory propounded by Max Planck in 1900, which asserts that the action of certain subatomic particles is inherently random. HPL accepted the theory only grudgingly (see *SL* 3.228), and in a manner that involved a fundamental misunderstanding of its true import. See S. T. Joshi, *H. P. Lovecraft: The Decline of the West* (Mercer Island, WA: Starmont House, 1990), p. 20.

81. *Crookes tube:* A device invented in 1878 by Sir William Crookes (1832–1919) involving an electrical discharge between two electrodes. The device later led to Röntgen's discovery of X-rays.

82. *ether radiations:* The phrase suggests that HPL, though making a bow to Einstein, was not entirely comfortable with the theory of relativity, which renders the notion of the ether (supposedly an undetectable substance in space that facilitates the transmission of light) obsolete.

83. The Germans used flame-throwers in World War I beginning in 1915, whereupon the Allies began using them as well.

84. Daylight saving time had first been introduced by Germany, Great Britain, and the United States during World War I. Opposition by farmers,

however, led to its repeal over a presidential veto on 20 August 1919; it was not adopted again in the United States on a national basis until 1942.

85. *Dutch oven:* In this sense, a brick oven in which cooking is done by the preheated wall.

86. The *Revue des Deux Mondes* is a leading French journal, founded in 1831 and still published. Franklin Chase Clark produced translations not from French but from Latin, notably the *Georgics* and *Aeneid* of Vergil.

87. HPL would later use such images of "geometrical confusion" in his conception of hyperspace in "The Dreams in the Witch House" (1932).

88. This sentiment is contradicted by a variety of narrators in HPL's stories. Cf. "Beyond the Wall of Sleep" (1919): "Whilst the greater number of our nocturnal visions are perhaps no more than faint and fantastic reflections of our waking experiences . . . there are still a certain remainder whose immundane and ethereal character permits of no ordinary interpretation . . ." (*D* 25).

89. Cf. "The Night Ocean" by R. H. Barlow (rev. HPL): "The lamp burned endlessly, yielding a sick light hued like a corpse's flesh" (*HM* 449).

90. *rugose:* wrinkled. The bodies of the Great Race in "The Shadow out of Time" (1934–35) are described as "immense rugose cones ten feet high" (*DH* 386).

91. Cf. "Facts concerning the Late Arthur Jermyn and His Family" (1920): "[Science's] reserve of unguessed horrors could never be borne by mortal brains if loosed upon the world" (*D* 73).

92. The Rhode Island School of Design Museum currently is at 224 Benefit Street. It originally was housed at 11 Waterman Street, where HPL visited it in his youth. He describes it as "an enchanted world for me—a true magick grotto where unfolded before me the glory that was Greece & the grandeur that was Rome" (HPL to Lillian D. Clark, 4 October 1925; ms., JHL).

93. The Providence Athenaeum is a private library at College and Benefit Streets, established in 1831.

94. *Hopkins Street:* A small street (named for Stephen Hopkins, an important colonial governor of Rhode Island) leading from Benefit Street to South Main Street. At the corner of Benefit and Hopkins is the Stephen Hopkins house (1755), originally at the corner of Hopkins and South Main Streets.

95. *carboy:* "A large globular bottle, of green or blue glass, covered with basket-work for protection, used chiefly for holding acids and other corrosive liquids" (*OED*).

96. *inane verses:* HPL wrote a large quantity of verse from 1913 to 1920. In 1918 he remarked of it: "What a mess of mediocre & miserable junk. He hath sharp eyes indeed, who can discover any trace of merit in so worthless an array of bad verse" (*SL* 1.60).

97. This image seems analogous to the conclusion of "Under the Pyramids," written only a few months prior to "The Shunned House" in February–March 1924. There, what the narrator takes to be a "five-headed monster as large as a hippopotamus" proves to be *"that of which it is the merest fore paw"* (*D* 243).

98. Cf. HPL to Donald Wandrei, 12 April 1927 (ms. JHL): "People not yet aged can recall the famous 'Yellow Day' of Sept. 6, 1881, & I have myself seen many strange illuminative anomalies which ought to be celebrated in weird literature." The *Providence Daily Journal* (Wednesday, 7 September 1881: 1) reported that the previous day, the atmosphere throughout New England was "pervaded with a yellowish light, which lends a strange appearance" to the landscape.

99. *hideous roar:* This conception coincidentally is similar to that found in Sir Arthur Conan Doyle's story "When the World Screamed" (1928), in which Professor Challenger and his colleagues probe deep into the earth's surface and find a living core there. Consider this passage, when a character plunges a dart into the core:

> . . . our ears were assailed by the most horrible yell that ever yet was heard. Who is there of all the hundreds who have attempted it who has ever yet described adequately that terrible cry? It was a howl in which pain, anger, menace, and the outraged majesty of Nature blended into one hideous shriek. For a full minute it lasted, a thousand sirens in one, paralyzing all the great multitude with its fierce insistence, and floating away through the still summer air. . . .

Sir Arthur Conan Doyle, *When the World Screamed and Other Stories* (San Francisco: Chronicle Books, 1990), pp. 25–26.

The Horror at Red Hook

1. HPL's original title for the story (as recorded on the autograph manuscript [New York Public Library]) was "The Case of Robert Suydam." His later "detective story," *The Case of Charles Dexter Ward* (1927), bears many resemblances to "The Horror at Red Hook."

2. Cf. *CB* 128: "Individual, by some strange process, retraces the path of evolution & becomes amphibious." HPL's explored this theme more thoroughly in "Pickman's Model" (1926) and "The Shadow over Innsmouth" (1931).

3. From "The Red Hand," first published in *Chapman's Magazine* (December 1895) and included in Machen's *The House of Souls* (London: Grant Richards, 1906). HPL owned the story in the Knopf (New York, 1923) edition of *The Three Impostors* (*LL* 578), where the quotation appears on p. 255. "The Red Hand" similarly concerns the survival of primitive rituals in a large city (London). HPL wrote in 1931: "'The Red Hand' was especially shivery to me because of what it implied concerning Those Who Dwell Beneath. Possibly the atmosphere impressed me more than anything directly stated" (*SL* 3.439).

4. Pascoag is a small village in the far northwestern corner of the state.

5. Chepachet is a town about three miles southeast of Pascoag; population in 1937, 1693. It was in this general area that HPL and C. M. Eddy went to look for "Dark Swamp" in October 1923; despite a long trek through the wilderness, they never found the supposedly haunted region (see *SL* 1.264–67). Earlier, in September, HPL and James F. Morton had gone into the Chepachet area in an effort to ascend Durfee Hill, but they failed to do so for lack of time. HPL gives his first impressions of the town: "Chepachet . . . is a veritable bucolic poem—a study in ancient New-England village atmosphere, with its deep, grass-bordered gorge, its venerable bridge, and its picturesque, centuried houses" (*SL* 1.251).

6. In HPL's original draft of the story, the preceding passage read as follows: "Picked up by ready hands, he was found to be still conscious, physically unhurt, & evidently cured of his sudden nervous attack. He apologised shamefacedly, keeping his eyes on the ground & ~~asking for a cab~~ begging one of his rescuers to find him a cab if such a thing was to be had in the village. When one of the two local taxicabs was called from the square beside the station he gave the driver a Chepachet address & rode away without once raising his glance. Later, when talking with interested villagers, the driver said that his passenger had recovered remarkably during the trip, displaying a brisk & paradoxically authoritative manner when alighting in the little hamlet of wooden Colonial houses which formed his destination. Inquiry at the drug store revealed much about him; but while revealing, only brought up new mysteries to heighten the enigma."

7. *anomalous:* "Unconformable to the common order; deviating from rule, irregular; abnormal" (*OED*).

8. *hamlet:* "A group of houses or small village in the country; *esp.* a village without a church, included in the parish belonging to another village or a town. (In some of the United States, the official designation of an incorporated place smaller than a village.)" (*OED*).

9. *thither:* "To or towards that place (with verb of motion expressed or implied)" (*OED*). Already deemed archaic or literary in 1919 by *OED*.

10. Woonsocket is a city in the northeast corner of Rhode Island; population in 1937, 49,376. In later years HPL expressed indignation that the city had been heavily colonized by French-Canadian immigrants (they made up three-fourths of the population in 1937).

11. Cf. "He": "My coming to New York had been a mistake."

12. *portion:* The word in this sense means "That which is allotted to a person by providence; lot, destiny, fate" (*OED*).

13. The name Red Hook derives from the Dutch *Roode Hoek* (Red Point), referring to the color of the soil. The region had been sold by the Indians to the Dutch in 1636.

14. Cf. the narrator's wry comment on Walter Gilman in "The Dreams in the Witch House" (1932): "Possibly Gilman ought not to have studied so hard" (*MM* 263).

15. *leprous:* Literally, "afflicted or tainted with leprosy"; here, "having a surface resembling the skin of a leper; covered with white scales" (*OED*).

16. *cancerous:* of the nature of "an evil figured as an eating sore" (*OED*). Cf. "The Lurking Fear": " . . . I felt the strangling tendrils of a cancerous horror whose roots reached into illimitable pasts and fathomless abysms of the night that broods beyond time" (*D* 189).

17. *rustication:* "The action of retiring to, or living in, the country; a spell of residence in the country" (*OED*).

18. *Dublin University:* HPL means Trinity College, Dublin, founded in 1591 and the only college in the University of Dublin.

19. *Phoenix Park:* A region in the western part of Dublin. The large eponymous park in the district is one of the most beautiful in Europe. "Georgian" refers to the architectural styles developed during the reign of the four Georges (1714–1830) in Great Britain.

20. *eldritch:* "Weird, ghostly, unnatural, frightful, hideous" (*OED*).

21. *polyglot:* "Of or relating to many languages" (*OED*). From the Greek *poly-* (many) and *glotta* (tongue).

22. Note that, in "The Festival" (1923), the fire under the church in Kingsport where the celebrants practice the primitive Yule-rite ("older than man and fated to survive him" [*D* 214]) casts a "sick greenish flame" (*D* 214).

23. The word "sacrament" in the epigraph by Machen may be defined as "A mystery; something secret or having a secret meaning" (*OED*).

24. Cf. HPL's comment to Frank Belknap Long on the inspiration of the story: "it represents at least an attempt to extract horror from an atmosphere to which you deny any qualities save vulgar commonplaceness" (*SL* 2.20).

25. *Dublin Review:* A magazine published in London from 1836 to 1906. HPL apparently did not know that J. Sheridan Le Fanu (1814–1873) was a longtime editor of and contributor to the *Dublin University Magazine*, where many of Le Fanu's famous horror tales and novels appeared.

26. The first sentence of "The Man of the Crowd," first published in *The Casket* and in *Burton's Magazine* (both December 1840) and included in Poe's *Tales* (1845): "It was well said of a certain German book that '*er lasst sich nicht lesen*'—it does not permit itself to be read." Thomas Ollive Mabbott, in his annotated edition of Poe's tales, states that the source of Poe's quotation has not been found, and remarks: "Here he [Poe] took this to mean that the book was too shocking for a reader to peruse it completely; but the meaning of the source may have been that the book referred to was execrably printed, or that no copy was available" (Thomas Ollive Mabbott, ed., *Collected Works of Edgar Allan Poe* [Cambridge, MA: Harvard University Press, 1978], 1.518). HPL, like Poe, probably favored the interpretation that the book was too shocking; cf. *CB* 56: "Book or MS. too horrible to read—warned against reading it—someone reads & is found dead. Haverhill incident." HPL was fond of "The Man of the Crowd," stating in "Supernatural Horror in Literature": "'The Man of the Crowd', telling of one who roams by day and night to mingle with streams of people as if afraid to be alone, has quieter effects, but implies nothing less of cosmic fear" (*SHL* 44). HPL imitated the tale in part in "Hypnos" (1922).

27. This sentence suggests that one of HPL's models for Malone is Arthur Machen, who, as a Welshman, could be considered a Celt. The use of the word "ecstasy" is perhaps a tip of the hat to Machen's study, *Hieroglyphics: A Note upon Ecstasy in Literature* (1902). Machen had similarly written poetry in youth (*Eleusinia* [1881; rpt. Necronomicon Press, 1988]), and had also

lived a life of poverty in London, as recounted in his autobiographies, *Far Off Things* (1922) and *Things Near and Far* (1923).

28. *phantasmagoria:* "A shifting series or succession of phantasms or imaginary figures, as seen in a dream or fevered condition, as called up by the imagination, or as created by literary description" (*OED*). *FFY* (1929–30) could be considered such a phantasmagoria.

29. Aubrey Beardsley (1872–1898) was a celebrated British artist and book illustrator whose stylized and occasionally risqué line drawings contributed much to the atmosphere of the "Yellow Nineties." HPL owned a volume of his artwork, *The Art of Aubrey Beardsley* (New York: Boni & Liveright [Modern Library], [1918] *or* New York: Modern Library, [1925]; *LL* 71). HPL refers in 1927 to the "glitteringly malevolent art of a Baudelaire, a Rops, a Beardsley . . ." (*SL* 2.133). Beardsley is also mentioned in "Medusa's Coil" (*HM* 172).

30. Gustave Doré (1832–1883), celebrated French illustrator. HPL was tremendously fond of his illustrations for Dante's *Inferno* (1866), Milton's *Paradise Lost* (1866), and Coleridge's *Rime of the Ancient Mariner* (1876). The *Ancient Mariner* illustrations, which he stumbled upon at the age of six, helped to nurture his interest in weird fiction (see HPL to J. Vernon Shea, 8 November 1933; ms., JHL), while the illustrations to *Paradise Lost* may have helped to inspired his dreams of "night-gaunts."

31. A common conception in HPL's work, as embodied in the celebrated opening of "The Call of Cthulhu" (1926): "The most merciful thing in the world, I think, is the inability of the human mind to correlate all its contents" (*DH* 125).

32. Cf. *The Case of Charles Dexter Ward:* "Upon us depends more than can be put into words—all civilisation, all natural law, perhaps even the fate of the solar system and the universe" (*MM* 181–82).

33. *Butler Street:* A very short street roughly equidistant between Brooklyn Heights (where HPL lived at the time he wrote this story) and Red Hook.

34. *Governor's Island:* A large island in New York Harbor used for a variety of military purposes; it is also a base for the Coast Guard. A large star-shaped fort, Fort Jay (for a time named Fort Columbus), was built there in 1794 and has been in use ever since. The channel separating it and the Red Hook peninsula is called Buttermilk Channel.

35. *Clinton and Court Streets:* Two long parallel streets that run northeastward from Red Hook to Brooklyn Heights. HPL lived at 169 Clinton Street at the time he wrote this story.

36. *Borough Hall:* A fine Greek revival building on Joralemon Street in Brooklyn, built in 1846–51 and the location of the government offices in the borough. It was the city hall of Brooklyn prior to its incorporation into New York City in 1898.

37. HPL did not care for the work of Charles Dickens (1812–1870), finding it sentimental and the characters exaggerated.

38. Cf. HPL's stanzas "The Canal" (24) and "Harbour Whistles" (33) of *FFY,* whose imagery derives in large part from scenes in New York. "The Pigeon-Flyers" (10) in HPL's draft of the poem originally was titled "Hell's Kitchen," after a region on the west side of Manhattan.

39. HPL's romanticized conception of former Anglo-Saxon purity and present-day mongrel degradation is the subject of two early poems, "New-England Fallen" (1912) and "On a New-England Village Seen by Moonlight" (1913).

40. *cupola:* A small structure built on top of a roof for ornamental purposes or to provide interior lighting or serve as a lookout. Cupolas serve this very purpose in "The Shadow over Innsmouth" (1931).

41. *loquacious:* "Given to much talking; talkative" (*OED*).

42. Cf. HPL's description of one of his neighbors at 169 Clinton Street: "once a *Syrian* had the room next to mine and played eldritch and whining monotones on a strange bagpipe which made me dream ghoulish and incredible things of crypts under Bagdad and limitless corridors of Eblis beneath the moon-cursed ruins of Istakhar" (*SL* 2.116).

43. A common conceit in HPL's fiction, especially in "The Call of Cthulhu" (1926), which HPL outlined on 12–13 August 1925.

44. *The Witch-Cult in Western Europe* (Oxford: Clarendon Press, 1921) by Margaret Alice Murray (1863–1963), a professor of anthropology at University College, London, is a treatise maintaining that the European witch-cult was the product of a primitive pre-Aryan race that lived on in remote areas. The theory was met with some skepticism when first broached, and it is now regarded as highly unlikely. HPL was, however, taken with it, since it offered a "scientific" confirmation of the fictional conception embodied in Arthur Machen's "Little People." HPL read the book no later than the fall of 1923, as it partly inspired "The Festival," written at that time. It is mentioned again in "The Call of Cthulhu" (*DH* 128).

45. *Black Mass:* a travesty of the Roman Catholic Mass, ascribed to worshipers of Satan. Cf. *CB* 75: "Black Mass under antique church." HPL re-

fers to the Black Mass and other forms of devil-worship (sometimes meta-phorically) in his fiction.

46. *Witches' Sabbaths:* meetings of witches, supposed by medieval Christians to be demonic orgies. Referred to occasionally in HPL's other fiction.

47. *Turanian* refers to a nomadic people believed to have preceded the Aryans in Europe and Asia.

48. Suydam is an ancient Dutch family that settled in Brooklyn in the seventeenth century. Many Suydam graves are in the churchyard of the Flatlands Dutch Reformed Church in southeast Brooklyn. There is a Suydam Place and a Suydam Street in the Williamsburg section of Brooklyn, northeast of Red Hook.

49. *Flatbush:* A section of Brooklyn southeast of Red Hook, on the other side of Prospect Park. Sonia H. Greene's apartment at 259 Parkside Avenue, in which HPL resided from March to December 1924, is in this section. See HPL to Lillian D. Clark, 29 September 1922 (ms., JHL): "Parkside Avenue, be it known, is not part of the original town of Brenck-lin—or Brookland—or Brooklyn—as the Long Island metropolis is variously known, but is a remnant of the early Dutch village of *Flatbush,* which was engulfed about a quarter of a century ago by the expansion of the great city. Most of the original village edifices have long been destroyed, & replaced by blocks of shops & apartment houses; but some benign fate has preserved the ancient village church, whose ivy-twined belfry & spire still dominate the local skyline. . . . As I viewed this village churchyard in the autumn twilight, the city seemed to fade from sight, & give place to the Netherland town of long ago. In fancy I saw the cottages of the simple Dutchmen, their small-paned windows lighted one by one as evening stole over the harvest-fields."

50. *Reformed Church:* The Flatlands Dutch Reformed Church (1796) at the corner of Flatbush and Church Avenues in Brooklyn. HPL first visited the site in September 1922 (*SL* 1.198); it inspired "The Hound" (1922).

51. *Martense Street:* A short street off Flatbush Avenue four blocks south of Parkside Avenue. There does not seem at present any structure corresponding with the mansion HPL here describes. Cf. the Martense family in "The Lurking Fear" (1922).

52. Cf., in *The Case of Charles Dexter Ward* (1927), Charles Dexter Ward's three-year European tour, during which he studied with a variety of occult figures.

53. *the Kabbalah:* A body of Jewish mystical teaching, much of it consisting of secret doctrines that were transmitted orally. In the Middle Ages debased forms of cabbalistic thought concerning the unity of all existence were utilized by alchemists in search of the philosopher's stone. One of the main sources of cabbalism is the *Zohar,* cited in *The Case of Charles Dexter Ward (MM* 121).

54. *the Faustus legend:* The story of Doctor Faustus, who made a pact with the Devil for eternal life and all-encompassing knowledge. The most notable literary treatments of the legend are Christopher Marlowe's play *The Tragicall History of D. Faustus* (1604) and Johann Wolfgang von Goethe's *Faust* (1808–32). The relevance of the citation is, of course, that Suydam is a kind of Faust figure. Joseph Curwen is HPL's most poignantly realized Faust figure.

55. Several of HPL's characters are accused of insanity because of their delvings into the bizarre; e.g., Joseph Curwen (when he has disguised himself as Charles Dexter Ward) in *The Case of Charles Dexter Ward* and Asenath Waite (in the body of Edward Derby) in "The Thing on the Doorstep" (1933).

56. *mendicant:* "one who lives by begging" (*OED*).

57. Sephiroth is the Hebrew word for "numbers"; in cabbalism, it refers to the emanations and manifestations of the Godhead. Ashmodai is a variant of Asmodeus, a demon of lust and drunkenness in the apocryphal tradition of the Bible. Samaël is the creator-god in the doctrines of Gnostic Christianity. Interestingly, like Azathoth, it is a blind god.

58. This is somewhat similar to the excuse Charles Dexter Ward puts forth to account for his increasingly peculiar behavior (which has included the resurrection of Joseph Curwen from his "essential saltes"): "He was seeking to acquire as fast as possible those neglected arts of old which a true interpreter of the Curwen data must possess, and hoped in time to make a full announcement and presentation of the utmost interest to mankind and to the world of thought" (*MM* 161).

59. HPL is in error in regard to the name Corlear, which does not exist in the history of the New York area. He may have been thinking of Jacob Van Corlaer, a seventeenth-century farmer after whom Corlaer's Hook (now Crown Point) in Manhattan was named. There were no Corlaers in New York in 1925. There were, however, a few Van Brunts. There is a Van Brunt-Cropsey house (c. 1715) in the New Utrecht section of Brooklyn.

60. *Ellis Island:* A small island in New York Harbor very close to the New Jersey coast. It was established as an entry port for foreign immigrants in

1892 to deal with the unprecedentedly large influx of immigrants occurring at that time. It is now a museum.

61. Not located.

62. *Atlantic Avenue:* A major thoroughfare in Brooklyn Heights running perpendicular to Clinton and Court Streets.

63. The church in question actually existed in Red Hook, although it has now been destroyed. See *Crypt of Cthulhu* No. 28 (Yuletide 1984): 9. The church was in fact used as a dance hall. HPL's Free-Will Church in "The Haunter of the Dark" (1935), based on St. John's Catholic Church on Atwells Avenue in Providence (nonextant), is similarly regarded by its neighbors.

64. Cf. *CB* 84: "Hideous cracked discords of bass musick from (ruin'd) organ in (abandon'd) abbey or cathedral. Red Hook"; "St. Toad's" (*FFY* 25): "'Beware St. Toad's cracked chimes!'"; and the strange cracked, infra-bass vocal sounds in "The Dunwich Horror" (1928).

65. *Nestorian Christianity:* A reference to the followers of Nestorius, a fifth-century monk in Constantinople who asserted that the human and divine Jesus were two conjoined but not unified aspects of his being. He was condemned as a heretic in 430, and his followers scattered to Persia, India, China, and Mongolia.

66. *Shamanism of Thibet:* A reference to the pre-Buddhist religion in Tibet known as Bon, in which shamanism (a religious system in which mystics cure the souls of the sick and perform other functions by the use of magic and talismans) is central. HPL refers to the "Bonpa priests" in "The Last Test" (1927; *HM* 19).

67. *Mongoloid:* A racial designation for the peoples of southeast Asia, China, and Japan, as well as Native Americans.

68. *Kurdistan:* An archaic term for a region in what is now portions of Turkey, Iraq, and Iran, inhabited by Kurds.

69. The Yezidis were a sect of Kurdish-speaking peoples in Iraq and Syria who worshipped a god who, they believed, was originally the creator of evil but who later became good. HPL appears to have derived his information on the Yezidis from the opening of E. Hoffmann Price's story "The Stranger from Kurdistan" (*Weird Tales,* July 1925): "'You claim that demonolatry went out of existence at the end of the Middle Ages, that devil-worship is extinct? . . . No, I do not speak of the Yezidis of Kurdistan, who claim that the Evil One is as worthy of worship as God, since, by virtue of the duality of all things, good could not exist without its antithe-

sis, evil . . .'" E. Hoffmann Price, *Strange Gateways* (Sauk City, WI: Arkham House, 1967), p. 52. HPL was not acquainted with Price at this time, although they later became voluminous correspondents.

70. Cf. HPL's rant at the dress fashions of the foreigners he saw in New York: "Certain lapel cuts, textures & fits tell the story. It amuses me to see how some of these flashy young 'boobs' & foreigners spend fortunes on various kinds of expensive clothes which they regard as evidence of meritorious taste, but which in reality are their absolute social & aesthetick damnation . . . And yet, perhaps these creatures are not, after all, seeking to conform to the absolute artistic standard of gentle-folk" (*SL* 2.28–29).

71. Prohibition (1919–33) was in effect at this time; cf. the later mention of "bootlegging."

72. Robert Olmstead conducts his investigation using similar techniques in "The Shadow over Innsmouth."

73. *tramp freighter:* A ship known as an "ocean tramp." "A cargo vessel, esp. a steamship, which does not trade regularly between fixed ports, but takes cargoes wherever obtainable and for any port" (*OED*).

74. Cf. "The Call of Cthulhu" (1926): "That cult [of the Old Ones] would never die till the stars came right again, and the secret priests would take great Cthulhu from His tomb and revive His subjects and resume His rule on earth. . . . Then the liberated Old Ones would teach them new ways to shout and kill and revel and enjoy themselves, and all the earth would flame with a holocaust of ecstasy and freedom" (*DH* 141).

75. *erstwhile:* former.

76. The *Brooklyn Eagle* was a long-running local newspaper (1841–1955). Walt Whitman edited it from 1846 to 1848.

77. Gerritsen is another ancient New York Dutch name. There was a Gerritsen's Mill on the west side of the Storm Kill in Long Island (destroyed 1934). Several Gerritsens married Van Brunts in the eighteenth and early nineteenth centuries (see n. 59 above).

78. *Bayside:* A region in the far northwestern section of Queens, bordering on Little Neck Bay. It is almost fifteen miles from Flatbush.

79. Suydam's marriage to Gerritsen as a means of repairing his reputation seems to have provided the model for Joseph Curwen's similar marriage to Eliza Tillinghast; although Curwen also wished for a descendent who he knew would resurrect him.

80. Cf. "The Haunter of the Dark": "The paintings on those windows were so obscured by soot that Blake could scarcely decipher what they had represented, but from the little he could make out he did not like them" (*DH* 100).

81. Cf. "Pickman's Model" (1926), of Pickman's paintings: "It was the *faces* . . . those accursed *faces,* that leered and slavered out of the canvas with the very breath of life! . . . [the paintings] repelled because of the utter inhumanity and callous cruelty they showed in Pickman" (*DH* 19, 21).

82. This incantation is derived from the article on "Magic" (by Edward Burnett Tylor [1832–1917], a leading anthropologist of the nineteenth century and author of the landmark treatise *Primitive Culture,* 1871) in the 9th edition of the *Encyclopaedia Britannica,* which HPL owned (hereafter cited as Tylor). In his discussion of Greek and Roman magic, Tylor writes: "The worship of Hecate, the moon, sender of midnight phantoms, lent itself especially to the magician's rites, as may be seen from this formula to evoke her: 'O friend . . .'" Tylor notes that "This magical record [is] preserved by an early Christian writer." *Gorgo* is a variant of *Gorgon,* a generic name for creatures in the shape of women with snakes in place of hair; chief among them was Medusa, who was killed by Perseus. *Mormo* is a female specter the Greeks used to frighten children.

83. As in the work of HPL's Richard Upton Pickman.

84. *Hellenistic Greek:* A reference to the period of Greek history from the death of Alexander the Great (323 B.C.E.) to the conquest of Greece by the Romans (146 B.C.E.). Alexandria was the leading intellectual center of Greece at this time.

85. HPL derived the following incantation directly from Tylor, who prefaced the quotation with the remark: "But in compelling the spirits he [the Jewish magician] can use Hebrew and Greek in admired confusion, as in the following formula (copied with its mistakes as an illustration of magical scholarship in its lowest stage)—. . ." The article did not translate the utterance. On one occasion HPL was asked to do so. His translation was published as "The Incantation from Red Hook" (*The Occult Lovecraft* [Saddle River, NJ: Gerry de la Ree, 1975], pp. 23–30), which is probably an extract from a letter, perhaps to Wilfred B. Talman. In the following notes, HPL's comments are given in quotation marks and with his initials attached (text silently corrected).

86. "*Hel* is clearly the Hebrew *el,* meaning Lord or Deity. Illiterate translations always take liberties with aspirates" [HPL].

"*Heloym,* by the same token, is *Elohim,* the Hebrew word for deity in its less tribal and more generalised sense" [HPL].

"*Sother* is simply bad Greek for *Soter*, meaning *Deliverer*" [HPL].

"*Emmanuel* is Hebrew for God-with-us, usually applied to the prophesied future incarnation of deity in the Old Testament, whose fulfilment Christ is assumed to be" [HPL].

"*Sabaoth* is an Hellenised form of the Hebrew *Tsebaoth*, meaning hosts found in the scriptures in the *Lord God of Hosts*. It was a favourite word with mediaeval occultists and with them probably came to signify *hosts* or *armies* of elemental spirits. I have often wondered if this, rather than *sabbath* (day of rest), is not really the parent-word for the term *sabbat* (*Witches' Sabbath*) applied to the hideous secret orgies of the witch-cult followers. Surely a word signifying *throngs* is much more appropriate for the obscene convocations of May-Eve and Hallowe'en than is a word signifying a weekly *rest* period" [HPL].

"*Agla* is a frequent word among occultists, being often engraved on the wands and knives of magicians. It is formed of the first letters of the Hebrew words composing the sentence 'Thou art a mighty god forever'" [HPL]. HPL derived this information from Tylor. The word is cited in an incantation by Joseph Curwen in *The Case of Charles Dexter Ward* (*MM* 170).

"*Tetragrammaton* is a Greek term of magical conjuration identified with a certain cabalistic diagram. It represents a mystical symbolisation of the four elements—air, water, earth, and fire, and is used for evoking their elemental spirits—respectively the sylphs, undines, gnomes, and salamanders. There are four generally recognised magical diagrams which recur repeatedly in occult rites. The other three are the triangle (equilateral), sign of the Trinity or mystical threefoldness of things; the double triangle or Sign of Solomon, representing the Macrocosm or Entire Universe; and the all-potent pentagram, or five-pointed star, which represents the star of Bethlehem and is the greatest of all conjuring forces. With one point up, the Pentagram is the sign of Christ and an aid to White Magic. With two points up it is the Sign of Satan and the Black Magicians' ally. But this is a digression" [HPL]. Actually "Tetragrammaton" is the four Hebrew letters usually transliterated YHWH or JHVH (Yahweh or Jehovah) to represent the name of God, for the reasons HPL gives below.

"*Agyros* is probably a misspelling of the Greek *agora*—an *assembly*" [HPL]. Actually, the word is derived from *aguris* (itself an Aeolian form of *agora*), meaning "a gathering, crowd" (Liddell and Scott, *Greek-English Lexicon*).

"*Otheos* is probably an even worse misspelling of the Greek *Othneios*, meaning *strange*" [HPL]. Possibly derived from the verb *ōtheo* ("to thrust, push").

"*Ischyros* is good Greek meaning *mighty*" [HPL].

"*Athanatos* is also good Greek and means *immortal*" [HPL]. Literally, "deathless."

"*Jehova* is the common modern pronunciation of the Hebrew *Yahweh* meaning the supreme and awe-inspiring tribal god whose name was too terrible to be pronounced save by a high priest once a year" [HPL]. Also cited by Joseph Curwen (*MM* 170).

"*Va?* I give up. Can't make head nor tail of it" [HPL].

"*Adonai* is the Hebrew alternative word for *Yahweh*—used commonly because the familiar use of the real god-name was forbidden" [HPL]. Also cited by Joseph Curwen (*MM* 170).

"*Saday* is another term beyond me, although I have seen it repeatedly in the many ancient formulae which I have copied from different sources as colour-touches for future tales" [HPL].

"*Homousion* is probably a decadent variant or compound involving the Greek *Homou—together*" [HPL]. HPL is considerably in error. The term means "of the same substance," and is generally taken to refer to the orthodox Christian belief that Jesus Christ is of the same substance as God.

"*Messias* is the Hebrew *anointed,* and under the more common form *Messiah* is a frequent term for Christ" [HPL].

"*Eschereheye* stumps me again—it being only a guess of mine that the barbaric word involves the Greek meaning *in a line* or *in a row*" [HPL]. HPL appears to be referring to the word *scheros* (found only in the dative case, *scheroi:* "in a line, one after another, uninterruptedly, successively" [Liddell and Scott]), but it is unlikely that this is a proper definition of the word in the incantation.

87. *Cunard Pier:* A pier on the southern tip of Manhattan where, beginning in 1840, the Cunard Line debarked for transatlantic voyages.

88. *Social Register:* A listing of the names and addresses of "prominent families" in New York, issued from 1887 to the present day.

89. *tramp steamer:* See n. 73 above.

90. *Chaldee letters:* A reference to the script (a kind of hieroglyphics) of the ancient land of Chaldaea in southern Babylonia near the delta of the Tigris and Euphrates rivers. Its capital was Ur.

91. "*LILITH*": A Sumerian goddess of desolation. In some traditions she is thought to have been the first wife of Adam, or the queen of demons and Satan's consort. According to Lewis Spence "*Lilith* was the prince or princess who presided over the demons known as succubi. The demons under *Lilith* bore the same name as their chief, and sought to destroy new-born infants" (*An Encyclopaedia of Occultism* [1920; rpt. Secaucus, NJ: Citadel Press, 1977], p. 251); *LL* 827.

92. See HPL to August Derleth, 26 November [1932] (ms., SHSW): "As to the 'grapevine telegraph' among niggers, it is pretty well agreed that *dreams & smoke columns* are responsible—both in Africa & in Haiti. This mode of signalling is traditional among the blacks."

93. *Gowanus:* HPL's diary for 1925 reports several occasions early in the year in which he walked along the Gowanus Parkway (now the Gowanus Expressway), which proceeds from southwestern Brooklyn and goes directly into Red Hook to the waterfront. The entry for 15–16 March reads: "Sonny [Frank Belknap Long] & H P walk Gowanus—waterfront—streets" ("Diary: 1925," ms., JHL).

94. *mitre:* "A head-dress forming part of the insignia of a bishop in the Western Church, and worn also by certain abbots and other ecclesiastics as a mark of exceptional dignity. In its modern form, it is a tall cap, deeply cleft at the top, the outline of the front and back having the shape of a pointed arch; the material has usually been white linen or satin, embroidered and often jewelled; but mitres of gold or silver have also been used" (*OED*).

95. Cf. "The Colour out of Space" (1927): "In February the McGregor boys from Meadow Hill were out shooting woodchucks, and not far from the Gardner place bagged a very peculiar specimen. The proportions of its body seemed slightly altered in a queer way impossible to describe, while its face had taken on an expression which no one ever saw in a woodchuck before" (*DH* 61).

96. Cf. Houdini's rationalizing comment in "Under the Pyramids" (1924): "But I survived, and I know it was only a dream" (*D* 243).

97. *Incubi:* Demons in male form who were thought to approach women in their sleep and copulate with them.

98. *succubae:* Very rare feminine plural form of a hypothetical word *succuba* (for *succubus*), demons in female form who would approach men in their sleep and copulate with them.

99. *Hecate:* The Greek goddess of the moon as well as the patron goddess of witches. Pronounced *Hec*-a-tee. See n. 82 above.

100. *Magna Mater:* Latin for "Great Mother," Cybele, the Phrygian mother goddess. Walter de la Poer invokes "Magna Mater!" at the conclusion of "The Rats in the Walls" (1923; *DH* 45)

101. *Ægipans:* Generic designation of the Greek Aigipan ("goat-Pan"), referring either to goat-footed Pan or to the son of Zeus and the nymph Aex

("she-goat"). In Greek art, Aigipan is represented as half-goat and half-fish. The word is not attested in *OED*.

102. Moloch is a variant of Molech, a god to whom human sacrifices were offered in the ancient Middle East. Ashtaroth is, properly, the plural of Ashtoreth, although taken by many to be merely a variant of it. Ashtoreth is a deliberate Hebrew mispronunciation of Astarte, the Canaanite fertility goddess.

103. *Walpurgis-riot:* See HPL to Margaret Sylvester, 13 January 1934 (ms., JHL): "Walpurgis-Night is the season of superstitious fear, when demons are supposed to be abroad, coming on the night of April 30–May 1. It was originally a prehistoric tribal festival, & in the Middle Ages became famous as one of the two annual meeting times of a secret cult of degenerate worshippers. It corresponds to Hallowee'n—& its name is that of a saint [i.e., St. Walpurga, d. 779] whose feast happens to fall on the same date."

104. *satyr:* In Greek mythology, a lustful figure with the head and torso of a man and the legs of a goat.

105. *lemur:* In early Roman mythology, the hostile spirits of the unburied dead (generally referred to in the plural, *lemures*).

106. *elemental:* Properly, an embodiment of one of the four elements (earth, air, fire, and water); more loosely, a wraith or specter.

107. Cf. "The Howler" (*FFY* 12), where the "howler" is an animal with a human face.

108. *Dionysiac:* A reference to the Greek god Dionysos, god of wine and intoxication who is frequently accompanied by satyrs and maenads (maddened and drunken women). The scene resembles that in "The Courtyard" (*FFY* 9).

109. *Tartarus:* A region in the Greek underworld.

110. At the end of "The Thing on the Doorstep" (1933), the body of Asenath Waite (into which she had thrust the mind of her husband Edward Derby while she herself occupied Derby's body) is similarly identified by dental work.

111. There are similar tunnels (based on fact) in the North End section of Boston in "Pickman's Model" (1926). Note also the tunnels in *The Case of Charles Dexter Ward*.

112. Cf. "The Rats in the Walls" (1923): "I found a terrible row of ten stone cells with rusty bars. Three had tenants, all skeletons of high grade,

and on the bony forefinger of one I found a seal ring with my own coat-of-arms. Sir William [Brinton] found a vault with far older cells below the Roman chapel, but these cells were empty" (*DH* 43).

113. The quotation translates to: "Have there ever been demons, incubi, and succubae, and from such a union can offspring be born?" HPL copied the quotation, obtained from Edward Burnett Tylor's article "Demonology" in the *Encyclopaedia Britannica*, in his commonplace book (*CB* 139). It derives from *Disquisitionum Magicarum Libri Sex* [*Six Books of Disquisitions on Magic*] (1603) by Martin Anton Del Rio (or Delrio) (1551–1608). The idea of offspring born of human beings and monsters is also the theme of "The Dunwich Horror" (1928) and "The Shadow over Innsmouth" (1931). See further *Commonplace Book*, ed. David E. Schultz, (West Warwick, RI: Necronomicon Press, 1987), 2:49.

114. Cf. the vast quantities of bones found in the cellar of Exham Priory in "The Rats in the Walls" and in the witch house in "The Dreams in the Witch House" (1932).

115. Cf. "The Well" (*FFY* 11), ll. 13–14: "And yet we put the bricks back—for we found / The hole too deep for any line to sound."

116. *Greenwood Cemetery:* An immense cemetery (478 acres) about a mile southeast of Red Hook in Brooklyn. It was constructed in 1840.

117. *hydra:* In Greek mythology, the Hydra of Lerna was a monster in the form of a water-serpent with a hound's body; when one of its several heads was cut off, two would grow in its place. It was killed by Herakles in the second of his labors. Cf. the reference to "Mother Hydra and Father Dagon" in "The Shadow over Innsmouth" (*DH* 337).

118. HPL derived the phrase from Poe, who in turn derived it from Joseph Glanvill. The epigraph to "A Descent into the Maelström" reads: "The ways of God in Nature, as in Providence, are not as *our* ways; nor are the models that we frame any way commensurate to the vastness, profundity, and unsearchableness of His works, *which have a depth in them greater than the well of Democritus*" (Mabbott 1.577). The phrase is also cited (without source) in "Ligeia": "something more profound than the well of Democritus" (Mabbott 1.313). Democritus (c. 460–370 B.C.E.) is the co-founder (with Leucippus) of the atomic theory and a significant influence on HPL's philosophical thought; his work survives only in fragments. Mabbott (1.332) believes the expression to have been based on a fragment that reads: "Of truth we know nothing, for truth is in the depths."

He

1. *Cyclopean:* An adjective used frequently by HPL. Its principal meaning applies to architecture, and refers to structures made of very large stone blocks; the Greeks used the word in reference to ancient Mycenaean architecture, which they took to be built by the Cyclopes, the race of enormous men invented by Homer in the *Odyssey*.

2. Cf. HPL's first impression of the Manhattan skyline as seen from Manhattan Bridge in April 1922: "Out of the waters it rose at twilight; cold, proud, and beautiful; an Eastern city of wonder whose brothers the mountains are. It was not like any city of earth, for above purple mists rose towers, spires, and pyramids which one may only dream of in opiate lands beyond the Oxus; towers, spires and pyramids that no man could fashion, but that bloomed flower-like and delicate; the bridges up which fairies walk to the sky; the visions of giants that play with the clouds" (*SL* 1.179).

3. See *The Private Life of H. P. Lovecraft* (West Warwick, R.I.: Necronomicon Press, 1985) by Sonia Davis, the woman who was HPL's wife: "One day while visiting Marblehead . . . we sat at twilight on the brow of a hill . . . overlooking a cemetery, watching the lights, one by one, appearing in the houses where fan-shaped doorways and diamond-paned windows reflected the lights. He was as delighted as any child to see this so-called phenomenon and enthusiastically called my attention each time a light appeared until the entire vicinity could be seen from where we sat" (p. 25).

4. Cf. "Harbour Whistles" (*FFY* 30): "The harbour whistles chant all through the night / . . . Fused into one mysterious cosmic drone."

5. *Carcassonne:* An actual city in the south of France. It was settled by the Romans in the first century C.E., and it became an important commercial center in the Middle Ages. Cf. Lord Dunsany's story "Carcassonne" in *A Dreamer's Tales* (1910; *LL* 273).

6. *Samarcand:* More properly, Samarkand. It is first mentioned by the Greeks in the time of Alexander the Great (c. 350 B.C.E.), under the name Maracanda, as the capital of Sogdiana. It was a center of the Arab and, later, Mongol Empire in the Middle Ages, especially under Timur (Tamerlane) in the late fourteenth century. The phrase "the golden road to Samarcand" appears in a poem by James Elroy Flecker (in his collection *The Golden Journey to Samarcand*, 1913), of which HPL was fond because of the image of the burning moonlight (see *SL* 3.57). Perhaps HPL's mythical city Sarkomand in *The Dream-Quest of Unknown Kadath* (1926–27) is meant to evoke Samarkand.

7. *El Dorado:* A mythical city (the name is Spanish for "The Gilded Man," referring to the putative ruler of the place), purportedly in South America, which many Spanish explorers attempted to find in the Renaissance. Cf. Poe's late poem, "Eldorado" (1849), about the California gold rush.

8. HPL spent much of his time during his two New York visits (April 1922 and August–September 1922), as well as his actual residence in the city (March 1924–April 1926), in exploring the remnants of colonial antiquity throughout the New York metropolitan area.

9. *elephantiasis:* Literally, "The name given to various kinds of cutaneous disease, which produce in the part affected a resemblance to an elephant's hide" (*OED*). HPL is using the word in a metaphorical sense (unattested by *OED*) meaning "unnatural vastness."

10. The expression clearly refers to the large numbers of "foreigners" of non–Anglo-Saxon origin whose presence in the city offended HPL.

11. *stridor:* "A harsh, high-pitched sound, a shrill grating or creaking noise" (*OED*).

12. Greenwich Village is a district of Manhattan on the west side of the island (from Broadway to the Hudson River); its northern border is 14th Street, its southern Houston Street. The court to which HPL refers is located at 93 Perry Street, just west of the corner of Perry and Bleecker Streets. See HPL to Lillian D. Clark, 29–30 September 1924: "I now sought Perry Street, in an effort to ferret out the nameless hidden court which the Evening Post had written up that day. (I sent you the cutting.) I found the place without difficulty, and enjoyed it all the more for having seen its picture. These lost lanes of an elder city have for me the utmost fascination, and I am constantly on the lookout for new ones" (ms., JHL). The article is reprinted in the Appendix.

13. HPL always expressed disdain for Bohemian artists. In 1923 he wrote: "Physical life and experience, with the narrowings of artistic vision they create in the majority, are the objects of my most profound contempt. It is for this reason that I despise Bohemians, who think it essential to art to lead wild lives" (*SL* 1.229). These views are expanded in "The Silver Key" (1926). Cf. HPL to F. Lee Baldwin, 27 March 1934 (ms., JHL): "Some regions—especially in the overtaken village of Greenwich, now infested with artists & litterateurs (mostly poseurs, but including a few genuine performers like Wandrei & his brother)—are quite definitely colonial; with slant-roofed brick houses in solid blocks, whose high stoops, pillared, transomed doorways, & projecting dormers mark them as typical."

14. *arcana:* Plural of *arcanum,* a word taken directly from the Latin: "A hidden thing; a mystery, a profound secret" (*OED*).

15. Cf. "The Shadow over Innsmouth": "Any reference to a town not shewn on common maps or listed in recent guide-books would have interested me. . . . All this, to the pious Miss Tilton, formed an excellent reason for shunning the ancient town of decay and desolation; but to me it was merely a fresh incentive" (*DH* 305, 313).

16. Dr. Muñoz of "Cool Air" and Joseph Curwen of *The Case of Charles Dexter Ward,* both resuscitated dead men, have "hollow" voices.

17. Cf. "The Nameless City" (1921): "It is only in the terrible phantasms of drugs or delirium that any other man can have had such a descent as mine. The narrow passage led infinitely down like some hideous haunted well, and the torch I held above my head could not light the unknown depths toward which I was crawling. . . . There were changes of direction and of steepness" (*D* 102).

18. *Ionic columns:* The Ionic is one of three classic orders of architecture evolved by the Greeks (the others are Doric and Corinthian). An Ionic column has a slender shaft, twenty-four semicircular flutes, and a small base.

19. See n. 7 to "The Shunned House."

20. A lintel is "A horizontal piece of timber, stone, etc. placed over a door, window, or other opening to discharge the superincumbent weight" (*OED*).

21. *fanlight:* "A fan-shaped window over a door" (*OED*). It is a specifically New England architectural feature.

22. *private estate:* A reference to the Warren/Van Nest mansion, built between 1726 and 1744 and torn down in 1865. It occupied the block bounded by Perry, Charles, Bleecker, and West Fourth Streets (hence across the street from the courtyard at 93 Perry Street). See Elaine Schechter, *Perry Street—Then and Now* (New York, 1972), pp. 4–6.

23. See n. 40 to "The Horror at Red Hook."

24. *pediment:* A decorative feature (usually triangular but sometimes semicircular) crowning the front of a building or placed above a doorway or window.

25. *Doric cornice:* A cornice is "A horizontal moulded projection which crowns or finishes a building or some part of a building; *spec.* the uppermost member of the entablature of an order surmounting the frieze" (*OED*).

26. See n. 24 to "The Shunned House."

27. *Chippendale:* Furniture designed by or in the manner of Thomas Chippendale (c. 1718–1779), the most famous English furniture maker of his time, whose works are largely in the rococo style.

28. *mid-Georgian:* See n. 19 to "The Horror at Red Hook."

29. *queued:* Participial form of the verb *queue,* "To put up (the hair) into a queue ['A long plait of hair worn hanging down behind, from the head or from a wig; a pig-tail']" (*OED*).

30. Cf. HPL in 1914: "Verily, I ought to be wearing a powdered wig and knee-breeches" (*SL* 1.4).

31. *sartain:* Dialectical variant of *certain.*

32. *desarving:* Dialectical variant of *deserving* (as also *univarsal* below).

33. *purpose:* Archaic for *propose.*

34. The area had in fact been settled by Indians: the Algonquins had established a port on the shore nearby and had called it Sapokanican ("The Place of Tobacco Pipes").

35. *choler:* Literally, "bile"; hence, "Anger, heat of temper, wrath" (*OED*). Generally archaic, although *OED* cites a usage as late as 1858.

36. *plaguy:* "Of the nature of or pertaining to a or the plague; pestiferous, pestilential, pernicious" (*OED*). Archaic.

37. *catched:* Archaic past participle of *catch* (for *caught*). Cf. the dialectical variant in "The Picture in the House" (1920): "Ketched in the rain, be ye?" (*DH* 120).

38. *larning:* Dialectical variant of *learning.*

39. *custom:* "The practice of customarily resorting to a particular shop, place of entertainment, etc. to make purchases or give orders; business patronage or support" (*OED*).

40. *States-General:* The Dutch equivalent of the British Parliament or the U.S. Congress: the chief legislative body of the Netherlands, consisting of two houses.

41. *afeared:* Archaic dialectical variant of *afraid.*

42. *salvages:* Archaic for *savages.*

43. *chymist:* Cf. *The Case of Charles Dexter Ward:* ". . . the close-mouthed 'chymist'—by which they meant *alchemist . . .*" (*MM* 119).

44. *in fine:* "in the end, at last; . . . also, in short" (*OED*).

45. Cf. a passage in "Hypnos" (1922), derived from the theory of relativity: "The cosmos of our waking knowledge, born from such an universe as a bubble is born from the pipe of a jester, touches it only as such a bubble may touch its sardonic source when sucked back by the jester's whim" (*D* 165).

46. The subsequent passage seems clearly reminiscent of chapter three of Lord Dunsany's *The Chronicles of Rodriguez* (1922; in the U.S. *Don Rodriguez: Chronicles of Shadow Valley*), which HPL read in the spring of 1923 (cf. HPL to Samuel Loveman, 29 April [1923]; *Letters to Samuel Loveman and Vincent Starrett,* ed. S. T. Joshi and David E. Schultz [West Warwick, RI: Necronomicon Press, 1994], p. 17). In this novel, Don Rodriguez and his associate Moraño scale a high mountain and enter the house of a wizard, who takes them to two windows showing, respectively, the wars of the past and the wars of the future. See S. T. Joshi, "Lovecraft and Dunsany's *Chronicles of Rodriguez,*" *Crypt of Cthulhu* No. 82 (Hallowmas 1992): 3–6.

47. Cf. "The Music of Erich Zann" (1921): "Yet when I looked from that highest of all gable windows . . . I saw no city spread below, and no friendly lights gleaming from remembered streets, but only the blackness of space illimitable" (*DH* 90).

48. Trinity Church, at Broadway and Wall Streets, was the first Protestant Episcopal church in New York City. The first church on its site was built in 1698, destroyed by fire in 1776, and reconstructed in 1787. A new church was built in 1839–46. St. Paul's Chapel, on Broadway between Vesey and Fulton Streets, is the oldest church building in Manhattan. Its cornerstone was laid in 1764; a wooden spire was added in 1794. HPL married Sonia H. Greene in this church on 3 March 1924. The Brick [Presbyterian] Church, at Park Row and Beekman Street, was built in 1767 and torn down in 1856.

49. *Puling:* "Crying as a child, whining, feebly wailing; weakly querulous" (*OED*). Archaic, although *OED* cites a usage as late as 1857. *Lack-wit:* Lacking in wit; a fool. Note that HPL once signed a letter "Epicurus Lackbrain, Esq." (*SL* 1.112).

50. The flying things are reminiscent of the "night-gaunts" of HPL's youthful nightmares.

51. *crotala:* Plural of *crotalum,* "a sort of clapper or castanet used in ancient Greece and elsewhere in religious dances" (*OED*).

52. *bitumen:* "Originally, a kind of mineral pitch found in Palestine and Babylon, used as mortar, etc. . . . In modern scientific use, the generic name of certain mineral inflammable substances, . . . including naphtha, petroleum, asphalt, etc." (*OED*).

53. *domdaniel:* "A fabled submarine hall where a magician or sorcerer met with his disciples" (*OED*). First cited in the French translation (1788–93) of the *Arabian Nights;* usually capitalized.

54. *vulturine:* Pertaining to or resembling a vulture.

55. This entity might be the ultimate origin of the protoplasmic shoggoths in *At the Mountains of Madness* (1931).

56. In "In the Vault," George Birch makes a stack of coffins to enable him to climb through a high transom in a locked tomb.

57. HPL himself, of course, would not return to Providence for another eight months after writing this story (April 1926).

In the Vault

1. Charles W. ("Tryout") Smith (1852–1948) was longtime editor of the *Tryout*, an amateur journal to which HPL had been contributing since 1916. HPL met him in 1920 in Smith's home at 408 Groveland Street, Haverhill, Massachusetts, and on several subsequent occasions.

2. *limitation:* "The settlement of an estate by a special provision or with a special modification or modifications" (*OED*).

3. *Dr. Davis:* Cf. HPL's young amateur friend Edgar J. Davis (1908–1949), with whom he explored Haverhill and Newburyport in 1923.

4. A rusty lock bars entrance to the burial vault in "The Tomb" (1917).

5. Cf. "Pickman's Model": "The fellow must be a relentless enemy of all mankind to take such glee in the torture of brain and flesh and the degradation of the mortal tenement" (*DH* 21).

6. *Matthew Fenner:* Cf. the frequent mentions of the Fenners (a family in colonial Rhode Island) in *The Case of Charles Dexter Ward* (1927).

7. In his notes for "The Cancer of Superstition," an uncompleted piece of ghostwriting for Harry Houdini, HPL made note of his intent to address "Good Friday beliefs &c". Superstition about Good Friday plays a part in *The Case of Charles Dexter Ward*.

8. See n. 4 to "The Shunned House."

9. In July 1923, HPL had stayed "in a quaint & modest house on a hillside on Front St." where an "old Mrs. Bixby, widow of the artist who designed the Town Seal of Marblehead, who will give a plain but nice room for *$8.00* per week" (HPL to Annie E. P. Gamwell, [6 July 1923]; ms., JHL). HPL also mentioned having his watch repaired by the "Bixby Silver Co." (HPL to Lillian D. Clark, 1 September 1925; ms., JHL).

10. *Asaph Sawyer:* HPL's great-great-grandfather on the maternal side was Asaph Phillips (1764–1829), whose grave in Foster, RI, HPL would see in 1926 and 1929. Sawyer is a name HPL would use again in "The Dunwich Horror" (1928).

11. *phlegmatic:* "Having or showing the mental character or disposition formerly supposed to result from predominance of phlegm among the bodily 'humours'; not easily excited to feeling or action; lacking enthusiasm; cold, dull, sluggish, apathetic; cool, calm, self-possessed" (*OED*).

12. *tenebrous:* dark.

13. *Tower of Babel:* A tower and city mentioned in Gen. 11 where God interrupted the construction of a heaven-reaching tower by causing the workers to speak in a welter of languages (until then, only one language was spoken), so that the tower was left unfinished. HPL uses the expression picturesquely to hint at the ultimate futility of Birch's tower of coffins.

14. In his youth, HPL had written a poem on "The Vanity of Human Ambition" (1902).

15. Recall HPL's Roman dream of 1927: "Then with utter and horrifying suddenness we heard a frightful sound from below. It was from the tethered horses—they had *screamed* . . . not neighed, but *screamed*" (*MW* 50).

16. In "The Colour out of Space," a team of frightened horses flees with an empty wagon.

Cool Air

1. *draught:* British spelling of *draft*.

2. HPL had married Sonia H. Greene on 3 March 1924, and moved into her apartment in Brooklyn. At that time, he was offered the editorship of *Weird Tales* but, because the magazine was deeply in debt and because it would have required his moving to Chicago, he declined. He also had some prospects of doing freelance writing for "The Reading Lamp" (either a magazine or a literary agency) operated by Gertrude Tucker, but nothing

came of this. As a result, HPL had no income aside from random sales of stories to *Weird Tales.*

3. HPL lived in two different apartments during his New York stay, 259 Parkside Avenue (Sonia's place) from March to December 1924 and 169 Clinton Street from January 1925 to April 1926. By the end of 1924, when it became clear that he would have to relocate, HPL began looking at small, cheap apartments in the New York area, and for a time he considered moving to Elizabeth, New Jersey; but he settled on the Clinton Street flat because of its price ($40 per month in rent, later increased slightly to $10 per week) and its apparent cleanliness in a once-respectable area of the city (Brooklyn Heights). On the latter point HPL later remarked: ". . . the house *had* until almost that precise time been of the quality I thought I had found. My guess is that its decay had just set in owing to the Syrian fringe (all unsuspected by me) beyond Atlantic Avenue. . . . Friends who came to see me—better versed in Brooklyn ways than I, for my metropolitan residence had been confined to the quiet section of Flatbush—were quicker than I to see and tell me what a wretched hole I had crawled into; but by that time I was all settled, and with my desperate finances the idea of a removal was quite impossible" (*SL* 2.114–15).

4. The house referred to (317 West 14th Street) was at the time the residence of HPL's friend George Willard Kirk (1898–1962) and one location of his bookshop, The Chelsea Book Shop.

5. See the Introduction for HPL's description of the house, made on the occasion of his helping Kirk move there. Rheinhart Kleiner notes that most of the meetings of HPL's informal band of literary colleagues, the Kalem Club, met at Kirk's bookshop: "George's ability and perseverance in brewing coffee, and his liberality with buns and sandwiches, left nothing to be desired. Nor need it cause wonder if certain individuals became so attached to proprietor and shop as to appear every evening, often with the expectation—which was never disappointed—of sleeping here. A host, whose bed in the rear room could accommodate five guests, if they did not toss much, was never at a loss when visitors declined to go home." "After a Decade and the Kalem Club" (1936), *Lovecraft Studies* No. 28 (Spring 1993): 35.

6. In expressing the wish that he might one day "really live again," the narrator establishes a critical link with Dr. Muñoz, who has literally done just that.

7. In fact, HPL's landlady at 169 Clinton Street was a Mrs. Burns, whom he describes as follows: "The landlady was a refined-looking woman with two prepossessing youths as sons, and with a British accent of such absolutely

authentic caste that there can have been no mistake about her tale of better days—the usual thing—and her claim of being the daughter of a cultivated Anglican vicar in Ireland, educated in a private school in England. Poor old Mrs. Burns! Only later was I to learn of her shrewish tongue, desperate household negligence, miserly watchfulness of lights and unwatchfulness of repairs, and reckless indifference to the class of lodger she admitted!" (*SL* 2.115).

8. *Barcelona:* One of the largest and most important cities in Spain. It is situated on the Mediterranean coast in the region of Catalonia, in northeast Spain.

9. A common theme in HPL, especially with respect to whole civilizations as opposed to mere individuals.

10. Surely a reference to HPL's own tasteful furnishings at 169 Clinton Street. Kleiner recalled seeing HPL's furniture at 259 Parkside: "I remember very well the arrival from Providence of a surprising mass of material intended for his new home. There were heaps of fine linen, quite a few pieces of heavy, old-fashioned silverware, and other items which had probably been stored away for years. . . . Dropping in to see him and his wife, I could not forbear commenting on the speed with which everything had been placed in order. 'Why, this looks as if you had lived here always,' I said. He looked extremely gratified and, while I cannot recall the exact language he used, he explained that this was one way in which a gentleman could be recognized; a gentleman always made himself at home no matter where he happened to be" ("A Memoir of Lovecraft," *Lovecraft Remembered,* ed. Peter Cannon [Sauk City, WI: Arkham House, 1998], p. 201). Cf. HPL to Bernard Austin Dwyer, 26 March 1927: ". . . visitors not infrequently commented on the virtual transition from one world to another implied in the simple act of stepping within my door. Outside—Red Hook. Inside—Providence, R. I.!" (*SL* 2.115–6).

11. HPL had a folding couch in the main room of 169 Clinton Street. Cf. HPL's "Diary" for 1925 (ms., JHL): "Two alcoves with portieres enable one to preserve the pure library effect"; i.e., one that does not contain a visible bed that would suggest sleeping quarters. Cf. also HPL's remarks prior to his return to Providence in April 1926: "I don't want any bedroom stuff visible in the main room, for that is first of all a *study*. You know how sedulously I exclude all such stuff at 169 [Clinton Street]" (HPL to Lillian D. Clark, [9 April 1926]; ms., JHL).

12. The physician in "The Tomb" (1917), Ephraim Waite in "The Thing on the Doorstep" (1933), and the man in "The Evil Clergyman" (abstracted

from the description of a dream in a letter of 1933) all have iron-grey beards, as did HPL's friend Charles "Tryout" Smith.

13. *pince-nez:* Eyeglasses clipped to the bridge of the nose. HPL once wore eyeglasses of this type but discontinued because they were uncomfortable.

14. *aquiline:* "Eagle-like; *esp.* of the nose or features: Curved like an eagle's beak, hooked" *(OED)*.

15. *Moorish:* Adjectival form of *Moor,* a reference to the peoples of North Africa (either Arab or negroid) who practiced the Islamic religion and settled in the Iberian peninsula beginning in the 8th century. They were gradually expelled from Spain beginning in the 11th century; they made a last stand in the Kingdom of Granada in the southeast corner of Spain, which fell to the Spaniards in 1492.

16. *Celtiberian:* Celtiberia was the term applied by the Romans to a region in north-central Spain. HPL uses the term to designate the non-Moorish peoples of the Spanish peninsula: the Iberians (south and east) and the Celtics (west).

17. HPL also visited the barber regularly, although in later years he purchased a device that allowed him to trim his own hair.

18. See n. 16 to "He."

19. Like HPL's Herbert West of "Herbert West—Reanimator" (1921–22).

20. A theme addressed in different ways in "Herbert West—Reanimator," *The Case of Charles Dexter Ward,* "The Whisperer in Darkness," and "The Shadow out of Time."

21. HPL, of course, had the opposite condition, which caused him to be unable to manage a pen when the temperature fell below 70° and to lose consciousness altogether if the temperature fell below 20°. This condition may have been the result of a lesion in the hypothalamus.

22. Cf. HPL to Lillian D. Clark, 7 August 1925 (ms., JHL), in reference to an air-conditioned theatre in Providence: "Glad you have kept up with the Albee Co., though surprised to hear that the theatre is *hot.* They have a fine ammonia cooling system installed, & if they do not use it it can only be through a niggardly sense of economy."

23. Cf. *The Case of Charles Dexter Ward:* "[Ward] stated that the papers of his ancestor had contained some remarkable secrets of early scientific knowledge . . . of an apparent scope comparable only to the discoveries of Friar Bacon and perhaps surpassing even those" *(MM 160–61).*

24. *Valencia:* A large city about 200 miles southwest of Barcelona on the Mediterranean coast. It was formerly occupied by the Moors (see n. 15).

25. *Galens:* A generic use (in the plural) of Galen (c. 130–c. 200), a Greek physician in Asia Minor (Turkey) who wrote prodigiously on medical subjects and was the greatest medical thinker in the ancient world after Hippocrates. Thus *Galens* is synonomous with *physicians*.

26. *Valley of Kings:* A region in the ancient city of Thebes in Egypt, on the west bank of the Nile, where royal burials took place.

27. Cf. *The Case of Charles Dexter Ward:* "Local dealers in drugs and scientific supplies, later questioned, gave astonishingly queer and meaningless catalogues of the substances and instruments [Ward] purchased" (*MM* 159).

28. "Great War" refers to World War I (1914–18). Cf. "Pickman's Model" (1926): "I'm middle-aged and decently sophisticated, and I guess you saw enough of me in France to know I'm not easily knocked out" (*DH* 20). The fictional Dr. Herbert West also served in World War I.

29. HPL and George Kirk communicated with each other by knocking on the pipes between their apartments.

30. A frequent motif in HPL's work. Cf. "The Shadow over Innsmouth" (1931): "Curiosity flared up beyond sense and caution" (*DH* 327).

31. Cf. Arthur Machen's "Novel of the White Powder": "There upon the floor was a dark and putrid mass, seething with corruption and hideous rottenness, neither liquid nor solid, but melting and changing before our eyes, and bubbling with unctuous oily bubbles like boiling pitch. And out of the midst of it shone two burning points like eyes, and I saw a writhing and stirring as of limbs, and something moved and lifted up what might have been an arm." *The Three Impostors* (London: John Lane; Boston: Roberts Brothers, 1895), p. 230.

32. The time would have been 1904–5. The death of HPL's grandfather, Whipple V. Phillips, in March 1904 and HPL's removal from his birthplace so devastated him that he briefly contemplated suicide.

Textual Notes

The Shunned House

The sole basis for this story is the version typeset by W. Paul Cook for his abortive Recluse Press (1928) edition of the story; this text clearly derives from HPL's typescript, which has now been lost. (A single-spaced typescript of the story at JHL was not prepared by Lovecraft and apparently postdates the Recluse Press edition.) All subsequent texts derive from Cook's edition. Listed below are editorial departures from that text.

C = Unbound sheets (Athol, MA: W. Paul Cook/The Recluse Press, 1928)

35.18	side-hill,] side hill, C
36.11	farm-like] farmlike C
37.9	shew] show C
37.11	gnarled,] gnarled C
37.11	grass,] grass C
39.2	overmantel,] overmantel C
43.8	death-certificates] death certificates C
43.38	shewing] showing C
44.39	connexion] connection C
45.17	shewn] shown C
48.22	Armoury,] Armory, C
49.5	connexion] connection C
50.1	connexion] connection C
50.15–6	half doubted] half-doubted C
50.18	shewed] showed C
54.18	Nature.] nature. C
57.18	ash-like] ashlike C
	forever;] for ever; C

The Horror at Red Hook

Both HPL's autograph manuscript and typescript (prepared by himself) survive; in the former, only the readings relating to textual variants have been recorded. The *Weird Tales* appearance made its customary departures from HPL's typescript in accordance with its house style.

All subsequent texts aside from the corrected edition of 1986 (*Dagon and Other Macabre Tales*) have followed the *Weird Tales* appearance.

A = A.Ms. (New York Public Library)
T = T.Ms. (JHL)
W = *Weird Tales* (January 1927)
Z = all readings

58.11	behaviour.] behavior. W
58.26	recognised] recognized W
61.7	*er lasst*] *er lässt* W
61.14	phantasmagoria] fantasmagoria W
61.16	in Beardsley's] in Aubrey Beardsley's W
61.24	humour] humor W
61.34	nineteenth century,] Nineteenth Century, W
61.35–6	flavour] flavor W
61.36	"Dickensian".] "Dickensian." W
61.41	harbour] harbor W
62.34	neighbourhood's] neighborhood's W
63.3	cryptical,] cryptical Z
63.8	shewed] showed Z
63.10–11	*Witch-Cult in Western Europe;*] "Witch Cult in Western Europe"; A, T; *Witch Cult in Western Europe* W
63.28	his] this W
63.30–1	old world] Old World W
63.41	clothes,] clothes Z
64.3	mediaeval] medieval W
64.12–3	neighbourhoods.] neighborhoods. W
64.19	"Ashmodai",] "Ashmodai" Z
64.19	"Samaël".] "Samaël." W
64.32	demeanour] demeanor W
64.38	shewed] showed Z
65.10	organised] organized W
65.29	Thibet.] Tibet. W
65.32	Yezidis,] Yezidees, W

65.32	devil-worshippers.] devil-worshipers. W
65.34	unauthorised] unauthorized W
65.36	harbour] harbor W
66.6	arch-fiend] A; arch-/fiend T; archfiend W
66.14	unlicenced] unlicensed Z pedlars,] pedlers, W
66.17–8	"bootlegging"] bootlegging W
66.22	canal,] canal Z
66.29	reasons] reason W
66.37	accommodate] accomodate A, T
66.38	harbouring] harboring W
67.4	folklore] folk-lore W
67.13	investigations] investigation W
67.36	demeanour] demeanor W
67.37	shewed] showed Z
68.20	translated,] translated: W
68.24	favourably] favorably W
68.26	organ notes] organ-notes W
68.30	neighbourhood.] neighbor-hood. W
68.37–38	clamoured] clamored W
69.6	cannot] can not W
69.9	cabbalistic] cabalistic Z
69.10	Hebraised] Hebraized W
69.11	daemon-evocations] daemon evocations W
69.15	ADONAI * SADAY *] ADONAL.SADY. W
69.17	Circles] ¶ Circles W
69.26	protégés] proteges A, T; protegés W
69.27	clamour.] clamor. W
69.34	Pier] pier W
69.35	five] 5 W
69.38	old world] Old World W harbour] harbor W
70.15	"LILITH".] "LILITH." W
70.34	"In] In W
70.38	ROBERT SUYDAM."] ROBERT SUYDAM. W
71.6	it.] it. ¶ W
71.12	odour] odor W

71.13	shewed] showed Z
71.20	apprised] apprized W
71.24	rumours] rumors W
71.25	Vikings] vikings W
71.33	mitres,] miters, W
71.34	melee,] mêlée, W hastily] hestily T
71.35	odours] odors W
72.2	centre] center W
72.3	odour,] odor, W
72.16	paralysed] paralyzed W
72.26	Odours] Odors W
72.36	foetor] fetor W
72.42	moon-calves] A; moon-/calves T; mooncalves W
73.6	mould.] mold. W
73.7	Nature] nature W
73.11	daemon-lore.] demon-lore. W
73.12	phantasms,] fantasms, W
73.25	daemoniac] demoniac
73.38	daemon] demon W
74.5	(*here . . . forth*)] [*here . . . forth*] W
74.5–6	blood (*here . . . shriekings*),] blood, (*here . . . shriekings*) T; blood, [*here . . . shriekings*] W
74.7	tombs (*here . . . occurred*),] tombs, (*here . . . occurred*) T; tombs, [*here . . . occurred*] W
74.8	mortals (*short . . . throats*),] mortals, (*short . . . throats*) T; mortals, [*short . . . throats*] W
74.8–9	Gorgo (*repeated as response*),] Gorgo, (*repeated as response*) T; Gorgo, [*repeated as response*] W
74.9	Mormo (*repeated with ecstasy*),] Mormo, (*repeated with ecstasy*) T; Mormo, [*repeated with ecstasy*] W
74.9–10	moon (*sighs . . . notes*),] moon, (*sighs . . . notes*) T; moon, [*sighs . . . notes*] W
74.10	favourably] favorably W
74.14	clamour] clamor W
74.28	laboured] labored W

75.21	neighbourhood.] neighbor-hood. W
75.32	sombre] somber W
75.33	*talī*] *tali,* W
76.6–7	Yezidi] Yezidee W
	devil-worshippers.] devil-worshipers. W
76.9	shew] show Z
76.21	connexion] connection W
76.25	folklore.] folk-lore. W
76.36	old,] old W
76.38	rumours] rumors W
76.39	centres] centers W
76.40	dance hall,] dance-hall, W
77.8	again,] again: W
77.12	favourably] favorably W

He

HPL's autograph manuscript does not survive, but his typescript (prepared by himself) does. The *Weird Tales* appearance made its customary departures from HPL's text in accordance with its house style. All subsequent texts aside from the corrected edition of 1986 (*Dagon and Other Macabre Tales*) have followed the *Weird Tales* appearance.

T = T.Ms. (JHL)
W = *Weird Tales* (September 1926)
Z = all readings

79.10	paralyse,] paralyze, W
79.13	flower-like] flowerlike Z
79.17	and itself] and had itself W
79.23	panelled] paneled W
79.24	realisation] realization W
79.27	shewed] showed Z
79.30	flume-like] flumelike W
80.7	wraith-like] wraithlike Z
80.26	two] 2 W
80.30	rumour,] rumor, W
	realised,] realized, W
80.39	practices] practises W
81.8	practiced] practised W
81.19	favour] favor W
81.30	marvellous,] marvelous, W

81.33	flaring-lintelled] flaring-linteled W
82.18	shewed] showed Z
82.22–3	well-furnished,] well-furnished Z
82.23	panelled] paneled W
82.24	eighteenth century,] Eighteenth Century, W
83.3	Sir,"] Sir", T
83.7	practiced] practised W
83.8	good-fortune] good fortune W
83.10	New-York,] New York, W
83.16	shew] show Z
83.25	ancestor—"] ancestor," W
83.31	time,] time W
83.33	shewed] showed Z
	plaguy] plaguey W
84.18	shew.] show. Z
84.40	whispered,] whispered; W
85.36	half blotting] half-blotting Z
86.3	mouldy] moldy W
86.21	panelling,] paneling, W
87.4	half swooning] half-swooning Z
87.5	shewed] showed Z

In the Vault

This is, textually, the most interesting of the stories here included. An autograph manuscript and typescript must have been prepared by HPL, but neither is extant. A typescript (prepared for HPL by August Derleth) survives, containing pencil corrections in HPL's hand. The first appearance in the *Tryout* must have followed HPL's original typescript, while the *Weird Tales* appearance must have followed the Derleth typescript. It appears, however, that many of the hand-written revisions on the surviving typescript were made after the *Weird Tales* appearance; they were therefore not included in any text prior to the corrected edition of 1984 (*The Dunwich Horror and Others*). The last pencil revision—

the underscoring of the final phrase of the story—is made in a pencil differing from that of the other revisions, and may just possibly have been made at a later time by Derleth rather than HPL. The *Tryout* text is riddled with typographical errors. All subsequent texts aside from the corrected edition have followed the *Weird Tales* appearance.

T = T.Ms. (JHL)
T^c = pencil corrections on T.Ms.
Tr = *Tryout* (November 1925)
W = *Weird Tales* (April 1932)
Z = all readings

Dedication] Tr; *omitted* T, W
89.6   bucolic] bucolitc Tr
89.7   thick-fibred] thick-fibered W
         village] *omitted* Tr
89.9   comedy.] comedy, Tr
89.11   darkest tragedies] darkes
         tragediest Tr
89.14   physician Dr.] physician,
         Doctor W
         Davis,] Davii, Tr
89.15   affliction] affiiction Tr
89.16   receiving tomb] receiving-
         tomb W
89.19   which] whieh Tr
         to whisper] towhisper Tr
89.21   someone] some one W
89.23   Valley;] Valley, W
89.25   practices] practises W
         unbelievable] unbelieveable
         Tr
89.26   least] least, Tr
89.27   known] know Tr
         debatable] T^c, Tr; *omitted* W
         "laying-out"] "laying out" Tr
89.28   degree] degrees W
89.29   an] a Tr
89.33   fibre] fiber W
         liquorish,] liquerish, Tr
89.34   story] story, Tr
89.37   practiced] *omitted* Tr; prac-
         tised W

90.3   receiving tomb.] receiving-
         tomb. W
90.3–4   bitter weather,] bitter winter
         weather, Tr
90.5   or] nor W
90.7   nonchalant] nonchalent Tr
90.8   harvests] harvest Tr
90.13   mortal tenement] T^c; soul T,
         Tr; body W
90.15   Birch] Brich Tr
90.17   till] until W
90.18   15th.] Tr; fifteenth. T, W
90.22   afternoon] aftrenoon Tr
         15th,] Tr; fifteenth, T, W
         then,] when Tr
90.23   Fenner.] Fenner, Tr
90.24   subsequently] sebsequently
         Tr
90.26–7 which . . . pawed] which
         pawed Tr
90.27   head,] head Tr
90.28–9 on that former occasion] on
         former occasions Tr
90.29   had vexed] T^c, Tr; had
         seemingly vexed T, W
90.30   shelter] shelter, W
90.32   concerned only] only con-
         cerned Tr
90.38   good,] good Tr
91.7   carelessly] caarelessly Tr
91.9   recognised] recognized Tr,
         W
91.11   transom admitted] transo-
         madmitted Tr
         feeblest of rays,] feeblest
         rays, W
91.11–2 overhead] over-head Tr
91.14   rattled the] rattle dthe Tr
91.15   portal] portals Tr
91.16   realise] realize Tr, W
91.18   unsympathetic] unsympa-
         thetc Tr
91.21   The thing] "This thing Tr
         three-thirty] 3:30 Tr
91.23   but] bnt Tr
91.28   rambler hither,] ramblre
         hither Tr
91.29   might have] migh thave Tr

91.31	unwholesome;] unwhole-some, W		94.14	consequence;] consequence, W
91.34	candle; but] candle, but Tr; candle; but, W		94.15	"oh,] "Oh, W

91.31 unwholesome;] unwhole-some, W

91.34 candle; but] candle, but Tr; candle; but, W

91.36–7 least to] least an to Tr

91.37 meagre] meager W
        under such] underlsuch Tr

91.39 hillside,] Tᶜ; side-hill, T, Tr, W

92.1 rested as] restedas Tr

92.3–4 rear—. . . use—] rear, . . . use, W

92.6 on] no Tr

92.9 piled] piied Tr

92.17 minimum] minimun Tr

92.18 utilise] utilize W

92.25 surface] surfice Tr

92.37 case] case, W
        appropriate;] appropriate, W

92.42 newly gathered] newly-gathered Z

93.3 midnight—] midnight; W

93.4 eerie] eery T, W; evry Tr

93.5 on the] on he Tr

93.5–6 philosophically] phllosophi-cally Tr

93.6 brickwork;] brick-/work, W

93.11 height;] height, W

93.13 might] would W

93.15 transom.] trasnom. Tr

93.17 strength] streugth Tr

93.21 age.] age. ¶ W

93.23 bespeaks] besepaks Tr

93.24 wholesale] wholesnle Tr

93.33 transom;] transom, W

93.39 pains,] pains Tr

93.42 breaking wooden] break-/wooden Tr
        rate] rate, W

94.1 automatically] automaticllay Tr

94.3 in his wriggle] to wriggle Tr

94.7 lodge;] lodge, W
       mould] mold W

94.8 responding] respounding Tr

94.11 answered] Tᶜ; responded to T, Tr, W

94.13 Dr.] Doctor W

94.14 consequence;] consequence, W

94.15 "oh,] "Oh, W
        ankles!",] ankles!" Tr
        "let go!",] "let go!" Tr; "Let go!", W
        "shut . . . tomb".] "shut . . . tomb!" Tr; ". . . shut . . . tomb." W

94.17 shoes,] shoes W

94.18 Achilles'] Achilles W

94.21 members;] members, W

94.25 least] last W

94.27 pile;] pile, W

94.28 dusk,] dark, W

94.28–9 distinguished] disringuished Tr

94.29 Asaph] Asanh Tr

94.32 Fenner and] Fenner aud Tr

94.33 funeral,] funreal, Tr

94.36 Dr.] Doctor W

94.37 caused entirely by] Tᶜ; due entirely to T, Tr, W

94.41 till . . . story;] until . . . story, W

94.42 then] rhen Tr

95.3 scarred;] scarred, W

95.4 response] Tᶜ; reaction T, Tr, W

95.5 "Friday", "tomb", "coffin",] "Friday," "tomb," "coffin," W
        concatenation.] contatena-tion. Tr

95.7 changed his] dhangedh is Tr

95.8 upon him.] uponhim. Tr

95.9 sort of] sort o Tr
       crudities.] cruditnes. Tr

95.10 it was meant] Tᶜ; he sought T, W; it sought Tr

95.11 Dr.] Doctor W
        Birch] Breib Tr
        night] night, W

95.12 receiving tomb.] receiving-tomb. W

95.13 marred] manned Tr

95.15 dissecting rooms,] dissect-ing-rooms, W

95.17	once,] once Tr	100.22	mediaevalists,] medievalists, TM
95.19	hurling at him] huring at bim Tr	100.42	I had originally felt.] *omitted* TM
95.22	Asaph's] Asapha's Tr	101.24	odour;] odor; TM
95.24	shew] show Z	101.36	death-daemon] death-demon TM
95.25	face. . . .] face! . . . W	102.18	neighbouring] neighboring TM
95.29	old Father Death himself.] old Father Death himself, Tr; time and death! W	102.26	a.m.] A.M. TM
95.30	what a rage!] his rage—W	102.32	whilst] while TM
95.31	it, Birch?] it Birch, Tr	102.39	install] instill TM
95.33	thing some] thing in some W	103.2	p.m.] P.M. TM
95.37	I've . . . sights] Iv'e . . . sfghts Tr	103.8	odour] odor TM
95.39	deserved.] deserved! W	103.36–8	and all . . . air.] and I sure hate the smell of ammonia. TM
95.40	*those . . . coffin!"*] Tᶜ, W; those . . . coffin!" T, Tr		

Cool Air

HPL's autograph manuscript does not survive, but his typescript does. The appearance in *Tales of Magic and Mystery* made various alterations apparently in conformity with its house style. All subsequent texts aside from the corrected edition of 1984 (*The Dunwich Horror and Others*) have followed the *Tales of Magic and Mystery* appearance.

T = T.Ms. (JHL)

TM = *Tales of Magic and Mystery* (March 1928)

Z = all readings

97.2	draught] draft TM
97.6	odour,] odor, TM
97.12	clangour of a] clangor of TM
97.25	splendour] splendor TM
97.29	regylar,] regularly, TM
97.33	criticisms] criticism TM third-floor] third floor Z
97.40	odour] odor TM
98.12	But] But, TM
98.13	a arm] arm TM
99.20	this] his TM
99.35	draught] draft TM

www.ingramcontent.com/pod-product-compliance
Lightning Source LLC
Chambersburg PA
CBHW020624250626
47154CB00004B/1648